THE BEST PEACE FICTION

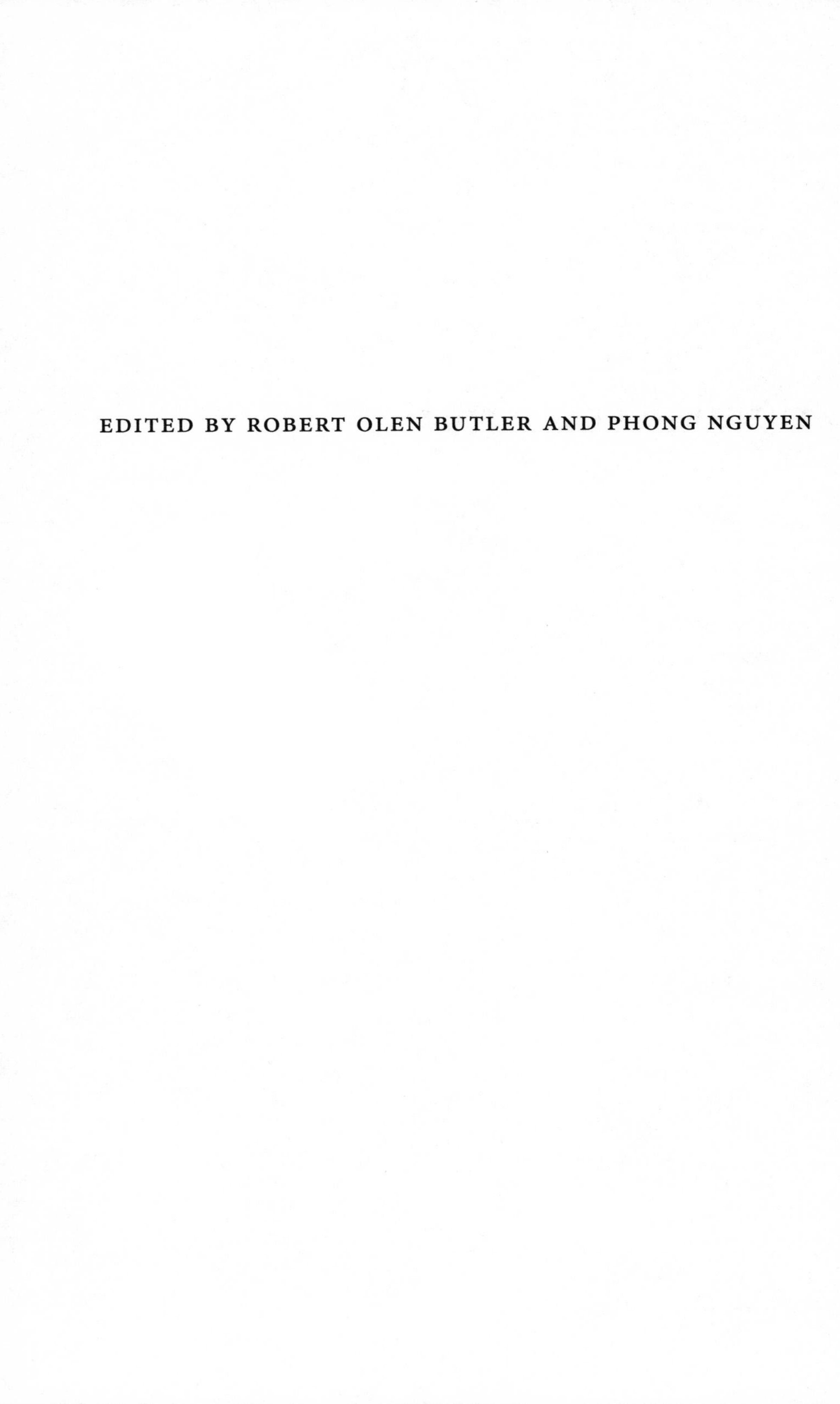

EDITED BY ROBERT OLEN BUTLER AND PHONG NGUYEN

THE BEST PEACE FICTION

A Social Justice Anthology

University of New Mexico Press Albuquerque

ISBN 978-0-8263-6303-9 (paper)
ISBN 978-0-8263-6304-6 (e-book)

Library of Congress Control Number: 2021937825

Founded in 1889, the University of New Mexico sits on the traditional homelands of the Pueblo of Sandia. The original peoples of New Mexico—Pueblo, Navajo, and Apache—since time immemorial have deep connections to the land and have made significant contributions to the broader community statewide. We honor the land itself and those who remain stewards of this land throughout the generations and also acknowledge our committed relationship to Indigenous peoples.
We gratefully recognize our history.

Designed by Mindy Basinger Hill

Composed in 10.2 x 14.5 point Minion Pro
and Masqualero Stencil

CONTENTS

INTRODUCTION

In an interview with Alexander Weinstein for *Pleiades: Literature in Context*, George Saunders said that "a story is an oomph-making machine, or it's nothing at all." That measure for a story's success—*Does it have the power to move the reader?*—is one that I adhere to as a writer and editor, and one that the selection team applied meticulously when narrowing down the submissions for our guest editor, Robert Olen Butler. But we needed to be moved in a particular way: toward empathy, toward awareness, and toward humanity. Especially the latter. In *Creative Quest*, Questlove wrote that effective creative endeavors demonstrate "proof of life." At the core, we need to know that our art is not manufactured by, say, artificial intelligence, but that it is the actual product of one human appealing to another, whether directly or over a span of time and space.

It is no surprise that humans appealing to one another would tell stories, and it is no surprise that they would tell stories about war and strife. But what is fascinating and unexpected are the manifold stories we tell about the periphery of war, the aftermath of war, the war-raging-within-a-self-or-a-society—the unstable "peace" that we live in day to day, which we know to be built on a foundation of luck and privilege. Americans, in particular, have lived so long with the paradox of being outside the war zone themselves yet, as participants in a democracy, being complicit in war-making throughout the world, that we have become immune to its depiction. In screen media, violence is inherently aestheticized, and we live at a comfortable remove from the horrific events playing out before us. Therefore, we need a different approach in order to become aware of our peculiar place in the global scheme.

"Peace" is a slippery, sometimes oily, term. Like any vast abstraction, it can conjure up associations with soaring oratory, much of which is utilized to manipulate. It is particularly hollow in the mouths of politicians (of all alignments), priests (of all faiths), and gurus (of all persuasions). Yet there is no better word in the English language for all-that-is-not-war. In this anthology, "peace fiction" means stories that are close enough to the fire to singe but not catch—depicting those moments when war is on our minds or in our hearts, not inflicted upon our bodies. It means: not a war story or an antiwar story, but a story that reveals the ripples of war that move over the surface of all our lives.

This conception of "peace fiction" is not naïve. It is not a utopian project. This anthology modestly poses whether literature has any role in furthering the ongoing pursuit of peace. If such a thing is possible, it requires the imaginative energies of creators to realize a future capable of great empathy. At its best, literature provides us with both the model and the means for achieving it. These fourteen stories are the most successful recent examples of such stories. Published in 2018 to 2019, they represent the current wave of fiction that looks outward and *observes* the world, rather than looking inward and repeating what we've already seen before.

We hope this anthology will be the first in a series of biennial anthologies that will have a different guest editor each time. Forty semifinalists were selected by me and interns at the University of Missouri, based on open submissions and the copious reading of published literary journals. These included individual journals with emphases in social justice and/or diversity, such as the Asian American issue of *The Massachusetts Review*, and the journal *Obsidian*, which is devoted entirely to works by authors of the African diaspora. These were then passed on to guest editor Robert Olen Butler, who selected fourteen stories for inclusion in the anthology.

We still have work to do to represent the true diversity of today's working writers. Future entries into the *Best Peace Fiction* anthology will prioritize and center our diverse population of authors, hopefully including works that highlight issues that came to the fore since 2020: the BLM movement, Indigenous rights, anti-Asian and anti-Muslim violence, and other issues that impact minoritized groups.

Literary journals are well represented in these pages: *Kenyon Review* has two stories in these pages. *Ploughshares* has four (!). The rest have appeared in *Bellevue Literary Review*, *The Massachusetts Review*, *Iowa Review*, *The Missouri Review*, *Obsidian*, *London Magazine*, or *Witness*. One story was selected from the story collection *All the Names They Used for God* by Anjali Sachdeva.

In "Coffins for Kids!" Wendy Rawlings's uses defamiliarization to reflect the absurdity of our twenty-first-century reality, where school shootings are a common, even weekly occurrence and where second-amendment activists rationalize the massacre of children by leveling blame at everyone but the firearms manufacturers. It approaches peace from the uneasy position of living in a violent society where war is an undeclared ethos.

"All the Names for God" by Anjali Sachdeva examines how the chaos of war swallows civilians and noncombatants and is inherently violent toward the innocent. The only peace to be achieved here is through the cathartic and fantastical exercise of dominance of will over the oppressor.

"Down to the Levant" by Joshua Idaszak conveys the texture of wartime in the periphery. "Ada, After the Bomb" by Alicia Upano looks at the periphery of war in the long view—throughout the mid- to late-twentieth century. Miranda Gold's "A Small Dark Quiet" explores the intricacies of grief and possibilities of hope in the aftermath of war. In Denis Wong's "The Resurrection of Ma Jun," the plight of ethnic and religious minorities in China is depicted as a state of perpetual war. Camille F. Forbes reveals what a tautology "war and peace" can be for slaves on a plantation during the Civil War.

Dan Pope's "Bon Voyage, Charlie" gets into how integrity can be compromised by the distortions of truth that war requires. In "A Woman with a Torch," Mark Powell explores the psychic violence of our contemporary moment, despite the persistent illusion of peace; and whereas "L'homme blessé" by Ron Rash shows the ambiguous legacy of war's victors, "The Man on the Beach" by Josie Sigler Sibara examines the legacy and inheritance of war's losing side, of history's villains.

"Letters Arrive from the Dead" by Rachel Kadish takes a haunting and lyrical approach to its subject matter. It tells the story of what lingers on in the aftermath. "The Blue River Hotel" by Stephen Henighan takes up the possibility of romantic love in wartime. Finally, "The White Spot" by Jonathan Blum registers the complexity of familial love in a time of strife.

I would venture to guess that none of the stories included in this anthology were written merely to provoke, but their provocation is valuable. Being driven to action is a literary effect. The literary cosmos isn't merely divided into *mirror* stories (reflecting our lives as lived) and *window* stories (giving us access to exotic and distant vistas); there are *water* stories too, which soak the reader in their brine and involve us deeply as participants in the narrative. Like the best stories out there, these fourteen pieces are not consigned to a "single effect," as Poe strived to evoke, but to a "multiple effect": they cause us to feel, to think, and hopefully, to muster the will to act.

PHONG NGUYEN, *editor*

THE BEST PEACE FICTION

Wendy Rawlings

COFFINS FOR KIDS!

The gunman didn't like redheads. Someone told Naomi afterward. The gunman didn't like redheads, okay, but he liked, I don't know, what? Blasting the brains of seven-year-olds across a wall map of the United States made out of construction paper?

Spraying bullets at kids shoving coats inside lockers? Maybe he just didn't like maps of the United States. Maybe he had something against lockers. When he was a child, had he cut the heads off rodents? That was a thing, wasn't it? An indicator of something gone wrong, early on? Naomi remembered her own childhood, stealing Mallomars from her mother's stash, learning to masturbate using Barbie's legs, shoplifting a lipstick from Macy's. Maybe she wasn't the numero uno best child in America, either. But growing up to blow away a bunch of second graders with a semiautomatic weapon? Picking off redheads?

Oh, and he also didn't like girls. So Emily'd had two strikes against her. If only Naomi had birthed a brown-eyed boy, now she and Rick and the brown-eyed boy could leave New England forever, go live in New Mexico and grow edible cacti, reinvent themselves, get perma-tans. But no. Now Emily, with her wrong gender, wrong hair, was in the market for a coffin: *Hey Mom, could you get me a nice box to be buried in? All the other kids have one!* Rick had suggested cremation, but what parent puts her kid in an oven? Not a half-Jewish parent, that's for sure. So a nice box it would be.

She Googled *children's coffins*. Up came an image of a tattooed guy wearing a safety mask and doing something with a blowtorch. Asterisked beside the photo were the words *Free Consultation with Master Craftsman Brock Hunnicut. We Send Your Little Angel to Heaven "In Style*. Naomi lingered on the site, scrolling down to a photo of the guy with his wife. His dark beard reached nearly to his shirt pocket. Why had he put "In Style" in quotes? Maybe that was a trademarked phrase. The "Custom Casket" gallery showed coffins made to look like trains, like boats, like surfboards, like zebras. One had a Teenage Mutant Ninja Turtle's face on the lid; another had butterflies painted on it; another was camouflage with a deer's head on top and, attached to the side, a child-sized rifle. The sight of a firearm made Naomi gasp; she hadn't seen anything even resembling a gun since the Thursday Glen Belson decided he didn't like redheads.

The deer's-head coffin could ship in twenty-four to thirty-six hours.

She wondered if Brock Hunnicut took American Express.

When Naomi was thirteen, her favorite cousin had died of leukemia. Watching her father and her uncle weep openly at the funeral, Naomi swore she would never have kids. Instead she would have birds. Maybe a dog. She liked lizards. But when she was thirty-six, Rick convinced her to "take the goalie out," as he put it, and half a year later she was pregnant. That a child could die of leukemia had made Naomi an atheist. Who was crazy enough to believe in a God who was a total shithead? But Emily's death, and the deaths of her classmates Paul and Eleanor and Eleanor (all parents these days, it seemed, named their kids Eleanor), made Naomi reevaluate her atheism. A gunman wearing chain mail shooting up a third grade class? That could only mean a God did exist, and He was a total jerk. And why hadn't anyone stopped a guy wearing freaking chain mail from entering a third grade classroom?

"We thought he was doing a presentation on the Middle Ages," the principal told her and the other bereaved parents. Miss Oslansky wore polyester sheath dresses in primary colors with birds printed on them. Always birds. Once Rick had remarked that Miss Oslansky looked like she'd been extruded from a School-Principal-Making Machine. "We always do a unit on the Middle Ages," she said forlornly. "One is on the Black Death."

"A unit on the Black Death," Naomi repeated. She and the mothers of the Eleanors stared at each other's shoes. One of them looked as if she'd taken about nine different sedatives. The other bit at her fingernails so vehemently she drew blood. Why did little kids need to learn about the Black Death? Why couldn't they learn about something cheerful, like—well, like what? Science had its cheerful topics—ladybugs and the eradication of disease and whatnot—but history was a toughie. The Inquisition, the Holocaust, Hiroshima, the Nixon presidency. Slim pickings in the cheerfulness department. But if the curriculum was the Middle Ages, what about knights and nobles? Were knights and nobles cheerful? Knights wore chain mail, and chain mail brought her back to Glen the Gunman. Glen the Gunman had worn his chain mail as if for the battlefield, and his enemies were redheads and girls. His enemies were kids who still wet their beds (that ammonia smell wafting from her *SpongeBob SquarePants* sheets), and sucked their thumbs, and refused for months on end to eat anything but mashed potatoes and chocolate milk. Even if God was a total jerk, how could he set up such a one-sided matchup? Gunman versus Bed Wetters! Heavily Armed Adult against Thumb-Suckers! Why couldn't jerk-face God direct Glen the Gunman to the middle of Kabul, where he could go head-to-blown-off-head with a suicide bomber?

Naomi thought about killing herself. *I kill me*, she whispered as she watered Emily's African violet. But first, she would order a coffin for Emily. The obvious choice would be *SpongeBob SquarePants*, though Emily had also been fond for a while of a TV show called *Pajanimals* that featured animals learning valuable lessons by traveling to whimsical lands. She had especially liked a character named Cowbella, a miniature pink cow who always seemed to be wearing the same pair of purple pajamas. But that had been when Emily was much littler. Hadn't it? Was it possible for a seven-year-old to have a period in her life when she was "much littler"? Naomi felt a burp of panic rise up in her. Soon she would forget what her daughter liked to eat, how her voice sounded, how her peed-on sheets smelled. That was why she had to kill herself. If she didn't go to heaven, she would just end up in a coffin underground right next to Emily, and the two of them could rot together. But if she, in her atheist cynicism, had been wrong all along, she and Emily would meet up at the Holy Gates or wherever the crossroads of heaven were, wear gossamer robes or whatever angels wore, eat manna tacos from some Nirvanian food truck, bed down on a cloud.

Naomi could braid Emily's red hair and make sure she learned about cheerful events in history, like *Brown v. Board of Education* and the Obama presidency. They could grow old together, or whatever you grew in heaven. Maybe you just grew wiser, and Emily could stay seven forever.

The coffin-maker had an 800 number. Good job: it wasn't something clever like 1-80-DEADKID. The grief counselor had told her she might struggle with a sense of unreality at times. At times? The grief counselor had told her to try to anticipate what might trigger feelings of grief. What wouldn't? "Grief produces a wide range of responses. Everyone expresses grief in his or her own fashion," the counselor said. "Really?" Naomi wanted to ask. Wouldn't uncontrollable weeping and suicidal ideation be pretty common ways? What were the others? Did some grievers go out and play a few rounds of golf? Drink a Mai Tai and watch the sun set? Go to Best Buy and price laptops?

“Would you be okay if I . . . weren’t around?” she asked Rick over almond butter on rice cakes for dinner. Neither of them had the presence of mind to cook, and they were between casserole deliveries from friends.

“If you went on . . . vacation?” Rick asked. In the context of Emily’s death, the word seemed obscene, like eating dog meat in front of dogs.

“Sort of. More like a retreat.” Naomi pictured her Hawaiian shirt turned into a noose. A nice New Mexico vista before she drove off the cliff.

“I could manage for a little while.”

“Okay, cool.” She tried to bring up the custom coffin thing, but the words clogged her throat. Certain things you should never have to say.

A woman answered the phone. “How can we help?” she asked. Naomi remembered a photo on the website of a woman with her hair dyed partly pink. The “family liaison.”

“I need a coffin,” Naomi heard herself say. “For my kid.” Immediately she felt she sounded too definite, too businesslike. *I should be crying*, she thought. *I should be keening, rending garments.*

“Honey, how soon do you need it?” the woman said gently.

“No giant rush,” Naomi said. “We were part of that school massacre . . .” She trailed off, unsure what to say next.

“Which one?”

Which one? Had more than one lunatic mowed down bed wetters and thumb-suckers this week? Naomi hadn’t been watching the news; Rick had thrown a towel over the television, and she hadn’t summoned the energy to remove it.

“Utah or New Hampshire? Or was it Vermont?”

“Utah?” Naomi asked. Didn’t they love kids in Utah? Didn’t Utah have a law requiring you to have kids? “New Hampshire,” she said.

“I’m deeply sorry for your loss. He was the one in chain mail, wasn’t he? Not the Darth Vader.”

“Not Darth Vader,” Naomi said. “He was the other one.” *Death is not the worst of evils.* That’s what General John Stark wrote after *Live Free or Die* to his comrades celebrating the anniversary of the Battle of Bennington. He had a cold or something and couldn’t go. Naomi had learned that in her seventh grade unit on the American Revolution. But you know what? Death actually was the worst of evils. Not your own death—nope, that wasn’t such a big song-and-dance. The worst of evils was your little girl’s brains sprayed across the construction-paper poster of the United States by some nut wearing chain mail and carrying his own personal arsenal into Plymouth Elementary School. The worst of evils was Wayne LaPierre crawling out of whatever swamp he lived in to decry the tragedy of "gun-free zones" (i.e., elementary schools).

The woman on the phone introduced herself as Jillian and said she would take down some information about the child's "final resting place." "How old was your little angel?" she asked.

Naomi felt a zap in her gut, like she'd swallowed a live wasp.

"Emily was seven." Seven years and three months and eleven days and four hours.

"And what sort of theme are we thinking about?"

It could be anything, Naomi told herself. You can get a life-sized statue of Wayne LaPierre with his head shot off and his eyes poked out, roaches crawling out his eye sockets, each roach with a little speaker attached to its back that played the words *mea culpa* over and over again. Wait, his head couldn't be shot off, because that might be seen as condoning gun violence. Maybe a double-life-sized statue of Emily slicing his head off with a sword. That would be effective. All the news media in the entire world would cover the funeral. But Jesus, that would be exploiting the memory of her dead daughter. What the hell was wrong with her? What was she even thinking?

"I was thinking maybe Cowbella."

"We do Cowbella," Jillian said. "We can do her with her buddies or without. Do you want the whole crew? Squacky, the whole nine yards?"

"Definitely Squacky."

"Maybe they could be singing 'Sleeping Makes Me Feel All Right.' Though it's a little extra for the audio."

"I'll spring for it," Naomi said.

* * *

"I'm gonna go pick up the coffin," she told Rick. They were eating another casserole.

"You want me to come along?"

"I'll just whiz over and get it. Be back before you know." She didn't tell him it was in Texas, 2,038 miles away. She didn't tell him the coffin theme was *Pajanimals*. She didn't tell him on the way she might take a sunset detour off a cliff.

The next day, she loaded up a Styrofoam cooler with kombucha tea and a lot of cheese. Since the massacre, cheese had given her more comfort than she would have imagined cheese capable of. Those French were onto something. Maybe if the chain-mail guy and Wayne LaPierre got to eat more brie. . . . Of course, Wayne LaPierre hadn't himself committed a gun massacre, but in his activist zeal he seemed like kind of an advocate for gun massacres. All this enthusiasm over assault weapons was kind of unseemly, like a Christian showing up at Bergen-Belsen and saying, "What a great facility."

Plymouth, New Hampshire, was 549 miles from the National Rifle Association headquarters. Naomi could do that distance in less than a workday. Not everyone knows that located beside the NRA HQ in Fairfax, Virginia, is a wheelchair-accessible shooting range open to the public. Fifteen shooting booths. More than nine million bullets had been fired at the facility. Did people in wheelchairs actually come to shoot AK-47s at paper targets? She could go talk to that square-headed LaPierre himself, shove Emily's blood-and-brain-spattered denim jumper in his face. Maybe she should get herself a gun to bring in—*Naomi, Get Your Gun!*—and scare the bejeezus out of everyone. Maybe she could dress in chain mail. Who knows, maybe they would welcome her if she showed herself to be one of them, a gun-totin' mama with attitude!

At a Cracker Barrel on I-95, Naomi wandered through the shop with its Mason jars full of gumballs, its Moon Pies and horehound drops in paper sacks (did anyone actually *buy* horehound drops in paper sacks?), its vintage bicycles and hacksaws hung from the ceiling. If Emily were here she'd want the lollipop shaped like a giant mustache. Naomi had refused, once, to buy it for her. How could she have forbidden her daughter the simple pleasure of a mustache lollipop? A wave of such rage and self-recrimination washed over her that she had to dig her fingernails into her palms to prevent an urge to crack a jar full of gumballs against her skull. *Go eat eggs*, she told herself.

She ate eggs. She played the triangular peg puzzle with the golf tees that sat next to the napkin dispenser. Emily had loved the peg puzzle. Why hadn't she bought Emily four hundred peg puzzles, four hundred mustache lollipops? And was that what grieving the death of a child in a consumer society came down to, hating yourself for all the crap you'd refused to buy your kid when she was alive and noodging you?

Fairfax was still four hours away. The FAQs page proved informative. Yes! Gift cards in any denomination could be purchased. No! No on-site instructors were available to provide firearm instruction, though the answer to this FAQ mentioned, helpfully, that a bulletin board with contact information for private instructors was available. Naomi could get lessons in firearm use right in the belly of the beast, inside the Holy Temple of the Right to Shoot Children at School itself! The facility was open seven days a week. Some FAQs she didn't even understand: *Does the NRA Range have someone to zero my rifle?* She was willing to bet that zeroing a gun didn't mean rendering it unable to shoot. Nope. It meant making sure the gun shot dead-center. You wouldn't want the aim to be off, though in the case of Glen the Gunman at Plymouth Elementary that didn't much matter, as he sprayed the room indiscriminately. A gunsmith could help you zero your rifle, but a gunsmith couldn't do anything about getting a hand or a handle on your gunman.

Gunmen, it turned out, run in any direction they want.

In the Cracker Barrel parking lot, she stretched her hips and drank kombucha, then turned on the radio and listened to a public station out of Philadelphia. The Quakers built their first meetinghouse in 1685. Those kooky Quakers with their beliefs that God resided in everyone and therefore you shouldn't commit violence because basically that was God you were socking in the nuts. Maybe being an atheist was too nihilistically lazy. Maybe she should become a Quaker. Could a Quaker learn to shoot at the NRA Range and then blow Wayne LaPierre's brains against the wall with the sign on it that reads NRA: EXPLORE THE POSSIBILITIES? What were the possibilities to which that sign referred? Did Emily's untimely death at ten in the morning, right after she finished playing "Do You Hear What I Hear?" and put away her recorder, count as a possibility to explore?

As she neared Fairfax, Naomi began to think maybe she should pick up the coffin first, then go to the shooting range. Maybe she could lug the coffin in there to show them her custom Cowbella. How heavy could a seven-year-old's casket be? She felt herself chickening, a word she and Emily and Rick had invented to refer to that shrinking feeling when you were about to bail on a plan. No, bringing the coffin would be too histrionic; it would get her thrown out. Better to go undercover. She would be the puffy-eyed warrior, the de-motherified mother of none learning to wield a gun.

The range was weirdly hidden under the parking deck, like a survivalist's bunker. Naomi paused in front of a large emblem of an eagle squatting on crossed rifles atop a badge printed with a United States flag. Could eagles actually squat? Maybe it was preparing to take flight, the crossed rifles gripped in its yellow talons. Maybe it was headed off to the suburbs to deliver some more firearms to psychotic personality types, angry white trigger-happy boys with Confederate flag collections.

The door opened onto a pristine lobby with a curved counter and glass display cases full of boxes of bullets bright as Good & Plentys and Mike and Ikes. A sylphlike blonde in something like a hacking jacket greeted her.

"I was hoping to see the range," she said.

"Are you looking to shoot?" the Sylph asked.

"Eventually. I was thinking I'd start by looking and then finish up with shooting. Shooting would be the finale," she said stupidly. "If I could borrow a gun."

"We don't lend. You didn't bring yours?"

"Mine's in the shop." Naomi offered what she hoped was a beseeching look. "You sell them? I could buy one, like, just a little one to tide me over." Till it comes back from the shop, good as new like a Subaru tune-up.

"You have to bring your own," the Sylph said. "Those are the rules."

So the NRA had rules. It wasn't the Wild West out here in Fairfax; you couldn't just show up and expect them to equip you with a firearm. Gunland had its own laws, no exceptions, not even if your kid had been blasted to eternity by a heavily armed kook!

"I just kind of wanted to see the place," she said. "It's been a dream of mine. I drove here from New Hampshire."

"Well, you should've said! It's quiet today—I'll give you a tour." The Sylph stepped from behind the counter. She wore black pumps with extraordinarily high heels, so she towered over Naomi in sneakers.

The. Sylph's name was Tina. The Sylph liked to shoot. The Sylph had been working for the NRA for nine years.

"Did you ever shoot anyone?" Naomi asked.

"I only shoot to kill," Tina said, which Naomi took to mean no.

They walked into a fluorescent-lit room with numbered booths separated by Plexiglas walls the size of doors, each one like a bathroom stall open at the back. Only one booth was occupied, by a man Naomi could only think of as furry. He wore safety glasses and blue earphones, and his bearded face looked more bearlike than human. With an enormous rifle he was blasting the crap out of a blue drawing of a person on a paper target. When they stepped into his peripheral vision, he stopped and took off his earphones. "Ladies," he said.

"What'd that guy ever do to you?" Tina asked. Both she and Furry laughed.

"That's Obummer," Furry said, and the two of them laughed again.

"I voted for Obama," Naomi said. "Twice."

"Sorry," Furry said, and Naomi knew he meant he was sorry she voted for Obama twice, not sorry for insulting her. This had all been a mistake. Her motives hadn't been clear. What had she thought she'd do, choose some random gun supporters and unload her grief on them? Use Emily to try to guilt-trip them into locking up all the guns and throwing away the key?

"My daughter was killed by a school shooter," she blurted. It was the only bullet she had.

The three of them stood looking at the pockmarked paper target.

"Well, that's a hellacious situation, and I'm very sorry to hear it." Furry put out his hand and grasped Naomi's arm for a moment. *That is an arm that just shot a gun*, Naomi thought.

"We all need to protect ourselves," Tina said, in a voice Naomi recognized as an NRA spokesperson voice, a commercial voice-over voice, a don't-you-dare-argue-with-me voice.

Protect ourselves? Naomi thought. She felt herself riding over the lip of sanity and into something uncontained: an ocean of toxic junk, a vat of dismembered body parts, a galaxy of creosote and ash. What had she neglected to do in the protection department? Get a pint-sized bulletproof vest for her kid? Tuck a hand grenade in her lunchbox? Hire bodyguards to follow her from art to gym? Why hadn't she thought of any of these things before Emily had her brains blown out? How could a mother be so negligent? Here she had been coaching her daughter on the intricacies of Common Core Math when she should have been teaching her how to dodge a bullet. Or a hail of bullets.

How did one dodge a hail of bullets?

For a long moment, Naomi pictured herself collapsing on the highly polished floor, making her messy grief the NRA's problem. Furry and the Sylph would kneel awkwardly beside her, and she'd let her tears and snot dribble onto their capable arms, those arms that were so good at aiming and shooting, loading and reloading. The Sylph would get her a Sprite while Furry stroked the side of her head. They weren't bad people, these gun-lovers, these rifle associators, these keepers and bearers of arms. They had just confused the importance of one kind of arms for another. From Naomi they would come to understand the nature of their confusion, would come to see how much more important than firearms human arms were—human arms with tattoos of anchors and nudes on them, and wiry black hairs, and warts, and blemishes, and carcinomas from too much tanning, and scars from cutting and suicide attempts. Once Naomi made them understand, all those arms wouldn't want to aim guns at anyone.

Those arms would lay down their arms and learn to knit. Or juggle. Furry laid a hand on Naomi's forearm. "What I would suggest for you," he said, "is the Glock 26. People call it the Baby Glock. It's subcompact."

The Sylph nodded. "It's not the most attractive, but you can't beat it for reliability."

Naomi gave her companions a close look. They wore twin expressions of concern. Even though a gun had killed her kid, and guns would continue to kill kids, these folks weren't joking; Furry and the Sylph wanted to give her good gun-buying advice. In the universe they inhabited, it was hellacious that her kid had been blown away, but they, like good Americans, were looking toward the future, when she might not be anyone's mother ever again but could protect herself with a Baby Glock—not attractive, not warm or affectionate, but reliable. *A reliable baby.* What more could you ask for?

Anjali Sachdeva

ALL THE NAMES FOR GOD

Abike stands in the doorway of my room and says, "I want to see my parents. Will you come with me?"

I don't answer at first. I meet her gaze in the mirror but keep wrapping my skirt. Abike's parents have moved to Abuja. My family is also in Abuja now. She knows this. Though I have called them and written letters, I haven't seen my family since Abike and I were captured, eight years ago, when we were just sixteen. She knows this also. It is not a small favor to ask. I finish dressing.

"All right," I say.

We hitchhike for two days, take a bus once we reach Karu. On Friday, at dusk, when the National Mosque is just lighting up against the sky, we arrive in the city. I haven't been to Abuja since I was a child, maybe nine or ten years old, when I came here on a weekend trip with my parents. I peer from the window of the bus at the towering buildings, the sheer volume of people.

"Let's have a night out," I say. "We'll do our visiting tomorrow."

"Sure," says Abike. Her relief tells in her shoulders. "Where do we start?"

We start at the Hilton. We are still in our country clothes, the same worn clothes we garden and market and fetch water in, and small ridges of dried mud fall from our shoes onto the polished floor of the lobby as we enter.

"Do you want to do it, or should I?" Abike asks.

"As you like."

She nods and heads to the reception desk. The man working the counter is wearing a black suit and a crisp white shirt and has the haughtiness so common among people who serve the rich for a living, as if they are superior just from being near other people's money. From across the room he has been scowling at us, with our dirty, rumpled clothes, but when Abike approaches and leans toward him, he becomes nervous.

"We'd like to check in," she says in English. "The name is Okonkwo."

He searches the computer for a moment. "I'm sorry, madam. I don't see anything under that name for tonight."

Abike frowns. "What kind of service is this? We've had reservations for months."

The man taps at the keyboard weakly. "No, I'm very sorry."

"Well, don't you have anything? Is the hotel full?"

"We have some rooms on the ninth floor with two queen beds."

"That's fine. But we're very upset. You should let us have it for free."

A family of white tourists has stepped into line behind us, a fat mother and father and two skinny teenage girls wearing torn jeans and pouts. The receptionist shifts uncomfortably from foot to foot and looks away, but Abike snaps her fingers and he turns back to her. One of the teenagers giggles, but the man shows no sign that he's heard her. He is eyeing Abike as though she is a dog and he is a cornered rat.

I've seen this face many times before, on many men. This man is used to difficult people, rich people, demanding foreigners. He is used to coolly and politely declining unreasonable requests, but this time he finds he can't do it. He looks as though he would like to cry. Abike taps her finger slowly against the stone counter and for a moment even I believe I can hear the click of manicured nails, though I'm looking at the blunt tips of her fingers. She's very good.

"I can't," he pleads. "I'm not allowed to give rooms for free."

"Really?" Abike's displeasure rolls out in waves. She sets one fingertip lightly on the cuff of his suit and he flinches. Another employee comes to ask him a question, but he doesn't seem to hear her.

"We would really like that room," Abike says, and she lets the silence accumulate between the two of them like a growing weight.

"Well, it's our mistake," the man says at last. He puts two key cards in a paper sleeve and hands them to Abike.

"Thank you," she says. She smiles at him and he smiles back idiotically. His relief is overwhelming him; he's so grateful that he has been able to give her what she wants. He nods his head eagerly and she turns to me and picks up her duffel. The tourist family stares at us as if we are museum exhibits, and Abike's eyes are laughing as we head to the elevator.

◆ ◆ ◆

Abike and I weren't close before we were kidnapped, but we come from the same village. She was the kind of girl who could be your best friend one minute and ridicule you without mercy the next. She thought she was special because she had cousins in Chicago who sent her tattered American magazines with articles about sex, and because during our lunch break at school she always put on more makeup than anyone's mother would allow and rolled up her uniform skirt until her thighs showed. So, of course, all the boys looked at her like she was a goddess when we sat outside, and somehow the teachers never caught her at it. Away from school she was always prim and proper. If she passed my family in the street, she would say in her prissy English, "Hello, Mrs. Layeni, Mr. Layeni. I hope you are well," and when she had gone my mother would say, "See? What a fine girl she is. So polite."

We were at church when the soldiers came, a group of us helping the Sunday school teacher get ready for her class. Abike was setting the bibles on the desks. My phone chimed, and I saw it was a text from my mother, who knew I was in Sunday school, who knew I was not even supposed to be looking at my phone. The message said, "Come home now." As I was staring at it, the phone began to ring, and then the door crashed open.

At first we thought the men were government soldiers, that it was some kind of emergency and we were going to be evacuated. Then one of them walked up to Mrs. Adeyemi and shot her in the face. We all screamed and tried to run, but there was another man blocking the door. The soldier who had shot our teacher looked at her body on the floor and kicked it.

"That's what you get for poisoning these girls' minds," he said.

I thought, *Why is he talking to her when she's already dead?* I had thoughts like that the whole day, very rational thoughts, like my brain was trying to throw weight on the other side of a scale against all the madness that was happening around me.

The men told us to go outside. We found trucks waiting, filled with girls our age and with more soldiers. The men took our phones and any money we had. They pointed with their guns and said, "Get in."

We rode for hours while the daylight faded into dusk, onto smaller and smaller roads, until we were moving through the forest. You could hear night birds and monkeys all around, calling to each other.

My friend Naomi was next to me and said, "We should jump out now, Promise. They might not even notice. We could hide in the leaves and they'd never find us in the dark." I nodded, but neither of us jumped. I had never been anywhere this remote, and the wildness of the place terrified me. If I had known what the next few years would be like, I would have jumped even if I could see a lion waiting in the shadows, but back then I was still hoping we would get to go home. Abike was in the same truck with us, crying and sniffling until finally one of the men said, "Shut up back there," and she was quiet. Later she told me she thought we would all be killed, that they would douse us in gasoline and set us on fire. I don't know where she got that idea. We had never heard of any such thing happening to anyone. But in a way she was not wrong; parts of us would be burned away forever.

* * *

Our room at the Hilton overlooks the pool, its cool-blue water undulating against the stifling blackness of the surrounding night. We take showers and ransack the minibar. Abike pulls a red dress and a pair of high heels from her duffel and starts steaming the dress with the iron. My dress is black and stretched too tight to wrinkle. We share a lipstick and look at ourselves in the mirror.

"My mother would shit herself," says Abike at last.

"Let's go," I say.

We walk down the street until we find a disco, packed with tourists and the girls who flock to tourists. We dance for an hour and then go to the bar to cool down. There are two girls chatting up some white men, Americans or maybe Brits. The girls have their long hair blown straight and look like they've been injecting themselves with some chemical to make their skin lighter. They pass a cigarette back and forth between them.

I stand too close to the nearest man. He looks up, surprised, but when I tap the bar with my finger he smiles at me and asks if I'd like a drink. I tell him I would. The party girls scowl. They can't understand how these men can even be looking at us, with our dark skin and our close-cropped hair. I smile at them; it's a look women anywhere recognize from other women, a dangerous shark look. They shrink back against each other and sullenly sip their drinks. Abike gulps a shot of vodka and orders another. I turn to the man beside me.

"Give me some money," I say.

"What?"

"Money," I say louder.

"You want another drink?"

"No." I hold his gaze and breathe deeply. The noise of the club disappears. The angry stares of the party girls dissolve at the edge of my vision. All I can see is this man, and all he can see is me. "Not for a drink. Not for anything. Just give it to me."

He doesn't reply, but he fumbles in his pocket, takes some bills, and presses them into my hand. I slip them into my purse without looking and blink. The music roars back to life. The party girls are gone, and Abike is sliding from her barstool, saying something I can't hear and pulling me toward the ladies' room.

The next morning, we get dressed to see our mothers. Abike has a green-and-yellow dress. The smell of our house is still lingering in the folds of the cotton; she pulls it over her head and begins to wind her *gele* around her temples while I put on my own dress, red and blue. We pleat our geles and pin them so we are crowned just so. Again we look at each other in the mirror. Abike nods. Already I'm beginning to feel uncomfortable. When we look like this it's too easy to see those girls we were—young, happy, helpless. These are the clothes our mothers would have dressed us in for holidays if we had finished growing up with them. We would have found them old-fashioned and complained that we wanted Western dresses. But now that we can dress as we please, we are more determined than ever to meet our parents in costumes they will find acceptable, to look something like the women they would have wanted us to grow into.

We go to Abike's parents' apartment first. Unlike me, she has visited before, so she has some idea of what to expect. We stand in the lobby of their building and she stares at the elevator doors with an expression I can't read. At last I reach out and push the button to go up. "There are worse things," I tell her, and she laughs and steps into the elevator. When she is gone, I go outside and get in a taxi to find my own family's place.

* * *

The first day after we were kidnapped, we stayed in the forest, and the men made us pray all day long. They did not give us food, and only enough water to keep our tongues moving. Their camp had a tall post that showed which direction Mecca was in, and we had to kneel facing it while a man named Bashir shouted out all the names they used for God and commanded us to repeat them: *the Compassionate, the Merciful, the Controller, the Strong, the Abaser, the Avenger, the Forgiver* . . . Ninety-nine words that were foreign and clumsy in our mouths. While we prayed, Bashir paced back and forth. If he thought someone was not saying the words correctly or not paying attention, he hit her with a stick or shouted in her face until she cried. We were so afraid of him then, as if being shouted at was something to fear.

Then we began to learn the long list of things that were haram, forbidden. Praying to Jesus: haram. Uncovering your head: haram. Laughing: haram. Whispering to the other girls: haram. Looking a man directly in the eyes: haram. Unless he told you to, and then: halal, permitted. Unless he didn't like the way you looked at him, and then, of course, you had to be punished.

They had a lot of punishments. If they were feeling lazy they would just slap you, or threaten to kill you. They would threaten to kill you for anything—too much spice in the food you had cooked, not keeping the camp clean enough, not smiling enough or smiling too much. But that was just when they couldn't be bothered to try harder. There was one girl who offered herself to one of the soldiers, thinking he would protect her. So he enjoyed her, but then he pulled her out into the middle of the camp, still naked, and shouted for the other men to come and witness what a brazen whore she was. They took turns beating her until you could not even recognize her face. She died three days later. And things like this happened all the time—to girls who tried to run, girls who were "defiant" or "shameless." After a while, you put your effort into learning not to see them while you looked right at them, into singing songs in your head so you didn't hear them scream.

Still, we thought someone would come for us. There were stories—girls ransomed by their parents, negotiated for by the government. Even if we wouldn't admit it to one another, we still had hope that there was a way out. And then, one night, we woke to hear the men shouting. There were torches moving in the darkness, the sound of gunfire. The next thing I knew, I was being pulled to my feet, dragged out of the tent where we slept. Abike was beside me, and I saw her grabbed by another man, his arm around her throat, a gun in his free hand. The men looked crazed; they were yelling and cursing at us to move faster, and all around girls were crying and asking what was going on. The men half pushed, half dragged us to the edge of camp, and there I saw what I had been wanting to see for the past four months: a line of soldiers in government uniforms, their guns pointed at the camp, shouting at the men who held us to drop their weapons. Except the men did not listen, and you could see that the government soldiers were panicked. The man holding me began to fire at the soldiers, his arm like a bar across my throat, holding me in front of him, and I struggled but could not get loose. In front of me the soldiers were dying, their chests and heads bursting, and soon any who were left turned and retreated, and the men in the camp shouted after them, triumphant. At last, the man holding me let me go.

It had probably been only five minutes since I was asleep, but I felt as if the shooting had been going on all night. I was half-deaf from the gunfire and I fell to the ground crying, trying to get my breath back, but the man who had held me pushed me with the toe of his boot and said, "Start moving those bodies. There. Pile them together." So I did. Because I knew they would not hesitate to kill anyone who displeased them that night. Abike and I worked together, grabbing legs, arms, dragging the bodies to the pile. One of them wasn't even dead, though he was bleeding plenty. He watched us and said nothing, his eyes moving slowly in his face. Probably he was hoping the same thing we had always hoped: that if he just stayed quiet, they would overlook him, and he would find a way out. But it was dawn, and all around us the forest was getting lighter. We knew in the morning the men would set the bodies on fire.

At last, they let us rest. I sat on the ground, my head against my knees, and Abike sat a little distance off. We couldn't even look at each other. My hands and arms were sticky with blood, my clothes soaked with it. The flies would not leave me be, but I was too tired to chase them away. Someone sat next to me and I lifted my head long enough to see that it was one of the men, the one named Karim. I knew I shouldn't disrespect him by ignoring him, but in that moment I didn't care; even if I died for it, all I wanted was to be left alone. I could hear him breathing, under the buzz of the flies. Then he put his hand on the back of my head. "Promise," he said.

They didn't often call us by our names. I hadn't even realized he knew my name. He patted my head in a way I imagine was supposed to be comforting, but it made me feel unclean to have him touching me at all. I flicked my eyes up past the tops of my knees and I could see Abike, watching us but not directly, her whole body tense.

"Did you not have any Muslim friends in your village?" he said to me.

I nodded, barely moving my head. It seemed like a trick question. They never asked us about our villages. In fact, my best friend had been a Muslim girl named Fatima. She was as shy as a dormouse, but we always understood each other. Sometimes on Saturdays we would ride in the back of my uncle's truck to the nearest town and walk through the market together holding hands, and half a day would pass where we would not say anything and be perfectly content.

Karim moved closer and looked at me earnestly. "Then you know what life you could have," he said. "You're upset, but if we hadn't killed those soldiers, do you know what they would have done? They would have killed all of us and taken you back to your village."

Yes, I thought. In that moment, I could imagine my village more clearly than I had in months: the smell of the incense in church, the passing breeze of the fan as I sat behind my desk at school, the taste of Abike's lipstick when she let me borrow it, of *akara* straight from my mother's frying pan. *Yes, they would have done that.*

"And then you would never have come to understand how great Allah is, and your soul would be lost. So these men had to die. Allah wouldn't allow it to be any other way. Don't cry."

I nodded my head again at this, but I hid my face in my knees and cried harder. Thinking about home, even for those few seconds, had torn apart some shell I had gathered around me over the months since our capture. Usually I didn't let myself imagine it. It was only some place I had known in another life, and might see again if I lived long enough.

A moment later Karim shoved me forward so that I went sprawling onto my face. "You're a stupid girl," he said. "All of you, stupid girls. Your crying only shows how ungrateful you are."

After that, we stopped waiting for anyone to come for us.

Several weeks after the government soldiers attacked, the men decided that our camp was too vulnerable; they split us up and took us to different towns. Before we left, most of us were married off—myself to Karim, Abike to Bashir—standing in the middle of camp while a man with a long white beard recited the same ceremony again and again.

Do I even need to say that we were raped? The only question was whether you were raped before or after being married. The men thought they had been saints for waiting a few months to "reeducate" us before posing this question; this proved to them that they were not just bandits but true followers of Allah. If you refused to convert and be married—you could refuse—then you were an infidel whore and they could do as they liked with you. If you were married, then of course you could not refuse your husband, or you couldn't expect him to care if you did. It was a choice of being raped by one man or many, not a very difficult choice.

I never saw most of the girls again, but Abike and I went to the same small village in Borno State. Our husbands were boyhood friends, our houses next door to each other. We frequently ate together, the four of us, Abike and I sitting silently while Bashir and Karim laughed and joked with each other.

One day, Abike called me to her house to eat lunch with her. Our husbands liked this, when we did normal wifely things, inviting friends over for lunch. It made them feel like maybe we were normal wives, like we had chosen them, rather than being forced to marry them. They were eager to believe this. For their own sakes, they should have been more eager to see the truth: that we despised them.

Bashir came into the room. "Husband," Abike said, "please sit down with us." He sat down and she smiled at him and looked into his eyes. She began tapping her hand on the table, gradually slowing her pace. At first I thought she was going to say something, but she didn't, just kept staring at Bashir. Her hand was resting on the handle of the teakettle but she didn't pour any tea. Her husband shifted in his seat, as though he had sat down on something that prickled, but then he was still again. After a long time, Abike said, "You should lie down on the bed and say the names of God a hundred times. Say them very slowly, and don't miss any. Promise and I are going to sit outside."

Bashir blinked and nodded. He got up and walked to the bed and lay down facing the wall, and we heard him start to say the names of Allah. I just stared at him for a long time. I was so shocked I could barely breathe. I didn't know any word for what she had done to him, but I could see that she had done it. "Come," she said, and she led me to the door and out into the sunshine.

◆ ◆ ◆

The young man who opens the door to my parents' apartment raises his eyebrows at me and moves more solidly into the doorframe, as though he expects me to push past him. For a moment, I think I've got the wrong address. In the past four years, in the many letters and phone calls I've exchanged with her, my mother has asked me dozens of times to come home. I've made any number of excuses about why I couldn't, and now I wonder if, when I've finally worked up the courage, they've moved somewhere else and neglected to tell me.

But over the man's shoulder, I can see a table and on it a blue-and-pink bowl of fruit, the same bowl my mother has had my entire life. I look at the man again and realize this is my brother, George. The last time I saw him he was eleven years old, scrawny and missing a tooth. Now he is nineteen, heavily muscled in his arms and chest, wearing a Che Guevara T-shirt and knockoff designer jeans. He leans against the doorjamb and says, "You looking for my parents? They're not home."

My hand flutters against my chest. "Promise. It's Promise," I say, though my throat is so tight I can barely speak.

Still, he stares at me for a second before he says, "Oh. Oh, you?" He hugs me tightly, lets go again, and takes my hand. "Come inside."

He walks into the room and there's a carelessness in the way he moves, a looseness in the joints. I realize he's drunk. He sits on the sofa and looks up at me without a trace of nerves, gestures vaguely at the other chairs in the room. I sit in one and he takes an orange from the bowl on the table and begins to peel it.

"So, you decided to come and see us."

"I felt like it was time." He nods as though this makes perfect sense, though it doesn't, even to me. "Where are Mom and Dad?"

"I don't know, I was sleeping when they left. Probably just at the store or something. Want a drink?"

"Sure."

He goes to the kitchen and comes back with two glasses, then to his bedroom for a bottle of Scotch. We clink glasses and throw the liquor back. I try to remember what I know about this grown-up George, what my mother has told me. He was supposed to be at the university this fall but couldn't be for some reason. He's been working somewhere instead—a restaurant? A copy shop? A week ago I could have told you, but right now my mind is blank. I don't know what to make of this man, how to connect him to anything I know about my brother. Whatever I expected coming home to be like, it was not this, my brother watching me with nonchalant amusement while we get drunk in the middle of the day.

Behind me there is muted conversation from the hallway, the click of the lock as the door opens. Before I can turn around, I hear my mother's voice, sharp, saying, "George, I have told you for the last time, keep your dirty girls out of my house." She walks quickly toward me and as I turn to face her, she is shoving a bag of groceries into my father's arms. Whether she was planning to strike this "dirty girl" or just shove her into the hallway I never find out, because when she sees my face, she says, "*Chei!*" and claps her hand over her mouth. Her eyes fill with tears and instead of trying to embrace me, she staggers back a step, for which, I find, I am grateful. I don't know how to put my arms around her; I need that little distance. I try to smile at her but I can't; I only want to weep. I say, "Hello, Mama, hello, Dad," and my father hugs me hard against his side with the groceries still cradled in one arm.

* * *

Without Abike's help, I would never have been able to go home. She taught me what she knew, that way of controlling a man for which I had no name.

"How did you learn it?" I asked.

"Do you know Onyeka, that woman who lives at the edge of the village?"

I nodded. Onyeka was a prostitute. Not that anyone said it, but she walked through town with her head uncovered, wearing makeup, laughing too loud. She touched all the men in ways we wouldn't dare. I often saw her in the market, but of course we were not supposed to talk to her.

"She can do it," Abike said. "She taught me. I thought she was just boasting. But it works. How else could she go around like she does in a place like this?"

"But why were you talking to her anyway?" I said.

Abike looked away. She nodded her head silently, as though replying to some other question I couldn't hear. Finally, she said, "I went to ask her how to get rid of a baby. Anyway, I'll teach you. How to do both."

So she tried to explain it to me. She said to start with simple things: make a man scratch his nose, or look away. Things he won't question, things he might do anyway. But for months I felt nothing, like I was just staring at Karim, and I worried all the time that he would ask me what the hell I thought I was looking at.

"It's like anything else," Abike said. "You have to practice."

So I kept trying. And after a while, I began to understand. It felt like reaching out with your hands in a dark room, feeling for something you knew was there but could not see, except the room you were reaching into was another person. After a year, if I concentrated, I could sometimes persuade Karim that he wanted to go out instead of staying home, that he was too tired to touch me when he lay down next to me at night. If I said I wanted to visit with Abike, he didn't object anymore, even if it was time for me to cook his supper or wash the clothes.

Abike and I started to spend more time together, to take longer and longer walks around the village, but we got too bold. One day, we were sitting in the kitchen drinking our tea when the door slammed open and my husband walked in. Abike grasped my leg beneath the table, but her face remained calm. She smiled at him and welcomed him and asked if he would have some tea with us. He pushed past her into the back room where Bashir was lying in bed and said, "Bashir, get up." Bashir didn't move, just kept talking quietly to himself. Abike and I stood behind Karim, huddled together.

"He's praying, you shouldn't disturb him. He tells me never to bother him when he is praying," Abike said, but Karim shook Bashir roughly by the shoulder.

"Get up!" he said. Then he turned and struck Abike hard across the face so that she fell to the floor. "You damned witch," he said in English, and I thought, *Yes, that is the word. That is what we are.* He took me by the arm and shook me. "You, too? You think you'll turn me mindless like you've done with him? This man is like a brother to me, and what have you bitches done to him?" He shook me harder. I screamed and wept but all the time I was thinking, *Just look at me. Just look at my eyes for one moment and I'll end this all.* Abike didn't make any sound and I was afraid for her; I wondered if he had killed her. He grabbed me by the chin and said, "Stop crying and answer me."

I looked at him, reached out into his eyes, deep, deep into him until I could feel the center of him, and what I found there I squeezed and crushed. I was too frightened to be subtle. He let go of me, but I leaned toward him, kept his eyes. "Go sit on the bed with Bashir," I said, and he staggered backward until he found the mattress. "Help him say the names of God." I went back to Abike. She was sitting up now. She looked up at me and smiled and her front tooth was cracked.

"We have to go," I said.

"We're taking them with us," she said. "You know what kind of evil they'll get up to if we leave them alone." She gathered all the money from my house and hers, and we took our husbands by the hands and walked out of the village.

We went to a new town, a place where no one knew us and big enough that no one had time to care who we were. We got a house where we could live together, mobile phones, new clothes. I could have called my parents right then. I hadn't spoken to them in three years and I knew they must wonder what had happened to me, even wonder if I was still alive.

And I know what you're thinking, what anyone would think: *Why didn't you run straight home?* The truth was that we couldn't bear to see anyone we knew, knowing the things we had done. We had killed babies and soldiers, had watched as girls wrapped themselves with bombs to go to the market where they would murder people like our mothers and fathers, and we did nothing to stop them. We had spat and screamed at the other girls in camp when they looked for comfort, had blasphemed, lied, spoken against everything we once believed in. We might have sold our own siblings to gain our freedom if someone had given us the chance. We had nights where we did not fight back the little bit we could have, where we did not even say, "Please, no," and where we imagined a new life that went something like this: Go along, praise Allah, have clean clothes and enough to eat, raise some militant's baby like any other woman raising a baby, forget about how it all started. When these things have never happened to you, you think, *I would rather die*. But the truth is that it is not so easy to decide to die. And when, suddenly, you have the option to live again, that is not so easy either.

◆ ◆ ◆

When my parents are finished crying, my mother cooks supper for me, all the recipes I haven't tasted since I was sixteen. I stand in the kitchen with her and chop vegetables while my father and George watch football in the next room. I know she doesn't need my help, but I don't know what to say to her and it feels good to have something to occupy my hands. As we work, she talks about George, raising her voice now and then when she wants to make sure he hears her.

"He's too busy for school," she says. "Busy drinking and chasing girls. You remember, he was such a good boy, and what happened? He's wasting his life."

"It's mine to waste," he says from the living room, and from the grim tone of his voice I can tell this is a fight they've already had many times, one where the heat of the argument has given way to simmering resentment. My father tells him to be quiet and my mother hands me an onion for the chopping board.

She makes enough food for a dozen people, and when she has it all on the table, my father claps his hands and breathes deeply before he says grace. He always did this, but I'd forgotten about it until just now. George and I would roll our eyes at each other just before we folded our hands to pray. I look at my brother and he meets my eye and, for a moment, he smiles, the same mischievous smile he had at eleven, and I can see him just as he was, as though no time has passed. My father thanks God for bringing me back to their house, and my mother squeezes my hand in hers as though she could knit our flesh together.

After we eat, my mother says, "I'll get some sheets. You can sleep on the sofa."

"I have a hotel room."

"No," she says. "You have to sleep here. What kind of mother lets her daughter sleep alone at a hotel?"

The cushions of the sofa are too soft, the night too full of city sounds. I lie awake, still dressed, listening to my parents' breathing in the next room for perhaps an hour before a wedge of yellow light spills into the hall from George's bedroom. He steps softly into the living room and stands looking down at me.

"You awake?"

"Yes."

"Want to get out of here? Have some fun?"

"Sure."

"All right, come on." He holds out his hand to help me up from the couch and I'm surprised all over again by the strength and size of him. When I'm standing, he looks me up and down and says, "Do you have something else to wear? Something less . . . you know?"

"Yes."

"Good," he says. "I don't want people to think I brought my aunt to a party."

"Shut up," I tell him, but I'm smiling in the darkness.

From outside I text Abike: *Need a break? Going to a party, meet me there.* I ask George for the address and send it to her, then we hail a cab and head out across the city.

The party is in a basement apartment in the far western suburbs. A few lamps with pink shades cast a dim light over the main room, where people are packed tight together and dancing. George disappears into the kitchen to get us drinks. I look around for Abike but don't see her. The people here are anywhere from eighteen to thirty, college students and office workers and new arrivals who've come to give the big city a try. They all look impossibly young to me. George presses a bottle of beer into my hand and says something I can't hear. Soon he is dancing with a girl in a low-cut dress, leaving me to my own devices. I retreat to the kitchen, where a man smiles at me and asks me where I'm from.

"Near Matazu," I reply, though the village where George and I grew up feels like it's several lifetimes away. I tell myself, *It's not that hard. It's just talking. Just talk to him.* But it's been a long time since I talked to a man for fun. I take a deep gulp of my beer and let the alcohol relax me, and soon we are chatting, like normal people. Others join us and an hour goes by before I go to look for

George, and I finally spot him on the far side of the living room, standing in a corner with Abike.

George is smiling but he looks dazed. He is staring down at Abike and opening his wallet. She stands with her hand out, smiling in a self-satisfied way, as George counts a pile of pink-and-blue bills into her palm. He stops and she taps the money with her finger, *more*, and he starts again. For a moment I stand where I am, unable to move, just watching them. Then I am across the room in three strides, shouldering my way through a throng of dancers and grabbing the money from her hand. "No," I say.

Abike laughs. "*Peche*, relax, don't we always share?"

I shove the money back into George's wallet and close his fingers around it. Abike looks at me like I have lost my mind, like she would be angry if she weren't so surprised. "No, no, it's George," I tell her. "It's my brother." What I want to say is, *He's different. He's not here to beat us or rape us or even lie to us. He's a good boy.* But he's not a boy anymore, and I can feel tears hot in my eyes and my fingers curling into fists, as though there were someone to strike.

Abike looks at the floor. "Sorry," she says, and she turns and walks away before either of us can say anything else.

George stands there blinking, clutching his wallet. "I think I've had too much to drink," he says. "Who knew it was possible?" He smiles his little-boy smile at me. "Is your friend here yet? We can come back later. Let's go get something to eat." He wraps his arm around my shoulders, and I let him lead me away.

By the time we return to my parents' apartment, the sky is turning from black to blue. George stumbles to his room and immediately falls into a heavy, snoring sleep, and I rush to the bathroom to change into my pajamas before my mother wakes up. But even when I've stuffed the black dress to the bottom of my duffel, I still feel anxious and dirty. I scrub my face and hands, but the smell of sweat and cigarette smoke sticks to my skin; the taste of stale beer lingers in my mouth. I can't sleep. When my mother comes out to make breakfast and finds me sitting on the sofa clutching my knees, she nods sadly and says, "You're ready to leave again."

"I'll come back," I tell her.

"I hope so."

I dress and get ready to go. My mother insists on doing my head wrap for me. I sit in front of the mirror and she smooths my hair back from my forehead and pulls the fabric of the gele around the back of my head so that she is holding the two long ends in front of me. In that cradle of cloth, my head suddenly feels lighter, my neck loose and limp. She wraps the fabric across my forehead and pins it in place while she gathers the rest into her hands.

"I wish I could come home for good," I say.

"We all wish that. You come whenever you're ready." She lays her hand against the back of my neck. Her skin is cool and soft against mine. She finishes pleating the gele and fans the folds carefully above my head. Then she takes a handkerchief from her pocket to wipe my face. "Don't cry," she says. "I'm proud of you. How many girls could survive what you have?"

As she says it, I wonder if it's true, if I have survived. Until today, I have never missed my old self, the self that could be abducted, bullied, raped, made to marry a man for whom I had no feelings but dread and hatred. I have rejoiced many times in the death of that girl, but now my mother looks at me in the mirror and I know that's who she is looking for. I can feel it in the way her eyes sweep across my face.

Abike and I ride home in the back of a millet truck. For most of the ride she is silent, but I can tell she is watching me when my eyes are closed. When we are almost home, she reaches out tentatively and takes my hand.

I press my thumb against hers. "I'm not angry at you. You didn't know," I say. We have reached our town, and I call for the driver to stop. Abike kisses my cheek. "I'm going to ride on to the market," she says. "I'll be home soon." I nod and don't look back as the truck pulls away.

The village is dusty and quiet. Stray dogs nap in the sun outside our house. When I go inside, Karim is at the stove, boiling water. He looks frightened when he sees me but tries to hide it. He pours two cups of tea and motions for me to sit down at the table.

"Go ahead," I say, and he sits across from me, resting his hands on the tabletop. The backs of his hands are dotted with the scars of old cigarette burns. For a while, this was something Abike and I liked to do. We could make him sit with his palms flat on the table while we pushed the lit end of the cigarette against his flesh. All his fear and pain would go across his face, but he wouldn't move his hands until we let him.

Now I look at Karim in a way I haven't looked at him in years, with no command in mind. For so long, he has been nothing to me but a curse I broke, a monster I hollowed out and made weak, but now it occurs to me how little I know about him: what his family is like, what he himself was like as a boy, how he came to be part of a band of ruthless men with guns. Whether he really believed in the Prophet or whether he just wanted three meals a day and something to do. His skin is bagged under the eyes, his hair patchy where he has worn it away with nervous scratching. He is only thirty-five years old. "Go and get Bashir," I tell him.

A few minutes later they return and sit side by side across the table from me.

"Bashir," I say, "my husband is going to divorce me. You are our witness. Karim, tell me that you are divorcing me."

He does it, without hesitation. To him this is no different from any other command, not freighted with meaning or emotion. He might as well be ordering food in a restaurant.

"Again," I tell him. "Again." And then it's over. He's not my husband anymore, he's just a man on the other side of a table. He sits quietly, watching me, waiting to hear what I'll say next. "I want you to leave. Go away from here," I tell him. "Never touch another woman as long as you live. If you do, you'll fall to your knees and never get up. Remember that." Even as I say it, I don't know if this is enough, if a man like this can ever be punished enough. But I am tired of being the one to punish him.

"Where do I go?" Karim says.

"Where do you want to go?"

He shrugs his shoulders weakly, but he doesn't look away. His gaze is the soft, searching gaze of a dog being scolded for a crime it doesn't understand. He waits for me to tell him what I want, what to do. What comes next.

And who knows the answer to that?

Joshua Idaszak

DOWN TO THE LEVANT

South of Van, Kamal switches off the headlights. Superstition, more than anything, but it makes me uneasy.

"Are there checkpoints this far north?" I ask.

He shrugs. "Possibly," he says.

It's supposed to be ten hours to Nusaybin, our destination, although that's in a bus, by day. Not by night, without headlights, on our way to kidnap his sister.

When I turn my head, I can see Lake Van fading from view, its surface gleaming in moonlight. *Who can be so lucky?* Mevlana asks. Who comes to a lake for water and sees the reflection of the moon?

I ran into Kamal by chance, outside the Migros in the center of Van. I had just returned from Munich and was on my way to buy drinking water for the first time in years. I had only met Kamal once, the night he arrived in Munich to visit his sister, when she still lived there, years ago. But Trifa talked about him sometimes, and so I felt, mistakenly or not, as though I knew him better than our brief acquaintance warranted.

He held a three-gallon drum of water in one hand and a black plastic grocery bag in the other, its handles stretched thin, lengthening. They ripped in front of me. Three bottles of Jack Daniel's hit the pavement. By some miracle, only one shattered.

I stooped beside him to help.

We stared at each other, the air around us pungent with spilt whiskey. He looked grim, eyes sunk into his skull, and when he turned away, I thought it was the reaction of a brother running into his sister's first lover. Stupid, I know. Trifa and Kamal were never close enough for her to tell him anything about us.

I said his name. It sounded rough, as though it no longer fit him, or as though, coming out of my mouth and not Trifa's, it didn't belong to him.

My greeting seemed to startle him, and he lost his balance. He grabbed my shoulder—to steady himself, I think—and I fell forward, bracing myself against the sidewalk. He offered a hand to help me up. When I reached for it, he pulled back. I looked and saw the gash. I pressed my thumb onto the wound to help staunch the bleeding, felt the throb of my quickened heartbeat as blood ran down my hand and spattered the bits of bottle on the sidewalk.

I accepted Kamal's offer to take me to his apartment and clean and dress my palm. I had spent my first two days back in Van staying on a friend's couch, and I did not want to show up bleeding and in need of additional aid. My parents did not know I had returned.

"How's Trifa?" I asked Kamal as we stood over his kitchen table, filling a plate with glass tweezed from my palm. I could see through the doorway that separated his kitchen from his windowless bedroom. A tangled heap of clothes and a half-packed duffel covered his bed.

"She's back," Kamal said. He seemed disturbed, and it struck me as odd that he would not welcome the news. As he worked on my hand, I tried to recall the nights I had spent with her in the years between Kamal's visit and her graduation, tried to picture her pressed against me in her apartment before she abandoned Munich and me for Heidelberg and a position in Germany's best hospital.

Kamal put the tweezers down, started dabbing at the dried blood streaking my arm with a damp washcloth. I wanted to ask him more about Trifa's arrival, but I was afraid of the questions he might ask me. Why had I returned? What would I do now? I could not go back to my parents until I figured out how to break the news—that I had been kicked out of Germany, that I had squandered the opportunity they had worked so hard to provide. I made my uncle promise not to call from Munich, not to tell my father they had taken away my residency permit for driving drunk and without a license. I told him I wanted the chance to explain it in person, and he agreed, admiring my honorable intentions. Now that I was back, I did not know how to start. The prospect of appearing unannounced was horrifying. What could I say? I had nothing to show for my time.

"Is she in Van?" I asked.

Kamal shook his head. "Nusaybin." He shrugged. "I think." He told me the rest of what he had heard.

As he spoke, I tried to layer this startling, new version of Trifa onto the old, to sift through my memory for clues that might explain how the student of medicine and poetry I knew could become a fighter. It seemed impossible.

"What am I supposed to do now?" Kamal asked. "What can I do with such news?"

When I didn't answer, he spoke again.

"I'm going to get her," he said. "I'm going to bring her home."

I took a step back to see what, if anything, his expression might betray. He had tried to bring Trifa home before, under different circumstances. I knew that much. I'd been Trifa's ally then, in Munich, if only out of selfishness, the need to keep near her. Now, I didn't know how I felt.

"Let me help," I said.

We left that night.

Kamal refuses to switch on the headlights and the car's speedometer is broken, so there's no way to judge our speed. I turn around in my seat to reach for one of the remaining bottles of whiskey.

"Wait," Kamal says, but I take a drink anyway, a long one, and think about pouring some onto my palm. It hurts. I can feel my hurried pulse pressed against the bandage, and when I look down at my hand I imagine I can see it glowing, giving off a faint light. *The wound is the place where light enters you*, Mevlana says. Trifa loved that line. I never understood it. But the words themselves were enough, to hear her speak them.

"For my hand," I say.

Kamal says nothing, stares ahead. The windshield is cracked and with the headlights off it's hard not to feel criminal, not to fear the ever-shifting checkpoints scattered across the highways here. The military has closed the border to stop Turkish Kurds from crossing into Syria to help Syrian Kurds fight or flee. Our ethnicity and destination implicate us. Why else would we be traveling so far south, if not to slip into the chaos just over the border?

It seems Trifa has been trapped in the same logic. Their cousin had called Kamal, told him he had seen her in Nusaybin, that she was involved.

"How can you be sure?" Kamal had asked. I imagined him straining to suppress his rising panic, embarrassed he was not the sort of brother she might have confided in, that he knew nothing more of her return to Turkey than this conjecture across a crackling cell connection.

"Why else would she be here?" his cousin answered. A wartime syllogism, his cousin's question crystallizing into fact in the lingering silence.

I try to imagine Trifa as a rebel, try to imagine her dressed in camouflage, or in black, hunched among a small circle of fighters in some abandoned courtyard. It doesn't fit the nurse I knew.

"Germany," Kamal says. "Now Syria." He pounds the steering wheel a few times with his fist, holds out his hand for the whiskey. I pass it to him. He struggles with the fullness of the bottle, putting it to his lips, motions for me to take the wheel while he drinks. He hands me the bottle next and I take a final drink before I cap it and put it in back. The road is mostly empty. I wonder if everyone out at this time of night has their own secret pushing them on. My hand pulses. When I close my eyes I can almost hear it. *What you seek is seeking you*, Mevlana says.

We pass into a curtain of rain, sudden and blinding. Kamal swears. Drunk now, warm and loose with whiskey, I'm not afraid. It doesn't seem much different than before, driving with the lights off on this empty piece of earth. We slow to a crawl.

"Use the wipers," I say.

"There are none," Kamal answers, face pressed toward the windshield, squinting into darkness.

I'm most hopeful, it seems, leaving places. That's how I met Trifa. She was next to me on my flight almost a decade ago from Istanbul to Munich. We couldn't believe we were both from Van. When she asked me why I was traveling to Germany, I said university.

"Which one?" she asked.

I opened my mouth but nothing came out. I could barely name a single university in Turkey, let alone Europe.

She laughed. "No," she said. "Really."

"To work at my uncle's döner shop."

"That's better," she said.

She was studying nursing at Munich University. Even then she hummed with purpose. Under the reading light in the darkened cabin, her hair looked either deep red, or black, or both. Loose strands had escaped from where she'd tied it. I knew immediately that I had to stay close to her in any way possible.

And I did.

I think she thought my clumsy lies were charming, that I was the kind of Kurd she wanted to help. She invited me to the meetings she organized with fellow Kurdish students at her university. They would discuss things that affected Kurds in Munich, and what was going on back in Turkey, and how they could help. She thought it would be good for me. I rarely went. I should have been ashamed, but I thought my helplessness was what I had going for me, that being a Kurd in Munich without friends was what drew her to me. It was as though she alone determined my presence. That if she ignored me, I would disappear.

The night Kamal arrived in Munich I came over to Trifa's apartment and got drunk with him on duty-free rakı. She had mentioned his visit the weekend before, when she stopped by the döner shop and asked me to meet him. "You'll like him," she said. "He doesn't know any German either." I wasn't sure who she pitied more—him or me—but I didn't care. I went to Trifa's as often as she would have me. She was the only person I knew in Munich other than my uncle, and I needed the time away from him. It was a lot, working beside him all day, going home with him at night to his apartment, where I slept on his couch. I could never escape his audible breathing—thick and wheezy at work, hacked in the quiet hours of the morning as he turned endlessly in his bed, the thin walls doing little to stifle his snores, his restlessness. It felt as though he was taking up all the air in my life.

The more we drank, the more Kamal talked about the rates he had seen at the airport currency exchanges. Even with higher rents, withheld wages, and whatever else Kurds here had to face, he would return rich. I let him talk, tried to seem as excited about everything as he did. Who was I to dispel his illusions? His glow reminded me of *my* first weeks in Europe, when I too imagined endless possibility. Besides, he might succeed where I had failed.

"Will you stay here?" I asked, when the rakı had sufficiently dulled the shame I felt in asking such a question. I was drunk enough to feel, wrongly or not, as though I could conceal my fear: that his presence would push me out of the space in Trifa's life I hoped to occupy.

Trifa laughed. Kamal blushed. Before he could respond, she spoke. "Look around," she said. "Do you think he could fit?"

She caught Kamal's eye and smiled, and Kamal looked away. I smiled too. I should have known what Trifa would say. It was written in the details of her life—what brought her to Munich, what drove her into nursing. She wielded space coldly, expertly. It kept her free.

"And tonight?" I asked.

Trifa laughed again, and Kamal mumbled something about a room nearby.

"Well," she said, slowly, as though the decision was difficult. "Maybe tonight." She looked at him. "But only tonight."

Kamal smiled weakly, and I recognized in him what I knew of myself. That he knew he would not make it here. That it was only a matter of time before he returned to Turkey, defeated. That all his talk stemmed from this unshakable awareness.

I stood up, relieved, and said good-bye. "I don't want to interrupt any more of your visit," I said when Kamal implored me to stay. Soon after I left he would be kicked out. He knew it, and I knew it, and that was all I needed.

Even when Kamal was in Munich, Trifa visited the döner shop most Saturdays. She sat behind the counter with me, watching Roj TV on my uncle's small television while I took orders from the men who floated in and out, exchanging Euro change in near silence. Some nights I dreamed of other men, the nameless men back home who formed and broke the crowds I now moved among, who turned people into vectors, who snatched days from bodies, men of epaulets and tactics, men with sour breath and wet wool coats and patent boots. The mathematicians of exile at their work. I awoke to the remainder. *Who are you?* I wanted to ask each. *Have you found what you were looking for?* They kept their eyes on the rotating lamb. Sometimes they glanced over at Trifa, wondering if I was lucky or just her brother. I was neither, until the day Kamal returned to Van. He had grown tired of sharing an overcrowded apartment with other newcomers, of sleeping on the floor, of having to pay for showers at the laundromat down the street. He was too proud to ever ask his younger sister about moving in after that first night, although after hearing Trifa I'm not so sure she would've let him. She seemed intent to retain control of her life, her space; needed to know she would always be able to move as she chose. Even then, she was expert at triage.

That night I was eager to hear how Trifa felt about Kamal's departure. I was excited to be in her apartment again without having to worry about him showing up unexpectedly and misreading the situation. We spent the night talking about Van. Trifa told me she missed it.

"You help me remember," she said. We were sitting side by side on her bed.

I started laughing. It seemed clear she was joking. When I saw she was serious, I tried to stop. She punched me in the arm.

"I'm going back," she said. "When I'm finished here, I'm going back."

“You’re a nurse,” I said. “When you’re finished here, you can go anywhere. Berlin. London. Istanbul, at the very least.”

“No,” she said, sitting up. She reached for her bag beside the bed, pulled out a slim book, leafed through it.

“What matters is how quickly you do what your soul directs,” she read. She looked up, with expectation and doubt, as though she might not have read it right.

I didn’t know what to say. I reached to touch her cheek, her hair. “That’s nice,” I said, resting my arm around her, waiting for her to move away, beginning to pull her uncertainly toward me when she didn’t.

She read another line.

“What is that?” I asked, more certain now.

“Mevlana,” she said, letting herself be pulled.

Kamal wakes me by pressing one of the whiskey bottles against my cheek. “Friend,” he says, moving the bottle under my nose. It smells poisonous. I take it from him, press my bandaged hand against my seat to sit up, inhale sharply from the pain. Kamal laughs, a gun on his lap. An old revolver, its handle held together by fraying duct tape. He sees me eyeing it and smiles.

“What’s that for?” I ask, after a sip.

“Protection,” Kamal says, his mouth twisting in a fearful grin. He reaches into the backseat, groping until he finds a packet of pastirma. “Are you hungry?” he asks, holding it out for me.

I take it. We haven’t eaten since we left Van, and the throb of my hand is now matched by something similar in my stomach.

“I wish there was bread,” Kamal says.

I nod, biting into the cured beef.

He laughs, gestures for the bottle. I pass it to him. He takes a long drink. He passes it back and I spill some on my shirt.

“Be careful,” he says, sliding the gun under his seat. “There’s only so much.”

He reaches into the back seat for more food, finds a chunk of cheese.

“We really need bread,” Kamal says, shaking his head.

We finish eating and pull back onto the highway. In the morning light the land looks pristine, but I know better. I’ve seen photos. The bullet-pocked walls of outposts, the scorched frames of vehicles. Strange, that some of the most beautiful, barren places are the most dangerous. As though their beauty could not exist without the added danger of a stray shot, highway bandits, a roadside blast stretching to meet the wrong bus. Unrest brings curfew to Diyarbakir. Thirteen Turkish soldiers die in a separatist ambush. Two women and a four-year-old are wounded in a roadside blast outside Siirt.

You have to be careful here.

The checkpoint appears suddenly. We've been driving all morning, mountains giving way to dry plains, country I have never seen before. *Forget safety*, Mevlana says. *Live where you fear to live.*

Kamal slows his approach until we are crawling, and we stop in front of a soldier, his finger on the trigger of the rifle clipped to his chest, his free hand outstretched, facing us. Kamal and the man eye each other. The soldier points with two fingers toward the side of the road. We pull over.

"Out," he says.

I leave the car, squinting in the sudden expanse of light, the earth rippling in a haze that confuses its details. Two more soldiers appear out of a khaki-colored tent beside the road, a man following in a dark suit. They lead Kamal away.

"Stay," the first soldier says, standing beside me, eyeing my bandage, as though waiting to tear it off, find whatever I am hiding beneath it.

A soldier returns from the tent, starts looking through the car. The soldier beside me lights a cigarette. *Who are you?* I want to ask. *Have you found what it is you're looking for out here?* I know, though, that he's the wrong man for this question. It's for the other soldier, moving through the back seat, the glove box, now reaching under the driver seat. He stretches purposefully into the car. I see him tense, and I know he's found the gun. What emotion is he living off, here, in the desert, on the side of the road, waiting for violence? He comes toward us, palming the revolver, a smile starting across his face. He tests its heft two or three times, brings it up to my face, boxes me with his free hand. He nods at the man beside me, who grips my arms and cinches them behind my back with plastic handcuffs. They lead me toward the tent.

Kamal is standing against the far wall, arms behind his back, his head covered with a hood. They shove me beside him. *Be alert*, I think. *Remember the details.* The man in the suit is conferring with the soldier who searched our car. I stare at his shoes, impossibly shiny for the desert. He gestures at Kamal. A soldier moves toward him, grabs him by his neck and drags him, stumbling, from the tent.

They cover my head with a hood. *I'm not a separatist*, I want to say. I'm hardly a Kurd; I have next to nothing in common with myself.

"Two Kurds," the man says. I feel his breath on my cheek through the cloth of the hood. His breath in my ear. "Traveling alone." It is not uncommon, two Kurds traveling on a highway in southern Turkey, but I know where he's leading with his questions. I wait for blows. "So," he says.

I start to speak and he boxes me, pain bursting in my ear, another blow landing solid on my jaw. I can feel the cut of my teeth, the warmth of the blood in my mouth, the inside of my cheek ragged when I tongue it.

He hits me again. When I fall he tells me to rise. Naïve to think this wasn't coming, this violence in this tent on this roadside. Men meeting the barren landscape the only way they know.

He feels my pockets roughly for my things. A lighter, some lira coins, my identity card. The objects, small and discreet, that explain my existence.

"What's this?"

His question curls into the blindness of my hood, and I know that what I've been waiting for, what has been inevitable since I entered the tent, is coming. He squeezes my bandaged hand and I feel a sharp pain leap up my arm into my body. *The cure for pain is in the pain*, Mevlana says, but I'm not thinking about that now, down on a knee, my cinched-together hands twisted in the grip of this man and his dustless suit.

I hear shots outside the tent, loud, as though they are exploding beside my ear. I strain for the sound of Kamal falling, hitting the ground, and wonder, whether the cracked earth would muffle the noise from the impact, or enhance it.

"He's an atheist," someone says.

"What?" the man asks. He shoves me forward and I fall onto my face.

"He must be."

The man yanks me up by my arm, asks if this is true.

"I like Mevlana," I say. One of the soldiers laughs.

Through the hood I smell something thick, and I realize that Kamal is back now, somewhere inside the tent with me.

"What's that smell?" the man asks, anger and disappointment in his voice.

"He shit himself," a soldier says. "When we fired the gun. We didn't even point it at him," he adds, as though attempting to head off some question not yet asked.

"Some rebels," someone says. Laughter, young and nervous, fills the tent. Relief: a threat neutralized. Nothing to do now but wait for the next one.

But the man does not laugh. He rips off my hood, pushes me by my face against the canvas wall, beside Kamal. The light from the entrance stings my eyes. He turns to Kamal.

"Where did you serve in the military?" he asks.

"Erzurum," Kamal says.

"You?" he asks.

"Erzurum," I say.

"Erzurum," the man repeats, as though testing the word for accuracy.

"Why the gun?" he asks.

"My sister has disappeared," Kamal says.

The man stares at him for what seems like forever. Time becomes details. The trickle of blood leaking from Kamal's ear down his neck, the man's spotless shoes, the reek of urine and sweat and shit and gun smoke. Finally the man speaks.

"Go," he says. "We will keep the gun."

Outside the tent a soldier cuts our hands free, throws our belongings in the sand. We stoop to pick them up.

The car is a furnace. Kamal turns the key and it comes to life and we edge out, slowly, onto the road. Figures shrink in the rearview mirror, where I find a cut above Kamal's left eye, swelling. Blood is seeping through my dirty bandage. The shit smell is unbearable.

As soon as the checkpoint is out of view Kamal pulls over, rummages through his pile of clothes in the backseat. Grabs a pair of pants, gets out of the car.

"When someone beats a rug, Mevlana says, the blows are not against the rug, but against the dust in it," I say through the open door.

"Fuck Mevlana," he says, bare-assed, shimmying into briefs and then a rumpled pair of jeans.

He gets back in, leaving his ruined pants on the side of the highway.

After Munich, Nusaybin looks like any other city in eastern Turkey. Gray brick streets, advertisements crowding the windows of mini-markets for Turkcell and Eker and Pepsi, swarms of power lines threatening to overwhelm crooked poles.

It takes two days to get Kamal's cousin on the phone. We sit in our hotel, waiting. When he finally returns Kamal's calls, he refuses to tell us his address. Reluctantly he agrees to see us, to meet us in an empty teahouse crouched on the edge of the desert, a humble structure tucked between abandoned cinderblock houses, the encroaching dust creeping through the crack under the front door. A rooster stands on a table by the entrance, clawing its rough surface. It eyes us as we move toward the back, turning in its stance to follow our path.

Kamal's cousin sits perched on the edge of his seat, as if poised at any moment to jump up, escape through the kitchen. He seems as cagey as the rooster. He and Kamal embrace, touch heads, temple to temple, and sit.

He eyes me, motions at the owner for three glasses of tea.

"I shouldn't be here," Kamal's cousin says. He has the same lean frame, the same slender nose as Kamal and Trifa. Unlike Kamal, he has an enormous mustache consuming his upper lip. It looks alive.

"I'm here," Kamal says, slowly, calmly, as though explaining something to a child, "because you called me."

Kamal's cousin watches the owner bring the tea, watches him return to the back room. He catches me staring.

"There's no one else here," I say.

"Who is this?" his cousin asks, nodding at me.

"My friend," Kamal says. "Trifa's too." He puts his hand on my knee, squeezes hard. I wonder at what might be behind the pressure.

His cousin reaches for his tea, knocks it over onto the wooden tabletop. Kamal nods at the glass in front of him, offering it.

"I saw her," his cousin says, taking Kamal's glass in both hands, sipping noisily.

"How is she?"

His cousin shrugs. "When I tried to talk to her, I was stopped." He raises his eyebrows.

"By who?" Kamal asks.

His cousin looks at his hands, pressed in front of him on the table. "A man," he says. He shifts, and creases deepen on his face. He opens his mouth as if to speak.

"Who?" Kamal asks.

"By a man who is not family. By a man with a gun. This is all I know."

"Why is this man protecting her?" Kamal asks. "Why does she need protection?"

"How would I know this?" his cousin asks. "I am not involved." He stares at Kamal. "Why aren't *you* protecting her?" he asks, pointing his finger at him. "She is alone here with strange men and you do nothing."

"Did you recognize him?" Kamal asks, ignoring the rebuke.

“Of course not,” his cousin says, standing, as though suddenly insulted. “I am not involved.”

“Tell me where she is.”

“On the street, in daylight, protected by strange men. I told you all I know.”

“Where can we find her?”

“By now,” he says, “who knows? Check the morgues, check the hospitals.” He drops some change on the table. “You should have never let her go to Europe,” he says. “You should have kept her home. Now, God knows what she thinks.” Standing, looking down at Kamal, his cousin looks admonishing, the gray streaks in his greasy hair adding a touch of authority.

They stare at each other, Kamal sitting calmly, as though attempting through stillness to will his cousin back down. “What do you think I’m trying to do?” Kamal asks, his voice uneven. He brings his hands down fiercely upon the table, upsetting the empty glasses.

“We knew she was gone when you came back from Munich alone,” his cousin says, almost wistfully. “Lost,” he says, with the air of an actor speaking his lines to an empty theater. “A younger sister shouldn’t dictate so much.”

“Help us find her,” Kamal says.

“There’s a fucking war going on,” his cousin says. “And I am not involved.”

We spend the evening wandering in and out of teahouses, hoping to overhear something about the fighting across the border. Each place is the same. Groups of unemployed men playing cards, loners staring vacantly at dirty television sets. I find myself trying to spot the undercover agents I assume are posted in each space, wonder what it is they are listening for, what it is we should be listening for. We order tea. Kamal puts his cigarettes on the table and glances around, waiting for someone to ask for one, to strike up a conversation. No one seems to register our presence.

“This is impossible,” Kamal says as we leave the last teahouse. In the car on the way down he had seemed sure of his plan, but here he seems lost, unsure where to begin, where to go.

The next day, we check hospitals, careful to avoid any police or soldiers stationed at each entrance. At every hospital, on every floor, each nurse seems to have a different list of patients. I search each tired stare for unspoken signs, hope to communicate wordlessly. *We are looking for one of you*, I want to say.

We check the refugee camp, edge past the gendarmerie at its gate. In front of tents, men sit or crouch beside open fires, boiling tea. Families stare out from unzipped entrances. The Trifa I knew from Munich would be here, I think, helping. *Where there is ruin*, Mevlana says, *there is hope for a treasure*.

We weave through row after row of the white Red Crescent tents, each indistinguishable from the next, wondering where to look as we look. I try to imagine how Trifa would feel about so many people displaced; try to understand how it might move her to pick up arms; try to see her as a fighter, crouched on a rooftop, her long fingers curled around a rifle barrel, scanning the street below.

We cover less ground the next day. It becomes harder for me to get out of bed. The throb of my hand has turned into a bodily ache. By the fourth morning in Nusaybin my legs won't work. I lie in bed, sweating, unable to rise.

"You go," I say.

Kamal looks at me, a mixture of helplessness and hate cross his face, and I know he will never find Trifa. Ours is a lost cause. He leaves. The pain is worse than ever. I'm convinced I'm dying. I close my eyes, my head pulsing with my heartbeat, red and anxious. I focus on each breath. I drift in and out. When dreams come, I can no longer tell what they are, whether I am in or out of the world. *Although you can see the pit, you cannot avoid it*, Mevlana says. It's something like that.

I awake in a new room, on a table, a damp sheet covering my body. Aside from a crooked standing lamp at the border of my vision, the room is empty. My hand lies at my side, unbandaged. In the faint glow it looks almost green, and I wonder if this is some sign of infection.

"You're awake." Her voice seems to emanate from the light. Trifa moves into my field of vision, into the glow. I close my eyes, hold them shut, and try to picture what I thought this moment would be like. When I open them, she is searching my face. "You're hurt," she says. Her words ring with a kind of practiced dispassion, like she doesn't want them to get too close, to be anything more than pure statement.

I want her to call me by my name.

"I want to fix your hand," she says instead. Against her touch it feels distant, not entirely mine.

"Trifa," I say. "What is this?"

"A hospital," she says. "My hospital," she adds after a moment, and the shadows on her face rearrange, and I can tell she is smiling.

"How did I get here?"

"The woman who cleans the rooms at the hotel," she says. "She brought you."

"Why?"

Trifa smiles. "She was worried you couldn't go to a state hospital. She thought you might be a fighter. You're Kurdish," she adds, after a moment. "That was enough." She turns my palm over, examines the back of my hand. "What are you doing in Nusaybin?"

"I heard you were here."

"You came from Munich?"

"From Van. We drove." I try to make a fist with my bad hand, but somewhere along the way the command dissolves in a loose and uncontrollable twitch.

"Who's with you?"

"Kamal. He thinks you're fighting," I say. "That you might blow yourself up."

"I'm a nurse."

In her tone I sense a kind of confusion, or perhaps disappointment in the fact that Kamal and I assumed the worst. That she, like those men in the tent, would only know one way, could only match emptiness with force. The false image of her on the rooftop returns to me, her fingers curled around her rifle barrel, and shame rises in me, a kind of regret that after my years of knowing her in Munich I still don't understand her, can't imagine her for who she is, who she has always been.

She turns my hand in hers, tests my wrist's rotation. "What happened?" she asks.

As I tell her, she moves her hands over my palm, rubbing it, I know, with some formula. Cleaning it. Efficiency in her touch, purposeful and direct. There can be no mistaking it, but I imagine something else, something useless and lazy, something like love. She takes out a scalpel, cuts away some skin. When I flinch, she frowns.

"Be still," she says.

"The wound is the place where light enters you," I say.

She stops. "You remember Mevlana?"

"You showed me."

She laughs.

"Do you?" I ask after a moment.

She turns her head. In her silence I understand her answer. I want to quote Mevlana on love, something about lovers being in each other all along, as the poet says, something to take her mind from this place, but I don't. She knows all the lines, has shared them with me. I close my eyes and let her finish. For the first time, the wound feels clean.

She stitches my palm, dabs it with gauze. "You can tell Kamal I'm not coming with you," I hear her say, feeling her firm grip as she wraps a bandage around my hand, but I'm not watching her or listening to her words. I'm picturing instead those moments in Munich: a rushed kiss in the stairwell of her building, her visits to the döner shop, the hope in her voice as she told me her plans.

"We were planning to kidnap you," I say. To my surprise, she laughs.

"And what about all the people who need me?"

A line slips into my mind. "A thousand half-loves must be forsaken to take one whole heart home."

Trifa smiles. "Okay, Mevlana." She squeezes my good hand. "You'll be better soon," she adds, but I already know that. Mevlana was wrong; the cure for the pain is not in the pain. The cure for the pain is in Trifa.

"You're leaving?" I ask, knowing she is, that she has to. Hating my body's uselessness. Longing to sit up, to delay her somehow.

"The half-loves," she says, moving toward the door.

Miranda Gold

A SMALL DARK QUIET

Had both of the twins made it out of the womb alive there wouldn't have been a name and a life going spare. The name was Arthur and the life waiting to be filled had been made in the shape of a proper little English man—a proper little English man and a proper little soldier.

MARCH 1945

Harry looked different in Mrs. Cohen's arms—he looked how a baby was meant to look. Sylvie's eyes turned from the tiny puckered face that had absorbed Mrs. Cohen's gaze, listening to the shush dusting the silence it kept. Just Harry's breath starting to slow now, slowing Sylvie's with it, an invisible cord winding her back to him again for the first time since he'd been born. She'd carried twin heartbeats, twin boys, but it was only Harry who came screaming his rude health into the world, slick with her loss. Harry and Arthur, tucked round each other, named the day Mrs. Cohen cracked the first egg of the year into the pan and proclaimed that a double yolk was a sign.

As Sylvie fell back onto the bed, two cold buds—one in her pelvis, one in her heart—tightened against the spring. The winter hadn't been as fierce this year, but, just as London's bones seemed to be beginning to thaw, Sylvie felt a second frost take hold.

Good boy, she mouthed in time with Mrs. Cohen, *such a good boy*, finding a stillness in repetition until a gulp of air shook the rhythm and Sylvie flinched back into her own skin. Mrs. Cohen's gentleness settling Harry filled the room, unlocking Sylvie's throat, hands, hips, letting her rock forward—

Such a good—

Her closing eyes opened at once by the pressure against the empty swell of her abdomen.

“Let’s put this little mite down now, shall we?” Mrs. Cohen said. Sylvie bent her head, sight glazed over her knees, the nod that was meant for Mrs. Cohen slipping unseen towards the floor. She pulled her chin in to her throat, sliding it hard across her clavicles as Harry’s cry began its crescendo—stop, it had to stop, before that cry unleashed her own.

When the bough breaks—

Sylvie followed Mrs. Cohen—

The cradle will—

Hearing herself aloud stopped her—was that her? It had been five days since her voice had been made to carry words. Five days that had left Sylvie behind in the body just split to the absence of Arthur, Harry’s collection of sticky limbs slapped against her, his chest fluttering with new breath and rich blood, but alien-cold without—

Arthur, she’d called out, *where are you taking my—*

Then bringing Harry home, passing the gashed city by—it was as though a mask had been dropped over her face, the air enough to choke her. She’d just wanted to get them into the house, cough London out of her lungs and breathe Harry in, breathe in whatever of Arthur might still be held in Harry’s skin—but, soon as she got inside, Harry’s head nuzzling between her neck and her shoulder, her throat closed. Couldn’t answer the door that evening, Mrs. Cohen’s knock—

Go away, couldn’t she just go away?

She’d sat with Mrs. Cohen most evenings from the day Gerald was called up till the day she’d gone into labour. Mrs. Cohen was always getting little extras for Sylvie; she’d known she was expecting before Sylvie did, reading Sylvie’s squeezed eyes and hands as fear that Gerald wouldn’t come back, rather than the fear that he would. The man who arrived home on leave never seemed to know her any more than she knew him—a little less of him returned each time, blotting out who each of them had been. She could almost hear Gerald’s voice in his first letters home, reminding her of the jugglers and tricksters that had sprung up in the dark that night they’d been caught in the crowd. The gathering roar of the city had seemed to melt under the sound of a flute rising and the voice of a flower girl calling—

Violets. Lovely sweet violets—

The flower girl had wished them luck, her hand tight round the florin Gerald had given her, and Sylvie had looked back but Gerald was already moving into the gauzy light streaming through an arch, beckoning for Sylvie to follow, their silhouettes thrown by a lantern swinging in the alley, those backstreets empty but for the boys playing marbles and a night porter's step—yes, of course—then what? Swallowed back up by the throng again, making it to the theatre just before the curtain went up and Sylvie humming the tune of the last song all the way to the river. They'd soon be having their walks by the river again, Gerald had said—she hadn't forgotten, had she, that evening over London Bridge? No, she hadn't forgotten—and for a moment the thought was enough to staunch the dread that crept up to the bedside each morning. But whatever echo of her husband she heard on the page was lost as soon as he came through the door: his eyes reaching past her, his few words, sharp and sudden, equal to silence. Somehow the odd tumbler knocked off the table or the box of records they'd collected kicked across the floor let her breathe, drawing the gasp that was just enough to cut the air thick with what was left unsaid. Gerald's mother had counselled Sylvie not to ask questions, to be attentive but not intrusive, bright but not loud. Articles snipped from magazines advised how best to placate the returning soldier—but Sylvie, just watching the clock tick until his leave was up, found herself bargaining with a God she'd never believed in to get her through each night without waking to the urgent burn of Gerald inside her.

"You're quite sure they're his?" Gerald's mother had asked, not waiting for a response. "Well, as long as they come out white."

Sylvie wasn't sure she wanted them to come out at all—until one didn't and then the want opened, widened, until it was all she was. Sleeplessness had made the days bleed into each other—it was only Mrs. Cohen's knock that struck an interval. Three times a day that knock, each hatching the same thought from collapsed time: if she slipped out just as Mrs. Cohen came in, left Harry there, found Arthur . . .

Good boy, such a—

"Sylvie dear!"

Mrs. Cohen, blurred by Sylvie's eyes, had taken her hand, insisting its warmth be accepted, careful not to sound anything but practical, crisp. *Only to bring a bite*, she'd said, quite sure Sylvie was managing just splendidly. But Mrs. Cohen couldn't do crisp, gliding down the hall, swiftly unpacking her string bag in the kitchen before going up to Harry, smiling as she lifted him from his cot.

"Precious little . . ."

Precious little—

Not without Arthur. She had to send Harry back into her body, find his brother, so that she could know them both. They'd taken her Arthur away before she'd held him but, dead or alive, her arms cradled the shape he might have taken.

Should count y'self lucky, the midwife had said when Sylvie asked where they'd taken her Arthur, *you've still got the one; war's taken all my boys.*

Lucky Sylvie. Well it could take her too. Let it have her. Be best for Harry if it took him as well. And Gerald. What had it all been for? Rushing for cover under a molten sky, the frantic hands of strangers dragging her down into the shelter, all only to wait for the same again. There was, of course, no interest in what would have been freely given. Aunt Cynthia had been right, should never have come to London—

London eats girls like you alive—

Others it might, Sylvie had thought, kissing Aunt Cynthia good-bye, but not her.

If only it had, swallowed her whole before she'd met Gerald and brought children into a world that wasn't made for children—is that what Arthur had understood? When the war had made a hell out of the skies and a pot-luck limbo out of the earth, the only heaven was underground.

Sylvie reached for her shoes, stretching them before she forced her feet in, Mrs. Cohen whispering as Sylvie got up—

"Are you alright, dear? Where are you going? Sylvie dear—"

Harry's cry, gathering force, was only steps away, but it felt distant, as though it was coming through the wireless. Mrs. Cohen was calling after her now—her coat, where had she put—never mind that, she'd do without it, only be a minute or two—

"Sylvie dear, the baby—"

Mrs. Cohen's voice only quickened Sylvie's step, legs taking her on: up Llanvanor, on to the Finchley Road, and into the park, not stopping until she reached the bandstand. She went a little further, paused by a branch of white buds nodding in the wind. She picked off a handful and scattered them, kneeled and pressed a cheek into the ground until a child's shout shook her into the cooling light. She didn't feel the rain begin to spit, only saw the first spots bleed into the petals that hadn't been turned and carried by the wind. That child's shout again. How long since she'd heard it? Weeks, maybe even months—certainly not since—but listen, yes—a laugh in it now too—a flurry of notes, high and light and clear. The wet petals seemed to be dissolving into the grass. *Wait for me!* the child called out, running, tripping, his hand on his tin hat. The image, unchanged, had become as familiar to her as the rhythm of the twins' kicks, appearing every time she felt her boys' insistent fists and feet. Queuing up at the grocer's the first time, digging around in her bag for the green ration book she'd been given. Never liked to get the book out, the way eyes would glance from the book to her belly pushing against the buttons of her coat, and then the comments, the advice, a look, distaste or concern or envy. Pregnancy had divested her of discretion and identity: a body to be prodded and measured by visiting midwives; an exhibit to be appraised and critiqued by the bored, the impatient, the wise. A woman in the queue had commented that Sylvie was *doing her bit* and gave her a wink. *One in the eye for Hitler*, she'd said. It must have been the closest she'd felt to patriotism—but it wasn't patriotism. She'd given an inward wink to each of the boys: *two in the eye*, she'd thought. No, that wasn't patriotism; it was her own dazzled sense of herself carrying two grand boys, inhabiting the body that had felt obscene and foreign moments before, making her native to the tiny world she was—and there, in that instant outside time, the only space was the shelter she gave and the shelter she took—but, just as she allowed herself to sink and settle, she found herself displaced: *not this world, it wasn't a world made for children.*

Remembering now how the boy in the tin hat had seemed to rush up to her and tug at her sleeve just as she felt Arthur test a foot inside her. *Be patient, Arthur!* she'd said, looking round to answer the tug, only to feel instead the relay of glances along the queue. *No telling with some*, came a mutter that encouraged others. Eyes down till she reached the counter, trying to make sense of the tug, verifying the identity of a foetal clench of fingers.

It had only ever been the one boy she'd seen, never two—and it was the same in that dream she had: pushing the pram up to the bandstand, the baby's face cut from glass shattered in a raid, the skin shredded and the face just a crying wound. Couldn't go back to sleep after that; just stood outside the room that would be for the boys, the blacked-out windows not letting her know how long it would be before the morning came to dim the fear of what she'd seen. She'd find a reason why she needed to go over to Mrs. Cohen's, always wishing she'd tidied herself up a bit. She'd spend as long as she could pretending to absorb herself in the patterns Mrs. Cohen had swapped, eyes caught by the needles crossing and clicking.

"You mustn't fret, Sylvie. A worried brow won't do the babies any good. Remember what Lord Woolton says?"

Lord Woolton's cheery lines on the wireless, parroted by everyone, never leave her head now:

Welcome Little Stranger.

Sylvie didn't mind it so much when Mrs. Cohen said it, but the click and cross of the needles kept catching her—no, no she would never do that—and it was only the blasts and the brawls and the throng of useless songs meant to drown out the sound of wasted lives—only that, not her. She'd known a girl who'd done it—only fifteen, could understand now how desperate she must have felt, how trapped. Everyone found out, whispering what a whore she was, some not even bothering to whisper at all. Terrible thing was it didn't even work. Local prophets cast the all-seeing eye: a girl born to a tart like that would come to no good. Aunt Cynthia had said they should pray for her. She was hidden away somewhere, which was probably for the best, some home for unmarried mothers. People didn't talk here like they did in Maldon, but they talked all the same. The little one must be six or seven by now. No, she wouldn't dare do it herself—she couldn't bring herself to. The girl seemed almost courageous to her in that moment. Was cowardice all that was stopping her? It was too late anyway.

Unbearable to think now that she might have wanted to get rid of them—how the sight of the needles had slid straight into the image of herself holding them between her legs, not even a breath as she stabbed—the violence of it so detached, so sudden. Thought so tangible it might be as brutal as the act itself—couldn't have been enough to take her Arthur, no of course not, ridiculous, smacked of the whispering gossipers back in Maldon. Yet the boys did seem to anticipate her fear before she felt it—their turning more restless, restless but weak—and she seemed to hear their jagged pulses—

Welcome little—

Would it have been love to have welcomed them into this? Into an ashen world that had to keep hoping because hope was all that was left?

Sylvie tried to pick the flecks of white still visible against the green, barely able to feel the grass beneath her—and there, for an instant, she felt as though she might have caught the flight of those high, clear notes. The sound drew her eyes up but the image of the boy in the tin hat wouldn't hold, his outlines dissolving, making him as far and unreal as he was—Arthur's laughing shadow. She looked over towards the gates and, securing a point of reference, saw again the automated steps she must have taken here—it was as though her legs had walked her away from the house. The sequence, returning to her in disordered fragments, resisted continuity until she could grasp how each action had given way to the next—leaving Harry in Mrs. Cohen's arms, down the stairs, out the door, and straight to the park, no intention or direction necessary—

No, not this world, this wasn't a world made for—

Cheek pressed against the ground again and closed eyes that wouldn't cry made her retrace her steps from Llanvanor—

Sylvie dear, you've left the door—Sylvie the—

Harry, she'd left—

Mrs. Cohen was lulling him as Sylvie came in, rocking from one foot to another, stopping as her eyes met Sylvie's, teeth pulling in her lip, "Oh Sylvie, your face," fingertips touching the cheek Sylvie had pressed into the ground.

"Gerald's mother will be round soon," Sylvie said, turning, "I need to get started on the washing."

"I'm right here if you need anything." Mrs. Cohen's hand opened towards Sylvie, a falling leaf for an instant suspended. "Do take care, Sylvie dear, do."

Sylvie dug her knuckles into her eyes, slapped her face, and went to the window to see Mrs. Cohen standing at the end of her front lawn, back to waiting for the post that would never come. Only the letters and parcels sent back. There must be some confusion, she used to tell Sylvie, the War Office mixed things up all the time. She'd waved the telegram at Sylvie three years after it was dated and asked her how they could make mistakes like this. Mrs. Cohen's husband had been taken from her before the war had even begun; the Lord, Mrs. Cohen was sure, would never let her son be taken from her as well. Her hand would float over the mantelpiece and she'd be wondering aloud how she would tell her boy what had happened to his father. She'd never have to now.

Sylvie closed the curtains and watched Harry's face scrunch and redden, touching it for traces of Arthur.

* * *

People would come to speak of two Londons: one gutted and one singing. Sylvie had found herself in each, straddled them, yet she struggled now to recall either. Dimly aware of the bodies trapped under rubble and talking to a woman, holding her hand until the stretcher came; of the jitterbug that had danced round her one night—yes, the ladies in the shelter had taught her, packed in as they were, and drafted her into their world. A gentleman had warned them not to excite a lady in her *condition*. The ladies' cheeks had pinched, laughter held in check until the gentleman's back was turned. Sylvie couldn't resist mimicking him, *to hell if he heard*, she'd said as the ladies covered their mouths and snuck glances in his direction, the ageless glee of midsummer fairies flushing their faces. *Oh you should be an actress*, one said. *No chance of that now*, another said, her eyes, mellowing, on Sylvie's belly—she had squeezed her hand then, holding it for a moment longer, pressing warmth into her palm as though it might be something Sylvie could carry with her.

But then, from Harry's birth to Arthur's death, the arc of life was crossed at once. Empty cradle had been twinned with empty grave and took all sense from the body she'd have to live in, from the city she was meant to call home.

The last all-clear wouldn't sound for another week and, while infant heads and hands and feet were blown from tiny bodies rendered nameless, Sylvie forged a tiny corpse of her own. Binding sticks and twigs, lined with moss and stuffed with stones, she wove her Arthur into deathless life and laid him in the ground, piling the warmth of the earth over him, planting him in a second womb. We'll visit, she promised, every Thursday.

Denis Wong

THE RESURRECTION OF MA JUN

Mother bends over Older Sister and hovers above Qian as if she is searching for a secret to keep from us: Father in his newly bought Li-Ning winter jacket and me, Little Brother, though I don't call myself Little Brother outside because my parents don't want to call more attention to us as a two-child household. It's good to be better than the people around you, but not too much better.

Mother's ear rests just below Qian's neck. Any minute now, Older Sister will rise up from the cot and shrug off Mother's touch. She'll tear the IV from her arms and say, "Mother, stop that. I'm not a little girl anymore," the way she always does. Or maybe Mother is counting the beats of Older Sister's heart, each one another two seconds lost.

Three days ago, Father stood at the doorway, half in and half out of Older Sister's room in Ward 6, after the two-inch gash on her forehead had been stitched closed, leaving only a deep bruise and her fractured leg set into a cast. "She looks like she's sleeping," I said.

"She is sleeping, for all purposes." The doctor seemed to be talking more to the nurses than to us. "It's tricky when the head gets hurt," she said. "We've cleared Qian of the most severe damage," she continued, speaking slowly at us, keeping her words simple because we looked like peasants—because we are peasants. "Her brain looks fine; all we have to do is wait for her to wake up."

I was surprised that the doctor was young and pretty. It was the first time I had seen a girl doctor. "It's remarkable that it wasn't worse. A miracle, you can say," the doctor said, and she waited for Father to respond, but he just stood there in his blood-covered Mao suit, unbuttoned at the chest to reveal a shirt yellowed with sweat. By this point, Mother was about to arrive; it took her a while because she had to find an emergency storage space for her pancake cart, which was usually parked outside the kitchen-knife factory. The thought that she would now miss the after-work sales crossed my mind. We would be out at least two hundred kuai because of that, and I would need to work more and skip school again. I was thinking about everything and nothing.

The nurse, an older no-nonsense type, tried to get Father to sit; they were probably scared of his silence. He hadn't washed his hands when he entered the hospital or worn a face mask, despite all the signs posted on the wall. Older Sister's blood, which had pooled into his arms and then streaked down his legs as he carried her from the road onto his motorbike, had dried into dark imprints of misshapen butterflies.

"You're a very lucky man, Mr. Ma," the doctor said. Father still didn't seem to hear her, and the doctor gave him a strained smile. "Excuse me," she said. "I have other matters to attend to, but I will continue to monitor your daughter's condition." Father nodded, and I couldn't help but be a little ashamed of his muteness and helplessness. Of his unblinking eyes, bared chest, oily hair, and stubble.

At the time, I didn't believe that it was Qian in front of me. It was some other girl who looked like her. It couldn't be her, because if Qian was gone, then I'd be alone with Mother and Father. I thought about talking to Father, but I couldn't remember the last time I had spoken to him without being addressed first. I tried to imagine the sound of our two voices together like we were some other father and son.

When Mother finally arrived that night, she collapsed right onto the tiles of the corridor. Father and the nurses rushed to aid her, and I no longer had to think about talking to Father.

Qian once told me that when I was a baby, Mother used to check on me every fifteen minutes, all through the night, to ensure that I was still alive. The four of us slept in the same bed then, and Mother would hold her face right next to my nose to capture my exhalations, to breathe in my used air. I was always so quiet that she thought I was half dead.

This is the way she takes in Qian now, even as the beeping machinery sounds every other second. We have to go home soon. Finally Mother lifts her head from Qian's heart and leads Father away. She's tired, which makes her look even older. She's only thirty-five, but people always mistake her for my grandmother. "This might be the best hospital we can buy, but it will still take us an hour to return home, and you have to be at work in the morning," Mother says to Father. She reaches for his fingers gently, ignoring the caked dirt, and I realize this is the first time I've seen them holding hands.

Father is proud of his work, though he would never admit it. Mother tells her friends that her husband is in "landscape management," a term she heard Qian use, except she didn't know that Qian was making fun of Father. "Far better than a migrant worker in a factory or in construction," Mother tells the other women in our building, whose husbands are migrant workers in factories or construction. But he looks the same as any other laborer, worn thin. The faint mustache above his lip makes him look somehow younger than Mother, when in fact they are the same age. He was seventeen, just a year older than Qian is now, when he married Mother. Even though he must have been different then, I cannot think of him as anything but the person I see each day: a sighing shadow slumped in our kitchen at dawn with a cigarette glowing brighter and then dimmer. And then he leaves for work. I am certain he has always been like this.

"Excuse me, Mr. Ma." A nurse has come in. Someone usually comes in to tell people visiting hours are over, but most days we don't stay that long. Some days, none of us come to visit Qian at all. "You need to fill out some forms before you leave," the nurse says.

"What?" Mother says. "Can't you leave us in peace for a moment?"

"I'll help." I put a hand on Mother's shoulder to calm her because I know Mother will go to extreme lengths to hide the fact that neither she nor Father can read much. "I'll be down soon," I say, and I stay for a little while longer after both Mother and Father are gone.

At the side of Qian's table is a small vase with flowers, still fresh after a week, and a stuffed bear from her coworkers at the clothing store in Trust-Mart. I take out her cell phone from my pocket and place it under the bear; by dumb luck I was able to see the cell phone lying at the side of the curb a few meters from where she was hit. The glass was cracked, but otherwise the phone seemed fine.

Older Sister never went anywhere without her phone. She was the first person in our family to own one. Some of the kids at school have them, but most don't. After watching her on the thing for an entire day, I asked her what she did with it, since she was always flipping the cover up and down, up and down, pushing buttons. "It's like magic, Little Brother. I can type a message to anywhere in the world."

She was sending messages all day, but I never found out who she was typing to. Now I take the phone and turn it on. There is a button for messages, and I press it. There's nothing in the sent folder. Was she talking to no one? I try pushing a few numbers, and characters appear. It really is like magic. It takes me ten minutes of constant stumbling and restarting, but I am able to type my first cell phone message to Qian: *I know you are awake. Write me back. I will keep it a secret.*

My parents tell me that my birth is why they moved to Jiufeng Village in Shanghai, rather than staying in their hometown of Ningxia, outside of Shaanxi. "Once we had a son, we knew we were meant to be in Shanghai. It was a sign," Father said last New Year holiday, after he was red and sweating from the cheap rice wine that I tasted and spat out immediately because it was like drinking cleaning fluid. Father didn't usually drink alcohol, but sometimes he made an exception. "We're ethnic minorities, you know, and it would've been easier to go back to where there are more Hui." Whenever my Father mentions ethnic minorities, he rubs the large grayish veins on his wrists. "Here in Shanghai, all people are allowed two children anyway! It's the law here. But you never know with officials. You never know when their itch for money comes." He must have felt really festive, because it was the most I had heard Father say in months.

Though I don't call myself Little Brother in public, I do keep the same surname as my family. Ma Jun, junior middle schooler and younger than my sister, Ma Qian, by two years, the same Ma Qian who was run into by a delivery van three days ago while she was riding a bicycle, after she swerved away from a foreigner standing in the middle of the road. She's been asleep ever since. A classic coma, the doctor said; at least there is brain function. The maroon bicycle we sold to a scrapyard for a few kuai.

Outside, I call Older Sister by her first name, Qian, and people know us as cousins rather than siblings. "What a pretty cousin you have, Jun," my classmates tell me when they see her after she returns from work. One day Meng Bo says, "It must be nice having a cousin like that living with you. What does she look like in the shower? Does she have big ones?" He keeps going on like that. "Come on, Jun, why don't you ever talk? That's why people take advantage of you. You're so fucking country. Don't you like girls?" Then I end up punching him, and we roll around the dirt for a while until we get too tired and decide it isn't worth the effort. "You're so fucking sensitive, Jun," Meng Bo tells me. "Are you in love with your cousin? Isn't that what you Hui do?" he says.

A sharp pain fills my chest. "What the hell are you talking about?"

"I saw your father wearing one of those Muslim hats last night! You can't deny it."

I don't know what to say because no one outside of my family has called me Hui before, and Father never told us what to do in this situation. "Your mother's cunt," I say to Meng Bo, and I spit on the floor. "I don't give a damn about Hui or Muslims or religion." And I don't, really. Meng Bo usually doesn't bother me because I'm big for a fourteen-year-old. That's why I can skip school sometimes and work without anyone asking questions. Just the way that Qian is only sixteen but can work at the clothing shop because they think she's eighteen.

"Fuck you, Jun; you Muslims are injecting Han citizens with HIV blood," Meng Bo says.

"That's Uighurs, and that's a horseshit lie." I pull myself up to my full height, almost a head above Meng Bo, and he backs away until he stumbles over the edge of the sidewalk. For a second I'm afraid he'll be hit by a truck like Qian, but he steps back onto the sidewalk and brushes off his jacket. It's a stylish military cut and not allowed as part of the school uniform, but he wears it anyway.

"I won't say anything because I'm your friend," he says, "but if people find out that your father is a Muslim, I bet he won't be able to work at that fancy international school, and your pretty cousin will lose her job too."

I almost hit him again so he'll shut up, but then I don't know if that will make things worse. Thinking about this stuff drives me crazy. Who cares about made-up ideas like God? *We can only rely on ourselves*, is what Qian and I have always believed. Not even our parents can save us. I look up at the sky and then back down to Meng Bo. He flinches as if he expects me to punch him. Instead I say, "See you in school." I mean it as a normal good-bye, but it comes out like a warning. I do want to see him. I mean, when I go to school, I always end up staring at the back of Meng Bo's head because I sit behind him, but maybe it's also because I'm trying to get a feeling across to him. I would say something to this effect if only everything I said didn't end up being dead on my lips. If only I hadn't punched him a minute ago.

"Yeah. OK." Meng Bo crosses the street in a hurry to his apartment building, which is not too far from mine.

The town around us probably looks like trash to the rich Shanghainese, the kind of people Older Sister sells clothes to. Nothing stands out here. Just little one-person stores, motorbike repairmen, empty shacks, and dogs and dog shit everywhere. You can't walk around without smelling garbage and dog shit. "Jiufeng is the toilet of the Shanghainese," Qian once said, when she was telling me about her plans to move closer to the center of the city. Xiujiahui was the area she was targeting. "We can't stay here, Little Brother. We can't be stuck here in a fourth-tier town with all the migrant worker children, lucky just to learn how to read." Qian always got excited about the future. "We'll become part of the new generation, Jun. Anyone with enough passion and determination can make money." *Leave the past behind* was another of Older Sister's mottos. She picked it up from an old propaganda poster.

Most people think there are only two kinds of migrant kids. The first are the robots who study all day and then study more all night, because if they get a perfect score on the local high school exam, they might be able to take the national exam and get into a good university, even though there are only a few places and millions of students fighting for those places. Hell, those standouts might even join the Party. Then there are the dropouts, the ones who smoke and get pregnant and have abortions and skip school to go to Internet cafés to play games. Most people put me in the dropout group, but I'm nothing like them. While the other kids are playing online games, I'm searching for novels on the Internet and whatever foreign stories I can find translated. Banned stuff, intellectual stuff; even bad comics will do.

Sometimes Older Sister brings me textbooks she finds in the garbage dump outside of Shanghai International School. They throw away books that easily cost forty or fifty kuai each! They could at least sell them to schools like mine, which have a lot of fancy banners and billboards from the local officials but only outdated textbooks that were probably freshly printed right after the Cultural Revolution.

Father calls us ethnic minorities, but no one would know us as Hui people unless we told them. Father does not wear Muslim clothing, and Mother does not cover her head with a scarf. There is a bamboo prayer mat under our bed, though—my and my sister's bed—and sometimes I take it out and lie face down on the smooth, worn fiber when no one else is around. It was my father's father's father's, and it's all we have left of being Muslim Hui, other than not eating pork. "What good is religion if we starve because we can't get work?"

Mother says, and though Father doesn't acknowledge that he agrees, he warns me and Qian not to talk about our religion, which is fine by us because we never knew what Islam was anyway. And even if I did, Islam would send me into a deep dark hell because of what I am.

I'm not surprised it's Meng Bo who found out about my family's Hui background. He was always waiting for me to walk to school, but I knew he really just wanted to see Qian. I tried to pretend otherwise, but pretending hurt worse than accepting reality. More than once I've noticed him jumping up and down by our building's fence, trying to peek into our windows, which you could just see into because we were only above the ground floor. Whenever I caught him in the act, he would smile from outside the window and mime breasts on his chest, and I would close the curtain to our bedroom window—mine and Qian's, I mean.

I decide not to tell Father about Meng Bo's threats to tell everyone that we're Hui, at least not until Older Sister is awake. She would be able to handle this better than I can. I honestly don't know why being Muslim should be so bad. I have memories, from when I was very young, of groups of smiling men sitting on low walls and wearing robes next to a mosque. They would pat my head and praise me when I performed Salat correctly. A few of the other migrants were Hui too. In the end, Hui or not Hui didn't really matter. Everywhere I looked, what was most important was whether you were rich or poor. And we were poor, until Qian was hit by a bus. Then suddenly we were rich.

When the foreigners came, it was a day after the accident. Father couldn't believe it, and Mother only said, "How can paper money be so heavy?" and "Father, what are we supposed to do now?" which seemed to embarrass the strangers in the room. But I couldn't read the expression on the white foreigner because his face moved too much. All of his expressions were like cartoon expressions. Everything was disgust; everything was anger; everything was outrageous surprise. It was as if he were a little child. The large white man turned out to be the husband of the woman who had caused the accident. He handed over stacks of hundred kaui bills like we were in a movie scene.

Two representatives from Shanghai International High School were with the foreigner, and they explained to my parents that the money was to help us through our hardships. "We hope you understand that the school is very conscientious," said the female representative, who was smiling the whole time. "And we would like to extend our hospitality to your daughter. When she is recovered, she can attend our school free of fees and tuition."

The other representative, who looked like an old Party official, added, "We are the number two school in Shanghai! Almost number one!"

"Mr. Ma, right?" they said to Father. "You work at the school, do you not? I was able to dig up your file. Imagine that, a laborer getting to send his daughter to such a prestigious institution. You would normally never be able to afford the fees in your lifetime!"

"What if she doesn't recover? What good is your offer then?" Mother asked, and the representatives and the foreigner blinked and looked at each other blankly.

"Mrs. Ma," the male official said, "the matter has already been settled with authorities. No compensation is required by law. Everyone who witnessed the *incident* noted that it was an accident. This offer, in fact, is made only because of the generosity of this foreigner, an upstanding teacher." The representative motioned toward the white man, who was unshaven and facing away from us.

I understood his Mandarin, but Mother and Father couldn't make out the representative's vocabulary, and I hated them for it. Hated them for their ignorance, their cheap clothes, my cheap clothes, for being Hui, for how small our lives were. They were like cockroaches digging through yesterday's scraps, happy to stay beneath the feet of everyone. Qian was right. What was the point of holding on to any of this?

"Get out of here!" Mother shouted, and I restrained her flailing arms.

A nurse poked her head in. "Quiet down, please. There are other patients in the ward."

"I'll shout if I want!" Mother said. "I have twenty thousand kaui. Put my daughter in the best private room you have!"

Why is it that all guys ever talk about is sex or girls or TV shows or money? Girl/Boy, Girl/Boy, Girl/Boy. I don't understand any of it. But I would still rather be in school than out of it, because at school at least I can look at Meng Bo.

Mother and Father don't know I skip school to go to work because they are never home when school calls, and I take all the letters from my teachers out of the mail before Mother and Father return from work. When Qian dropped out of school, they had a monthlong argument about it. Screaming and yelling and throwing furniture around, even my father. Only when Qian threatened to move out did my parents give up. Despite Qian's victory, I still made sure to be discreet about cutting school. Qian is the one who set me up with a part-time job unpacking DVDs on Baise Lu, down the street from the clothing store she works in. "Better use of your time, Little Brother," she said, though Qian actually believes in education and was a star student herself before she dropped out. For Qian, being self-made is even more important than education. *All of China's new millionaires are self-made* is one of her favorite sayings. *I will become the new fashion business mogul!* is another thing she says.

I come into the DVD store and work once a week. Just enough time for me to reboot my mind. Mother and Father take the money Qian and I offer them without so much as a word to us, so actually they might know I skip school, because where else would I be getting that money?

It's been ten days since the accident, and I've gone to school less and less. Mother and Father do not spend any time at home other than to sleep a few hours before dawn, when they prepare for work, so I'm left to do whatever I want. During the day, I pick up more hours at the DVD store. The owner there, Zai Zheng ("Ivan. Call me Ivan."), likes Qian and feels sorry for me. Ivan's orange-dyed hair hangs down from a side part so that it covers his right eye. He chain-smokes and takes pride in the long nail of his left pinky. He can be anywhere from twenty to forty years old, but I've never asked. Today, Ivan takes a drag from his cigarette and says, "I saw it happen right in front of me. Damn foreigners walking like they own the road."

"Uh-huh," I say.

"Go unpack the box of concert videos downstairs."

"Downstairs?" I didn't even know there was a downstairs. Ivan tips his cigarette ash into a white mug and shows me a trapdoor in the back aisle, by the cartoons. The stairs lead down to a musty, dark basement. There's easily enough room here for four or five bodies, I think. Or ten boxes of unpacked DVDs.

Sometimes while I lie awake, I hear my parents arguing about the money. Usually it's Mother who begins. "Father, let's leave Shanghai. It was a mistake to come here. This is what happens to us. This is the result. Let's go back to Shaanxi and open up our own store with the money."

And each time Father says the same thing. "We cannot go back now. We are already here."

"I can't understand you," Mother says. "We can take Qian with us and move her to another hospital."

“We can’t move Qian without hurting her. And if we go back now, what was the use of coming here at all? We cannot go back and forth. We are not *migrant* workers,” he says.

“You are too stubborn. You still have a son! And he’s becoming a delinquent in this rotten city! I don’t care about what we are; I want to save what’s left of our family.”

“That’s enough.”

Standing there, a meter away from her bed, I start to feel drowsy from watching Qian. Since the accident, I’ve hardly slept at all. I can’t get used to the quiet of our room at home. When she was still there, most nights I would wait until she fell asleep, and then, from the top bunk, I would listen to her steady breathing. Without the rhythms of Older Sister’s heart, it’s as if my own consciousness refuses to let go. Like a part of me is convinced that if I wait long enough, Qian will appear.

Here, in her hospital room, I stop listening and take out Qian’s cell phone. The green light from its screen bathes my face. I took it home a few days ago because I didn’t want someone to steal it at the hospital, but also because it was almost out of power and I had borrowed a spare charger from Ivan.

I write a message to Qian about the new space I found when I was unboxing the concert DVDs, old classical and jazz and blues, covers with foreign names I couldn’t pronounce. There was music playing with a deep drum that echoed into me. I asked Ivan what the name of that instrument was, and he said *timpani*.

When I finish typing the message, I decide to go to school the next day. I think I’m getting better at tuning out the noise and the expectations. I’ve become like a radio dialed into the perfect song, an ideal antenna. Reception steady and strong.

At school, everyone turns to look at me when I walk into homeroom. Even the teacher is surprised and stumbles with calling roll. The gang is all there, all my friends, though more and more I can’t really make out why I should call them friends any more than I can would a cat a friend, or the rubbish bin down the street a friend. Meng Bo is the first to greet me, and I feel an odd pain. “Hey, Jun! I thought you were dropping out or in jail or something.”

“Why would you think that?” I’m happy to have the chance to talk to Meng Bo again, but I make myself sound like I don’t care.

Meng Bo laughs and gestures for the rest of the gang to laugh.

I don't know why they're laughing. I've never been good at jokes, at knowing when to laugh or when something was supposed to be funny.

"This is why we love you, Jun. You just don't give a fuck."

The homeroom teacher tells us to be quiet. He comes over to my table and raps it with a rolled-up notebook. "Ma Jun, you and your parents have some explaining to do. See me after school!"

The rest of the day is uneventful. Even after missing one week, the lessons sound the same. Everything is the same, except my sister is lying on a white hospital bed with stiff rough sheets, and my parents have a pile of money. Nurses come and go probably a few times an hour and talk over her like she's not there. I'm glad Older Sister doesn't know how dependent she's become. I stare at the back of Meng Bo's head and wonder about his hands.

Meng Bo accused me of being in love with Qian, and I suppose that's true, but not in the way he thinks. I don't have perverted thoughts about Qian like some guys have about their sisters. In fact, I don't think I want to have sex with anybody; the thought of sex just makes me want to throw up. Yet before the accident, Qian was more than a sister. If I had to explain it, I guess I would describe her as my idea of the future. Without her, I didn't have a feeling that the days could continue. One day could easily be the next, one night's sleep becoming two. Once I lost sight of the day, things like school fell by the wayside pretty quickly. Without any care for the future, what was the point of the routines and responsibilities we lived by?

I mean to visit my homeroom teacher to explain why I've been absent so much, but Meng Bo and two of my other friends tackle me and drag me away before I'm able to make it to the teachers' offices.

They let me go when we reach an empty stairwell next to the athletics field. My vision is unfocused, and I can't look at them directly. Their voices blur together and cut in and out like static; then they grab me again.

"Jun! Hey, Jun. Come here. Where are you going? Don't leave your friends. We thought you were dead. Holed up with your cousin. Get that, holed up? Holy shit, Jun, stop moving already. We just want to talk."

Am I moving? I can't tell. Maybe my body is going forward. If it is, then it must be inertia, which was the science lecture today. My body must be in motion, and I can't stop it. Part of me is actually glad that Meng Bo would take the time to tackle me like this and push my face into the dirt.

"Fuck, Jun, you're a damn bull. Hey, Meng Bo! What should we do?" The voices are panicking a little. "Hey, Jun, Jun, we're not trying to hurt you. Fuck! Meng Bo, I'm not getting into a fight with this bald monster!"

Bald? I touch the top of my head and scratch at the stubble on my scalp. When did I shave my hair? Was it the last time I visited Qian? Did I do it after work one day? I'm faintly aware of the opposing forces of my friends, but their force is not equal to my own. Eventually I pull away. They try to hold me down and end up scratching long welts along my arms.

"Damn it, Jun!" It's Meng Bo talking. Now I notice more of my surroundings, maybe because of the pain. "I'm gonna tell them, you know. I'll tell my father, and the teachers, and the neighborhood representative about your father. I'll tell them how he's probably a terrorist and he tried to recruit me. That he's a separatist. And that you're skipping school to do terrorist training."

By now I'm completely free from anyone holding me. My inertia takes me across the grass of the field.

"Just introduce me to your cousin! I know she's in a coma! Bring me in and show me her tits and I won't tell!" Meng Bo shouts, but I do not stop my body. Meng Bo's voice is farther now but not far enough away that I can't hear him. "You wouldn't even know what to do with her, you fag! I've seen you looking at me, Jun, you disgusting pervert. Fucking homosexual."

And this is where I turn around. I think of myself as a radio again, and I've tuned into a classical station, 94.7. I don't know anything about classical music, except I watched one of those DVDs one day in the store, when it was slow, and Ivan just waved his hand at me when I asked if I could put on a classical DVD. I watched the conductor's hands cut through the air and then chop down violently, the same way my hand, my fist, must be coming down on Meng Bo, and the crash of the symbols, the beat of the timpani and then another thrust down, into Meng Bo's windpipe, so he can't speak anymore. Meng Bo, whose lips I've thought about sometimes. At a certain point, the conductor even closes his eyes because he feels the music so close to his heart. And I close mine too, because I don't need my eyes to shrug off the hands pulling at my waist and legs, to mash my knuckles into Meng Bo's lips. A few more beats of the drum, into their faces, and the arms stop, too. The strings, the woodwinds, the brass.

When I've come back to my senses and my reception is clear, the music is gone. I can see that the skin on my knuckles is peeled back white, the kind of white that holds until blood seeps through. Meng Bo isn't making any sound. My two other friends are groaning and holding their heads. I let my instincts take over. I go past the school, on my way to the main road that leads to the south of Shanghai, to Baise Lu. I don't know why I'm going there, but that's where I'm going. Walking to Baise Lu will take me a couple hours, but time doesn't matter to me anymore.

On my walk over, I hear a strange call of a bird. Then I remember when I shaved my head.

After work, last night, when Ivan trusted me to close the store for him. The other employees had left already, and Ivan had an important meeting that day. "What kind of meeting?" I asked.

"An important one," he said. "Didn't anyone tell you not to ask too many questions?"

"No," I said, because I didn't usually ask any questions.

Just before I locked the doors, I heard a knock. It was a kid, actually close to my age, but smaller and messier, like he had been lost in the woods for days without food and a change of clothes. His skin was so dark that I almost took him for Middle Eastern or something. Uighur, maybe. "Sorry, we're closing."

"Please," the guy said. "I need a DVD."

"Can't it wait?"

He shook his head. "It really can't."

I couldn't imagine why someone would need a DVD so badly, but he looked desperate and I let him in. I flipped the light switch. On the flat screen mounted to the ceiling, a Russian symphony's performance of Chopin flickered back on. "So what is it?"

He kept his head down. "Thanks," he said, like he was more tired than grateful. He held out a scrap of paper with curling letters. *Le Petit Prince*.

"I can't read that," I said. "Is that English?"

"French," he said. "This was in her plan book; it was the last movie my girlfriend saw."

I was getting confused. "Did I miss something? Who?"

"Never mind. Never mind who. Do you have this movie? It's old, 1974. Can you search the computer?"

I grunted. "No computer, but I know every movie in here by now. I'm the one who put them on the shelves, and I don't recognize that title."

The guy seemed drained, like he was about to collapse.

"Sorry," I said, "but I have to close." It was the truth; I was planning on going to school the next day and didn't want to be up so far past midnight.

"Wait, wait. What about the English name? It's an English movie. *The Little Prince*, how about that?"

I thought back, and there was something in my memory. "Yes," I said. "It's in the basement."

"Really? Thank God!"

What an odd person to thank was what I thought.

When I found the DVD, I was surprised to see the movie was based on a children's story. From the guy's expression, I expected a more serious film.

"Here you go."

"Thank you," he said. "Thank you. You have no idea what this means to me. I'm Andrew, by the way."

"Andrew? Are you a foreigner?" His Mandarin didn't sound like he was from Shanghai, but it was too perfect for a foreigner.

"I guess so. Taiwan."

"That explains it."

I took his money and put his DVD into a black plastic bag.

"Hey," he said suddenly. "Did you see that accident here about a week ago? It happened right in front of your store."

Why would he ask me that? I told him I'd been in school, even though at the time, I was really on my way to visit Qian and still a few blocks away.

"Oh, you're in school? I thought you were graduated."

I almost told him my real age but stopped myself. I liked that he thought I was older.

"I didn't mean to ask you out of the blue like that about that accident. I was just curious, I guess, to know what happened."

"I wasn't here at the time," I said.

Andrew looked at me directly for the first time. There was a blankness to his gaze. "Sorry," he said.

"It's fine."

"Do you know anything about the girl in the accident? Is she OK?"

"She's alive."

"It was someone from my school," Andrew whispered. "The foreigner who was in the street, the one who caused the accident. The woman lives at my school."

"You go to that fancy school next door?" I found it hard to believe. That was the school Qian had a full scholarship to when she woke up. Andrew looked like he was a homeless beggar, but then again, homeless people didn't buy foreign DVDs.

"Yeah," Andrew said. "Shanghai International High School. Do you want to see it?"

It was half past midnight, but I said yes.

Andrew snuck me in through an unmanned side gate. It wasn't that difficult; anyone could have broken in if they wanted to. Inside, I was amazed at the expanse of fields. Evenly spaced lampposts illuminated rows of trees, more trees than I've ever seen before. Within the forest, buildings arose like out of a fairy tale.

"This is a school?" I said.

"Something like that."

Andrew took me to his room. Again, I was surprised that it was so easy. I had never been inside another person's bedroom before, boy's or girl's—other than Qian's, that is.

"This late, the guard is usually asleep," Andrew said. "The former guard was more on top of things, but since he's been fired, a new one has taken over, and all he does is smoke and sleep."

Andrew's room was like him: a complete mess. It was also empty of decorations. Not even a picture. A family of six could have lived here, yet he had the room all to himself. He brushed a heap of clothes away to reveal an old-style TV set with a built-in DVD player. He pulled at the plastic of *The Little Prince* for a while before I took it from him.

"Here." In one motion, I ran my thumbnail down the side and opened the case.

"Thanks."

He put the DVD into the tray, and we sat on his bed as the disk loaded. I started sweating, even though the room was cold enough to be a refrigerator. For the entire movie, neither one of us said anything or moved. It wasn't that I was attracted to Andrew, but I couldn't have moved even if I wanted to.

I found it hard to follow the movie, even with subtitles. The man and the boy talked a lot about odd things like roses, but even though I didn't get it, I felt the pull of their relationship on the screen. Why did the movie have such an effect on me? Who was I thinking about? Who was my body moving toward? Was it my own father? Was it Qian? Was it someone I didn't know yet?

"Want a beer?" Andrew asked when it was over.

I had never had beer before, so I said no. "No, thanks. I don't drink. I never thought to drink alcohol before."

"All right," he said slowly. "That's fine." Then he laughed. "Jun, right?"

"Right."

"We're kind of the same."

"How?"

"We're both the ones in the background. Just scenery. We'll never be the heroes of any story."

I didn't get it, his talk of stories and heroes. It was as if he was completely caught up in another world.

"Never mind," he said. "Never mind." He got up with an energy he had not had before. "Look," he said, "can you do me a favor?"

"What?"

He handed me a pair of scissors and a razor. "My hair's horrible," he said. "I'm done doing this thing. Being left behind. I don't give a shit if I'm just a nobody. I'll help you do yours, too, so you can stop hiding too."

He cleared a circle in the middle of his room and placed his desk chair in the center. He sat, and I stood behind him and started shaving away his hair, using scissors where the hair was too long or tangled and the razor on the rest. Large swaths fell away onto his shirt, the floor, and he flinched once or twice. "Sorry," I said. "Did I cut you?"

"No. This is perfect."

When I was done, Andrew rubbed his scalp a few times. He looked like a newborn. "Like I'm in the military or something," he laughed. "All right, your turn."

"Me?" I blinked, and the next thing I knew Andrew was calling my name. I had fallen asleep on the chair and my hair was gone.

That night, the night after Meng Bo and the others tackled me, I expect the police to come and arrest me. For all I know Meng Bo is dead and I'm a murderer. Why did it have to be Meng Bo? I prepare myself for the consequences and resign myself to my fate, but nothing happens. The street is more silent, if anything—clear of motorbikes and late construction work. I turn around in my bed and think about Andrew, how he reminds me of Qian a little, and whether I'll see him again. I wonder if he and Qian would be friends if they studied in the same school, and it comes to me that if they were to meet, they would instantly recognize themselves in one another.

Near dawn, I hear my parents come home, and as usual they argue about the money.

"Father, how can you say that we shouldn't use the money? It's the only good thing that has come from all this. We can't give it to Qian if we're not sure she'll get better!"

"Then we'll wait until we're sure. Until then, the money's hers and we don't touch it."

"Father!"

"She will get better, and the money is hers."

They stop shouting earlier than usual, and I'm able to enter something like sleep, where I'm awake but my body is numb, other than the tingling in my fingers.

IVAN'S ADVICE

The next morning, I have an early shift so I skip school, even though part of me wants to go to school to see what will happen. At the sight of me, Ivan stubs out his cigarette and comes out from behind the counter to face me. "What the hell happened to your hand? No wait, don't tell me. When I was your age, I was always a day away from killing myself. I challenged myself to invent new ways of doing myself in: pills, cutting wrists, poison gas, burning charcoal, you get the idea. But time and time again, I came back to jumping into the Huangpu River from the Bund side."

"Why the Bund side?"

"Because the Pudong side is just too . . . tacky."

"But, why would you die from jumping in the river?"

"Yes, of course you're right. I thought of that too. There are so many boats that one would be bound to notice me. Or a foreigner with a camera would take a photo of me and then shout for help. Even if I cursed at them to go away, they'd still want to save me; that's how foreigners are."

"And it'd be pretty easy to swim back to the shore."

"But not if I tied a weight to my legs, and I could jump in before dawn, so there would be fewer people."

"I guess you've thought this through."

He raises a finger to his temple. "Oh, you bet I did. I had the perfect plan, but I'm not young and stupid anymore."

"What changed?"

He gets close to me and smiles. His teeth are whiter than any teeth I've seen, and I notice that his skin is clear and smooth. "Jun, all I can say is that when you are older, you'll see that the world is bigger than this little DVD store. Bigger than the people walking down the street, bigger than Shanghai. More than big enough for people like you and me to survive." And then he kisses me, and for the most part, I let him.

Mother and Father aren't able to visit Qian today. Father did lose his job after all, but not because of Meng Bo or for being Muslim. Meng Bo and the others are away from school, but there's no news about what happened to them. Instead, my father was fired because the school decided that the money they gave to Father was enough to break the rules of his contract. It would be unfair to the other laborers to treat him with such favor. These days, Father does not interrupt Mother when she talks about making plans to return to Ningxia. They look for suitcases and strong canvas bags. They do not mention me, or if they do, I do not allow them to.

When I get into the hospital room, I see that Qian's hair has gotten longer. How strange it will be for her to wake up and see her own hair spontaneously longer and mine completely gone. I've already decided to stay in Shanghai. There's enough money to last for months, even with Qian's bills, and I could always work more at Ivan's. He hasn't kissed me since that day and he only raised his eyebrows when I told him I'll be living alone in my family's apartment.

From my backpack, I take out the rolled-up prayer mat slowly and lay it beside Older Sister. I begin Salat in a calm manner, like I've seen Father do when he thinks we are all asleep. I check the position of the sun. This is the correct time, I'm sure; chest facing the west, I stand upright. Then I bend into a bow, then to my knees, my forehead to the mat, so that I smell the same fibers of my father, and his father, and his father. Then again, and again.

Camille F. Forbes

THE TIME IS NIGH

Didn't know that I needed to be grateful for this jaw, this deep skin, these hands. With these hands, I worked shoulder to shoulder with any man on McIntyre's land. I plowed, hoed, and picked cotton. Cut wood and hauled it in with oxen. Saunders, the overseer, said I was about made for hard labor, the way I handled things. I could yield a portion of cotton more than most folks and not say a word. A good thing that was, he said. A female who'd seen fifteen harvests like I did, with a body that never crossed from girl to woman, didn't serve for much else. If they could have, they might have tried to make a breeder out of me like they did some others. 'Stead, they studied the breadth of my back more than the width of my hips.

Toughness. Without it, no way to make it out of hell. No way to face what the devil heaps on your plate long past where you can hardly stomach the sight, let alone the taste, of what you're getting.

I fixed myself on what that life demanded, and met it with all I had. Some say it was better to work a man's land as a slave provided for than to be left to make it on your own, knowing nothing. But they didn't know the McIntyres.

Didn't know a man like Uncle Morris, the carpenter, neither. He gave me something no one else could or would. That gave me a start, even though it looked like we were all at zero—less than zero, being property of somebody. Didn't know it then, but it wasn't in me to give up. More like me to fight. I took after my Mam, though they all tried to scare it out of me.

When the new girl got to McIntyre's, it had already been seven harvests without Mam. I was carrying a yoke holding two buckets of water when the mama bell rang back at the big house. Fast as I could, I put down the yoke and started on my way. Being back by Peterson's field, I had a long haul.

I held up my large, shapeless shift so that my legs were free as they could be.

Why womenfolk didn't wear pants like the men, I never understood. I tried to fly, racing past the barn and the shed for storing cotton.

Mistress Louise must have known I was getting nearer, 'cause she hollered, "Calli! You come now, and I mean it!" Wasn't a time she called that she didn't act like the house was on fire. That was truer than ever now, in this time of war.

I skirted by the shed that was Uncle Morris's workplace, went through the quarters, and finally came up the stairs at the back of the house to the dirt porch where Mistress Louise stood. She had that puffed-up look that came over her when she was about to "make her point."

"Yes, ma'am," I forced out, panting.

She let go her chest full of air. "You took your time."

"Sorry, ma'am," I said. Head low, eyes low.

"Put another pallet in your cabin. New girl's here. She'll be toting water up to the cookhouse with you. Then send her to Mr. Saunders."

Mistress Louise took a moment to look out over the land, squinting at the brightness of the midday sun. Might have been satisfied with what she saw—colored hands worked the field in a rhythmic, endless pace—but her little chin was set, and the mouth above it was a hard line. Without turning her beady eyes away from the fields, she hollered toward the house, "Girl, come! You had enough time to put that baby down."

Wispy footsteps came close, then closer, till a wheat-colored, narrow-backed girl appeared. She hunched so much that it looked like her shoulders were trying to meet each other in the front, and they probably would have, if it wasn't for her full bosom. Every step she took was with her head down, almost touching her chest. She just about floated into the room and came to stand across from Mistress Louise and next to me. About my age, the girl was a tiny little thing, but full in the hips. Her voice was a whisper. "Yes, ma'am."

Her ways weren't a good sign. While Mistress Louise didn't care for bold, she didn't take kindly to simple, neither. These times meant that all new hands had to get to work, but quick. If the girl needed training, the job would come down to me, with Mistress Louise standing over my shoulder. That was one piece of trouble I could do without.

"Calli, take the new girl, and you make sure she gets back here before she's full again. John Junior's not to miss a drop of his milk."

Which was it? Take the girl to Saunders, or bring her back? I knew better than to ask. Ever since her brother died in the war, Mistress Louise had been extra rageful.

New girl and I stepped off. She kept up but stayed silent. I led her past the first stretch of the field, dust kicking up under our feet. In the distance, hogs roamed McIntyre's, searching for food, or sat themselves in a wallow, hiding out from the sun. Nearer by, hands kept themselves focused on the rhythm of their work. If they wondered about the new girl, they didn't show it.

As we walked, something tugged at me inside, like when a body has a mind to remember something that's all the while slipping away. Bothered me. It was something about that girl, but I wasn't sure what. I looked at her, sly, but she was looking at the ground, so I turned away and kept walking.

I had her follow me to the back of a shed, and I passed her straw she'd use to stuff the sack she'd lie on at night. She took the long, tough bundles from me with small hands. Those hands looked so soft, I wondered what kind of work she did on her old plantation. I asked myself how she'd fare at McIntyre's, where there wasn't much softness to be found.

I stepped into the hot little room and dragged a pallet out. "She probably not going to keep you in the quarters by the field long if you taking care of John Junior," I said. "Either that's the most cryingest baby I ever seen, or she just never give him a minute's peace. Seem the second more likely right, and if that's so, you won't get peace, neither," I warned. Still, better than being in the fields.

She stared back at me with her light-brown eyes, dumb. I wasn't surprised.

We were about forty-five of us, holding steady, working the plantation. New folk didn't come too often, but sometimes when they did, they had that same glazed look and slackish jaw the girl had. It might mean they'd never say much, or it might mean they needed time to wake up to everything being different.

Nearly all of us'd never been anywhere else, but Uncle Morris had seen everything. Master John let him hire himself out to other plantations, just like Old Master did. So when Uncle Morris said that out there was maybe even more hurting than a soul and body could take, I believed him. Figured maybe the new girl had seen it all and wasn't going to be coming back to her whole self. There was no point in wishing for the girl to change—I knew that. But, looking at the sorry little thing, her eyes now staring up at mine, a piece of me started to anyway.

When we got to the cabin, the door was swung open like usual. With no windows and the cracks between the logs filled with mud, the cabin sealed in stale air. We were forever trying to bring in the fresh.

Aunt Liza squatted on a low stool set up against the back wall. Her steady hands sewed a bag for a poultice. She stopped and looked at us as we stepped through the door. "Who dis?"

"New girl," I said, leaning the pallet against the log wall. I dragged the others across the narrow room to make space. "Gonna be tending John Junior, look like." I focused on rearranging, thinking about the passing of time. I'd meant to tote water to the cookhouse. Now I was going to slow up the cooks' work. And I still had to get to my row for that day.

"Lord, tending John Junior. You gonna need some prayers for handling that one and the mistress together." Aunt Liza shook her head and returned to her sewing.

I passed the new girl a bag to put the straw in. She took it with fumbling hands, her eyes still big and fearful. Wanting to ease things, I found myself softening my voice. "Make sure you pound it down good after you get it in there," I said, pointing. "If you lie on that tough as it is, you'll wish you were sleeping on a rock instead." I returned to rearranging the room.

She started stuffing the bag with straw. Then she murmured something.

I didn't notice what she said. *How long will it be before her breasts are full of milk?* I thought. I had no children. Didn't even bleed. About such things, I could only guess.

She mumbled again.

I was still working things out. On top of the toting, Mistress Louise wanted her to see the overseer. But it was probably better to get her back to the big house on time.

"Cissy," she said.

"What you say?" I asked, turning to her.

"The girl say her name Cissy," Aunt Liza said, not looking up from her sewing. "Short for Cecilia."

Not dumb after all. That was good. I nodded at her and felt myself warm a little. Then I set all that aside and turned back to thinking about how to get done what I had to without catching hell from Saunders or Mistress Louise.

In the end, Cissy made it back to John Junior in time to get nothing more than a tender-place pinch from Mistress Louise. It made her holler, but if it didn't send a body to Aunt Liza for healing, it wasn't worth mentioning.

Myself, I was beat down by the day. My shoulders ached from the yoke, having toted water twice to each of Cissy's returns. My back was sore from the bending and picking of harvest time, and the hauling of it all back to storage.

Truth is, though, it wasn't so much the day's work that beat me down. That I could do. I threw my body into it, left the rest of me behind. After a day like that, I was worn out, but not like this. It was something about that girl, so slight and soft-looking, big eyes staring up like a child. I saw her narrow shoulders trying to carry that heavy yoke, and it made me uneasy. A part of me did the work, and another part fixed on that girl, who was struggling and looking lost. Wasn't anything special about a body having troubles like hers, especially being new on the plantation. Still, thoughts of her gave me no peace. I wondered about her, and that wondering became a worrying.

On McIntyre's, I knew to mind my business. I'd been kin to the bad slave, the problem female who'd been the example to everybody, who showed what happened when one of us came to have her own mind. Fretting about other folks did a body no good. Told myself that again and again on the way to Uncle Morris to get my learning.

It was close to bedding-down time, but there was a half-moon that gave off enough light for us to see by. Away from the livestock, on the side of McIntyre's where Uncle Morris did a good piece of his woodworking, I stood scratching the dirt floor with a stick. Copied him motion for motion.

Old as he was, Uncle Morris still stood straight. He was long and lean—almost scrawny—and although he wasn't as tall as me, he reached for the skies like a tree. Standing beside him, I pulled myself up taller.

"You see the new girl?" I asked, looking at my scratchings. By night, Uncle Morris's blue-gray eyes looked almost see-through. Made me a little jumpy. I turned away and kept on with my stick, making the bridge that turns the two L's into an H.

"Umhmm," he said, finally. "Saw her when she was at the market." He looked down at the finished letter and pointed to it. "Both sides need to be just as tall."

I went to fix my mistake and stopped to talk. "She's wet nurse to John Junior, about to jump out her skin, she so scared. And so slow I had to carry water for her and me. Can't figure out what she did on the plantation." I took a breath. "You saw her on the block?" I fixed the letter, and when I stopped my scratching, he tapped my stick with his own. Time to move on to the next.

"Yep." He sighed and went to sit down on his stool.

I scratched out an E before he talked again.

"Screaming and carryin' on," he said. "Not much different from before." He frowned and tugged on his beard.

While I worked on my next letter, I went on. "The girl, her name Cissy. Didn't think she'd have a word to say, but then there it came." I kept writing. "Still, not much sign she'll be all right, though. What you think?"

Under his breath I heard him say, "I don't know."

"Don't know if she'll be all right?" I shot back.

He looked at me. "Gal, why you fixing on that new girl? You got matters to mind, nothing to do with her." His voice carried a hardness I never heard before.

I clamped my lips together and looked down, wishing I could disappear.

Uncle Morris's head stayed down, but he looked at me. Might have thought he was cutting his eyes, but I knew somehow that he was weighing things. He looked at me a while longer. "Calli-girl, sometimes not to know about things is what keeps you safe. I can teach you all this," he pointed at the letters with his stick, "but you best learn first the things that will keep you alive and the things that won't. Mind your own doings. That keeps a body alive." He broke his stare and shook his head.

Confused, I stole a glance at him. What was he talking about now? How could not knowing a thing keep a body safe?

"It was restless about the market, even the business as usual." He paused. "Calli-girl, seem like the time is nigh. Things gonna touch us."

My insides twisted tight. "What you mean? The work on the land's same as always, and Mistress and them are all about—"

His hard look stilled my tongue. "Calli, you got to see what's missing—not just what's there. Slim pickins on the block when the harvest is about to come in. Not much shouting in town square, but a lot of whispers. Folks more likely to pass through than visit with each other." He nodded to himself. "The war was in the distance, but it won't stay that way long." He rested, as if to make sure I followed.

When he spoke again, he'd smoothed the rough edge from his voice. "Calli-girl, when you live like we do, you need to see when a thing is moving. Nobody's there to tell you—or warn you—but look close enough, and you'll know."

"But what does—"

"Girl, hush!" He stabbed his stick into the ground.

Something was happening, all right, and now I was scared. Part of me was glad Uncle Morris stopped talking. I hadn't known that I was so settled with things till he told me something was moving. Even though everything inside me was jumpy now, I held myself still.

Eyes fixed on the ground, Uncle Morris started working things out inside himself. I knew it 'cause his mouth was moving, and I might as well have disappeared while he fought with what I couldn't see or understand. Snatches of this and that fell on my ears when he couldn't keep all the thoughts inside. Words like "strongest," "best chance," "what it takes." I lapped them up, but I didn't know what to do with them. All the while, he hardly blinked, didn't look in my direction.

After a time, he tapped the ground with his stick and stood up. "Lesson have to wait, Calli-girl. You go round to the spinners circle, and tell them there's gonna be moving. The time is nigh. Stay in there a while, then go to the storytellers. Find your way here before you bed down." He turned his back to me.

The moon, bright and big, lit the main path back to the quarters, but I kept to the bushes farther away. Though only Uncle Morris and me, because of him, got leave to be anywhere else on the plantation at night, that didn't mean I could do as I pleased. Going to see others in the quarters, I had to sneak my way.

It wasn't the first time I'd carried a message. Most times, it was about having church in the woods, or the goings-on at a nearby plantation: folks sick, dead, or sent away, who had ties to slaves on McIntyre's land.

This here, though, was bigger than anything before, I could tell. It made me skirt my way around, lying lower than ever, 'cause I wanted to do right by Uncle Morris.

After Mam got torn down by Saunders, only Uncle Morris could settle me. Over the years, his sure ways gave me something I could hold on to. I watched him woodworking in the barn and pressed my feet into the ground. Now I wanted to show him he could rely on me.

When I reached the spinners' cabin, I tapped on the door twice. News was to come.

I stepped in and closed the door. A wall of heat slammed into me, setting me off to sweating until I just wanted to sit, to try and catch my breath. But three women sat before me, waiting. They looked at me even while their hands worked cotton, combing big fluffs of it on two card cloths and smoothing it out.

"Find the kettle in the back of the far pallet," Mattie, the leader of the spinners, said in a rasp.

Mattie's voice had been like that ever since Saunders choked her nearly to death years before. He only stopped 'cause Master John caught him showing one of his fancy guests the land. It made Master John madder than hell. He hated when Saunders forgot who was what: McIntyre, the boss; Saunders, the worker.

I wove my way between Mattie and her sister, Cora, to get the iron kettle they used mostly for dyeing cloth. Cora watched me, her bony face looking as scared on the outside as I was trembly inside. The third woman, Hester, had a dull and lingering stare like always. She might not have had her wits about her, but her knowing hands never stopped moving.

I reached behind the pallet, laying my hands on the heavy pot. Pulling it across the dirt floor, my body's aches reminded me of how brought-low I was by the day. The spinners kept their eyes on me and didn't stop their work.

By the time I got the pot to the center of the room, Mattie had set aside her card cloths and pulled herself to her knees. She helped me set the pot upside down, then she pushed and I pulled so that a bit of the pot's lip raised off the ground. We held it there, sweating and breathing deep as Cora propped the side up with a block of wood. Now we knew our voices would be safe from traveling out the cabin. The kettle would catch our murmurings.

Mattie returned to her pallet and took up her card cloths. I dropped myself down on the floor across from her, taking in the thick air. While she now shaped the bits of airy whiteness into smooth, tight rolls, I stared at her long fingers, wishing I had some such thing to busy mine.

I cleared my throat. "Uncle Morris say the time is nigh."

The fingers stopped. "When?"

"Didn't say. But the market changed. Things gonna touch us soon."

Mattie looked at the ground and bit down. She turned to look at Cora. Her sister's face had crumbled, and tears ran over the cracks mapped on it. But not a sound came from her as she shook her head over and over.

Mattie bowed her head and nodded. Closing her eyes, she reached for her sister and Hester's hands and started the women in calling to God.

First she started to rock, her eyes still closed. Time passed. She began to hum, low but strong. Where I sat on the floor, I felt a vibration go straight through me.

With a face full of pain and need, Mattie opened her mouth to half sing, half pray, "Ah Lord, Lord, draw near, draw near."

The women called back with voices that already knew this song: "Draw near, Lord, draw near."

"We call on you, blessed Lord—" Mattie continued, her voice deep, the rasp smoothing out as she glided from one word to the next.

"Draw near, Lord—draw near."

They raised their voices, and the room warmed even more. These three women, rocking and singing, held more power together than I'd ever felt or seen. I'd been to prayer meetings before, but this here was something else. I joined in as they kept on, Mattie still leading.

"Guide us Lord, through the darkness—"

"Draw near, Lord—draw near."

"Give us strength, to meet the trials—"

"Draw near, Lord—draw near."

I don't know how much time passed with us singing, lifting up our hearts, but that whole time, it pushed back fear. Together, we started building something bigger than the I-don't-know-what we were maybe about to face. I soaked that in.

In time, our voices came down to a hum. I got up without speaking, leaving the pot where it was. They wouldn't likely talk more, but I knew the song would continue. By the time I got to the door, they'd quieted a little more, but there was still emptying and reaching to do. They would go on. Mattie opened her eyes and nodded at me before I left.

I stepped back into the night and walked around to the end of the long row of cabins. I tapped twice like before, now on the lead men's cabin.

Three of them sat in a circle. Different from the womenfolk, though, they didn't stop their talk on account of me. Ned, the oldest in the group and nigh Uncle Morris's age, sat at the far side of the cabin. He raised his chin at me, so I sat on down right away.

Wes, the work leader on McIntyre's on account of his size, was at the tail end of a story.

"When Isaiah left out of that place, he knew he wasn't never going back, no how!"

The men laughed, low and long, their heads bowed.

"That fool was crazy," Wes said finally, shaking his head. The bass of his chuckle added to the sweetness.

I wanted to stay in that sweetness. Finally, though, the men turned to look at me.

At first I just stared back, and then I heard myself say, "The time is nigh. Things are moving, and gonna touch us. It'll take the strong to make it, and the strongest of us to take us through these times."

A quiet stretched out for a while.

Wes spoke up. "Yes," he said. "The strongest." He looked at Ned, who flared his nostrils as he took in a deep breath. 'Zekiel, always Wes's shadow, opened his eyes wide.

The silence returned, and soon, I knew: We all had been waiting, not just for the times to touch us, but for us to have a chance to reap part of what we sowed. To have the best chance, like Uncle Morris said. Couldn't be scared; it was for us to be strong before whatever came. Maybe we had something to do, 'side from being swept by a tide.

After a time, I said, more like a question, "Uncle Morris called on me before bedding down."

"Then you go on and go, Calli-girl."

The men started leaning toward each other in the circle before I closed the door behind me.

When I reached the barn, Uncle Morris was sitting on his stool, whittling.

It didn't feel right for me to talk, so I stood there a while.

"You finished?" he asked. He stopped and looked at me.

His eyes bore into me. I looked away. "Yes. It was like they already—"

"That's good," he said, and put down his whittling. "It's time for you to go on back to your cabin, before it gets so late you'll have to pay for it."

"Yes, Uncle Morris." I wished that he let me finish what I was saying.

I was about to turn away, but I saw him cross his arms and look at the ground. I waited. He didn't look up. "Calli-girl, you may be young yet, but you likely gonna be called for more than you know. Time comes for that, I need to know that you'll remember what all I tried to teach you. And I mean every bit." He looked at me with those clear eyes, and I knew like never before that I needed to look at him.

"Yes, sir, Uncle Morris," I said. I didn't wait for him when he waved me off—just turned back out into the night, my head full of thoughts and my heart weighed down as if he'd passed some of his burden to me.

Back at the cabin, Aunt Liza was sleeping hard and Cissy was on her pallet. Although she was still, her breathing wasn't slow or deep. I lay my weary body down.

Cissy started to sobbing, and I lay still, hoping it would pass.

"My baby must be missing her mam now," she said, her voice thick with tears. "Abel, your mam ain't 'bout to forget you. She'll find a way back to you."

When auction time came, hardly a slave saw her folk again. Seemed to me better not to think of such things when what's gone was gone.

But it squeezed my insides when Cissy took to rocking like holding a baby in a dream. A shaft of moonlight threw her into shadow, and I saw the outline of her, hunched and shielding what she held in her hands. I wanted to say something that softened it all, but I knew nothing could.

"How far you come to get down this way?"

She kept at it. I didn't want to raise my voice, but I needed to make her stop.

"I say, how far you come to get down this way?" My voice was sharper.

I could tell she didn't want to leave that special place where she saw the baby and held it. It took a while for her to come back.

"Don't know how far. I'm from North Carolina. We stopped for a night 'long the way, but just so the traders could get others, looked like."

"That's a long way." I knew that from Uncle Morris. She was sure enough pulled up from everything she knew, and that was tough. But the day felt longer than most, and I was ready to shut my eyes.

I couldn't close my ears, though.

"Daniel said it might be hard, to get to be together. We had to ask, and wait. Asking and waiting. Everything in our lives waiting for someone else to tell us, 'Go on.' But they don't never do that. Never." Her little face broke into a grimace.

I turned away. Lord, what she had was heavy. Too heavy. We all lived these stories. Lying in the night, letting it ripple out of you like you had some right to something else than what you got, didn't change a thing. But she wasn't done.

"I need to get back my Abel. I can't stay here. I need to get back to my baby." Her already-ragged voice got tore apart with her sobs.

I closed my eyes. "That's past, Cissy. This here's Mcintyre's. You get to learning the way of things here. Your old master— "

"Arthur Wesley. His name Arthur Wesley. He the one took my baby. The one wanted to get me when all I wanted was Daniel. To be with Daniel. Have his babies." Her voice was half sorrow, half anger, getting louder.

"Cissy. You need to quiet down. Too many stirrings at this hour, and Saunders make us pay. You do your work, you step to it, you OK. But when Saunders make you pay, you pay. Hear me? Quiet now."

The sorrow won out. She bit her hand to keep in the sobs that tore through her.

I thanked the Lord that she didn't open her mouth again that night. But it was already too late. She'd given me a piece of her trials, and I could feel myself getting ready to tote it as my own. A heaviness took up space inside of me, and between her and Uncle Morris, that night I didn't get a snatch of sleep.

Dan Pope

BON VOYAGE, CHARLIE

Charlie Company was shipping out. Blair arrived for the send-off ceremony at the community center a few minutes before 11 p.m. and set up his gear—the softboxes and reflectors, the backdrop for portraits—in a corner of the gymnasium. The enlisted men were spread around the bleachers and banquet tables in their fatigues, chatting with wives and girlfriends, mothers and siblings. Along the opposite wall, VFW old-timers were serving hot food out of trays, wearing their ceremonial caps.

Blair was on assignment for the *Hartford Courant* to get a pictorial for the Sunday magazine. He had been drinking since morning, and this was his second shoot of the day. He'd spent the afternoon outside the police station in Hartford, waiting on a perp walk. Five hours with a half-pint of Jack Daniels, a gas-station grinder, and a can of Pringles. At last the guy had come out with a navy-blue windbreaker over his head. Blair always liked that shot: you cover your head, you've got something to hide. After that, he'd had a couple of drafts at the Half Door and fell asleep in his car. He'd woken in the dark parking lot around 10 p.m., shivering and dry-mouthed, and raced to Plainville in the oncoming sleet in time for this shindig. *Why a midnight send-off?* he wondered. Why keep the kids up so late on a school night? He could see no good reason, as was the usual case with all things relating to the US Marine Corps.

After getting his screens in place, Blair grabbed his 200 mm and walked over to the banquet tables for a plate of chicken and mashed potatoes, spooned out by the red-faced VFWers. There was no beer, only soft drinks. He took a few pictures of the coots in their caps, just to give them some attention.

Paper plate in hand, he mixed among the crowd, examining faces, looking for something to spark his camera. For Marines, they didn't look like much—more Lil Wayne than John Wayne. A motley bunch of white kids, Latinos and Blacks, a stray Asian—mutts, all of them. Blair was six-two in height, and he was probably the tallest guy in the room, although the pudgiest as well, going on 225 or thereabouts with the beer weight.

The enlisted men—it seemed mendacious to call them Marines; they were children, really, just a year or two out of high school—all said pretty much the same things. They had joined because it was better than working at a convenience store or some other dead-end job. "I signed up to pay back the evildoers for what they did to my brothers," one genius expounded.

"Your brothers?"

"The firemen, sir," he explained.

Blair tried to keep his face sympathetic. He wanted to tell the kid: You're fighting for oil, dumbass. That's the best-case scenario. But it's probably worse than that. You're probably fighting for Dick Cheney's cronies. You're fighting for Halliburton. You're fighting to line the pockets of some fat-bellied midland Texans who never served a day in their lives. Those are the evildoers. Those rich fucks and their lapdogs in DC, humping their bibles and wide-eyed interns, they're the ones you should target.

At midnight, the kid told him, the bus would take them to the air force base for transport to Twenty-Nine Palms. Then, after six week's training, to Iraq, the company's first deployment.

Blair asked, "Do you feel like a hero?"

The kid shook his head. "We've got a job to do and we're going to get it done."

Another brainwashed child with a rifle. Hell, Blair had spouted the same horseshit, not too long ago. He had spent a couple of years in the Suck himself, back in '91, in the first Gulf merry-go-round. He had been with the 1st Marines, a gunner in an M2 Bradley, part of a three-man crew. They'd come into Kuwait right behind the lead companies, the three of them yelling at each other the whole time, he blazing away with the machine gun. There were lines upon lines of bull-dozed trenches, some with arms and legs sticking out of the sand on top. That's what he saw in his sleep to this day: the limbs in the sand, some still twitching. Since then, since breathing in all that burning oil, he hadn't felt right, not for a single day. Some days he could barely get out of bed, with the room spinning under him. Whenever he turned too quickly, a sort of alarm went off inside his head, like a coach's whistle. Other times he would hear a sudden whooshing sound, like a wave coming to shore. When he told the VA doctor about the sounds, the woman looked at him blankly and scribbled on her prescription pad: *Risperdal*. There were other meds, prescribed by other doctors over the years, all of which sounded like the names of sci-fi planets:

Klonopin. Paxil. Celexa. He had a cabinet filled with little orange-brown bottles, the meds long expired by now. But Jack to start the day, a couple of Coronas for lunch, Guinness for dinner, vodka on out—this helped. Buzz management, he called it. He'd seen some TV show that said you could survive forty days on beer alone. He vowed to test that out someday.

For the past decade, since his wife had left him, he'd been working as a photographer. He'd started taking pictures in Kuwait City with a Hasselblad he'd found in the trunk of a blown-up Mercedes, four burned bodies sitting patiently in the front and back seats. Back home, he got a freelance gig with the local paper. Now he worked full time at the *Courant*, trying to survive the cutbacks and layoffs. He'd passed on the first round of buy-outs. He didn't want to consider the prospect of having nothing in front of him but his apartment couch and 35-inch Sony. Days off were bad, sometimes very bad, listening to the voices of the invisible and the dead. Best to keep busy, he figured.

Blair spotted a corporal with an interesting look, acne-scarred and bug-eyed. He asked if he could take his picture, and the corporal stood in front of the screen and posed stone-faced with his father's bible in one hand and an Arabic dictionary in the other. "I like to know my enemy's language," he said.

Good luck with that, buddy, Blair nearly responded. *Allahu Akbar*, he wanted to say. *As-salāmu alaykum.*

The corporal suggested that Blair get a shot of Hernandez.

"Who's Hernandez?"

Hernandez was his sergeant, the corporal explained. This would be his third deployment. He had volunteered to go with the platoon, even though he'd already done his requirement. "None of us have been over there, except him. I wouldn't go in his shoes, not a chance."

"Why not?"

"He got married yesterday. You want to meet him?"

"Sure," Blair said. It sounded perfect, just the sort of pablum his editor loved.

The corporal returned with a short, wide-shouldered Hispanic man. He had small black eyes, a nose that looked like it had been broken once or twice, and a fierce expression. "Yes, sir," said the sergeant; he'd be honored to take a picture with his bride. They'd met just three weeks ago, he explained. "She served me a burrito at Chipotle. That's all it took. One burrito, one smile."

"Which Chipotle? Here in Plainville?" asked Blair, scribbling in his steno pad.

"East Hartford," he said. "Angela," the sergeant called out, and the woman turned and came out of the crowd.

At the sight of her, Blair straightened up, assuming his old military posture. She was eighteen or nineteen, wearing a bright-red skirt and tight woolen sweater, her long dark hair covering her shoulders. Blair took his camera from his chest and raised it, studying her through the lens, pretending to check the focus, trying to keep his hands steady.

"We were going to get married in May," the sergeant said, "but then—" He looked at his boots and shrugged. "I figured we might as well do it now, just in case."

"I'm so proud of him," said the girl.

Blair directed the two to stand in front of his screen, trying not to stare. "Pose any way you like," he said.

The girl offered her profile, gazing up at the sergeant with adoration. Blair caught her expression at that moment, the shot they published the following Sunday: wide-eyed, aflame with love. He took a lot more pictures than he needed to.

Soon after that, he packed up and left, tossing his gear behind the seat, cursing, his gut aching. He got lost trying to find the highway on-ramp and pulled into a strip-mall bar a few minutes before last call and downed two quick vodka tonics.

By the time he found the interstate it was past 1 a.m. and he still couldn't get his mind off her. It made no sense, getting married. What was the point? The more he had to come home to, the more he risked. Why volunteer for another trip to see the elephant? Why fly off to Iraq when he had her warming his bed? Talk about stupid. Sergeant Stupid.

On I-84 eastbound, he came up on a Greyhound, and there they were—*Charlie Company, 2nd Battalion, 25th Marines*, according to the banner on the side of the bus. The interior lights were on, and he could see a couple of kids with their heads resting against the windows. In the center aisle, one stooge was doing some kind of goofball dance.

"Moron," Blair said aloud, honking his horn. He stuck his arm out the window and flipped them off. "Fuck off, Charlie Company. Company of fools and misfits. Company of cocksuckers. Company of buffoons. Company of dead men. Die well, Charlie Company. Die holding your guts in your hands. Die crying out for your mother."

He kept on like that all the way back to Hartford. "We've got a job to do and we're going to get it done," he said, the speedometer inching past eighty. "Keep dancing in the aisles, you ignorant children."

He thought he was done, but then he started up again. "Dick Cheney's dancing right now. He's shooting duck and dancing a jig. The man has no heartbeat. Did you know that, you cockeaters? He's a fucking zombie. He's eating your skin. He's sucking your blood and you don't even know it. Off to the slaughter you go. Kill well, my little darlings. Kill your darlings. Kill yourselves."

And all that dumb beauty waiting at home.

"Screw it," he finally muttered.

That night, bleary-eyed, he wrote the piece, trying to fit in every cliché he could: *For love of country . . . protecting our freedoms . . . newlyweds in love in a time of war . . . a company of heroes.* He titled it "Bon Voyage, Charlie Company." Next to the picture of the broad-shouldered sergeant with his arm around the girl he penned the caption: "Hero and his heroine."

His editor ate it up.

Two and a half years later, Blair was out of a job. He'd walked away with a three-month salary bonus and two-month vacation pay. Four times he trekked out to the Chipotle in East Hartford, gorging on guacamole and salty margaritas. She wasn't there. The fourth time, he didn't even go inside. He just nipped his Jack in the parking lot, watching the taxpayers going in and out the front door. A waste of time, he told himself. Even if she remembered him, would she smile at him that same way, her eyes wide with adoration?

His ex had looked at him like that, once. He could still see it, the joy in her face, that day on the tarmac in his dress greens, back from nine months in the sand. His high school sweetheart, the love of his life, a girl who would do anything for him. She came running out of the crowd, threw her arms around him. And what did he say, his prior self, the brainwashed fool? *Keep your hands off the uniform.* Within a year they were divorced. That's what the Suck did to him.

That last night, coming back from East Hartford, Blair pinched a curb and slammed into a guardrail. He managed to get home without arrest, but the next morning he reconnoitered the damage to the front end of his pickup—the right tire, wheel well, front shocks—two grand with labor, said the mechanic. His cushion gone, he had to go begging back at the *Courant* for freelance gigs, as well as a couple of crappy town papers.

He spent a lot of time on the couch. His excitements were take-out Korean and RedTube featurettes. Often he was too dizzy to piss standing up. Many mornings he found himself on the bathroom floor, his head atop a pile of clothes next to the laundry basket. The slab of porcelain, he dreamed one morning, was his gravestone: *A piece of shit, now and forever.*

When the email arrived he didn't, at first, recognize the name: Angela Roman.

You probably don't remember me. They told me you don't work at the newspaper anymore but gave me this email so I hope you don't mind . . . The email went on and on, the stray Spanish word mixed in, one long paragraph. It was *importante* that she get in touch with him because her computer had crashed and she had lost all her photographs. Did he still have the pictures from that night? Would it be possible for him to send the pictures he'd taken? She apologized for the trouble, but it was *importante* for her, now that her husband had been wounded in the war.

He read over the email a few times and pondered his response. Best to delete it, he figured. Head out to that new place, the Tilted Kilt, where the barmaids and waitresses wore mini-tartan skirts like schoolgirls and didn't mind dirty talk when you ordered a beer and didn't cut you off after four rounds. All this appealed to his half-Scottish heritage.

Instead he poured a vodka and tonic and mulled. An hour later, he had an idea. He emailed his old editor at the *Courant* and pitched a pictorial for the Sunday magazine, titled "Wounded Warriors." There would be no text. Just photos of GIs with their families. The caption would feature three pieces of information: the soldier's name and the manner and place of injury. *Private So-and-so, Mortar attack, Balad.* Et cetera.

His phone rang half an hour later. "Dynamite idea," said his editor. "We can run it on Veteran's Day."

He parked outside the apartment building, a noisy side street off Park Street, just a few blocks from his old offices at the *Courant*. Some kids were sitting on the front stoop, playing the radio way too loudly. He went through the outer door and pushed the button marked *Hernandez*, and a moment later the buzzer sounded. He took the stairwell—elevators ignited his dizziness—and climbed the steps to the fourth floor with his camera and satchel, inhaling cat piss and a burnt-meat smell, which made his stomach turn. He hadn't had a drink all day and it was almost 3 p.m.

A short, squat woman answered the door. She was wearing a stained housecoat. Late fifties, he guessed. He introduced himself and she waved him into a kitchen that smelled like ammonia. She left him at the table, calling out in rat-a-tat Spanish.

Blair placed his camera on a chair, listening to the chatter in Spanish from the back room. He stuck his head around the corner, spying the hallway photo gallery, which included his Sunday magazine spread, the newspaper a bit faded now, framed in black vinyl. Next to that were various shots of Hernandez in states of youth (child in carriage, preteen in baseball uniform, high school senior in prom tux), culminating in his Marine portrait, wearing his dress blues, hands clasped behind his back, his cover too big, tilted down on his brow.

The woman came back with an older man, stooped and bald, wearing heavy corduroy pants and a black shirt buttoned all the way to the top. He was carrying an accordion folder, papers sprouting from the top.

Blair stepped forward to introduce himself, but the man waved him into a seat. "Sit, sit. I am Javier."

"I'm from the *Hartford Courant*," explained Blair. "I'm here to take some pictures."

"Yes, of course," said Javier. "They are getting ready. I have some information to share with you."

The woman offered coffee, and Blair said yes, gracias, that would be nice, and she busied herself at the counter.

The man explained that he was Hector's uncle. His sister—he nodded toward the woman—wished to explain the problems they were having with the government. His sister did not speak English, you see, so he, Javier, had been reviewing the correspondence, making the phone calls, visiting the VA offices. "This has been going on many months now," he said. "They tell me to fax the forms to them. Fine. I go to Staples and fax the forms. The next day I call back, I stay on hold, I wait an hour. Finally I speak to the lady and she tells me, no, no, they did not receive the fax. They never receive anything."

The woman said something and Javier put his hands up. "*Calmese, calmese*," he told her. He took some papers out of the file and moved his chair closer to Blair's. He smelled like cigar smoke and body odor. "You see, here is the problem . . ."

While the man rattled on, Blair became aware of a rhythmic beeping coming from the back of the apartment, some hospital gadget, it sounded like, measuring blood or oxygen or other vital function. The mother placed a mug before him and he sipped the coffee, which was excellent.

When Javier finally stopped speaking, Blair asked, "Is Angela here?"

"Yes. I told you. They are getting ready. It is very difficult."

He started up again on the VA and Blair cut in: "Would it be possible to take your picture? You and—" he gestured toward the mother. He hadn't gotten her name. He didn't need their names. He just wanted the old man to stop talking.

"It is shameful, the way they treat Hector. They say they have no record of his marriage. How is this possible? You have the papers right there."

Blair said, "I'm just the photographer. You understand?"

"Yes, of course," said Javier, and he and his sister disappeared down the hallway. Blair heard a door opening, and the beeping intensified.

Blair poured himself the remainder from the coffee pot, looking out the window, the view obscured by a hanging fern—a shadowy alleyway, another brick apartment building just a few feet away, some kids standing on the fire escape, leaning over the rail.

Back at the table, he thumbed through the military reports while he drank his coffee. It had been two years since it happened, in July 2006. An IED had exploded beneath the sergeant's Humvee in some place called Al-Iskandariya. The other three soldiers in the vehicle died at the site, but Hernandez had somehow rolled onto the ground, bleeding and burning. He burned until another soldier extinguished him. This soldier was one of his friends, but he did not recognize Hernandez at that moment. He realized the burned man was choking so he reached into Hernandez's mouth and pulled out what he found there—his teeth, the shattered pieces. They got him to the air force base, then to a hospital in Germany, then to Walter Reed. There, he spent months in intensive care, undergoing multiple operations and burn treatments. He had lost one leg above the knee and another at the hip (*guillotine amputation at thigh*), his entire right arm (*limb burned away, bony stump visible*), his left hand, and part of his face (*fist-sized hole in the skull*).

Jesus, thought Blair, *the poor bastard*—burnt to a crisp and sliced off at the thigh: a half-man.

At the squawk of a baby, Blair glanced up. She came into the kitchen, holding a fat little boy, maybe two years old.

"I'm sorry," she said. "I didn't mean to keep you waiting."

Blair lowered the papers, as if caught in the midst of some wrongful act, and stood, knocking over his coffee cup. The transformation astounded him. She had put on weight, cut her hair. Sallow complexion, big freckled bags under her eyes. She was someone like any other—damaged, tired-looking, unremarkable. She could order a drink at the stool next to him at the Half Door and he'd probably not even notice her. All that crazy fire he'd felt that first night, that seemed absurd to him now.

"Oh God," she said, grabbing a napkin to mop up the coffee. "I can't believe he bothered you with all that. It's sort of an obsession for him."

"I know how it is. It's all red tape, the Marines."

"You were in the service?"

"A long time ago."

She bounced the baby on her hip, but the kid wrestled away from her and grabbed Blair's leg. "Teto, no," she admonished. "Leave the man alone."

"I don't mind," he said. He rubbed the kid's head. "Teto? That's . . ."

"Hector Junior."

"Of course."

The boy made a grab for his camera and Blair pushed it out of his reach. "I brought these," he said, digging into his satchel for the manila envelope. "I thought you might like them. I use the machine at work for free . . ."

This last part was untrue. He was embarrassed now, the time and money he'd spent on this little project at the photography store. He'd printed the shots he'd taken that night, a first-rate job—8 × 10s, some in color, most in black and white: the beautiful couple, she in her tight sweater, he in his desert camos and brown combat boots. A Marine recruitment poster: Join the Corps and get the pretty girl.

Angela sat and sifted through the pictures, staring intently, lingering on certain images. Meanwhile, the kid pawed at his leg, grinning like a maniac.

"He's got a lot of energy," Blair said dumbly.

Without raising her head from the photos, she said, "Come here, Teto," and the kid obeyed, crawling into her lap.

Blair picked up the empty coffee mug and put it in the sink. In the kitchen window, the late-afternoon sun was fading.

She slid the prints back into the Manila envelope, sniffing, tearing up. "That was—" She took a deep breath. "That was a different life."

He paused, unsettled by her tears. "The Marines ruined me too."

She didn't seem to hear him. "I've seen soldiers on the news with double amputations, even triple amputees like Hector. They have prosthetics. They go sky-diving, they run marathons. Some of them even rejoin the army."

"It'll take time."

"No," she said. "The head injury. It's not possible. He's like a child now. He has to be taught everything. The names of things. He gets frustrated so fast."

She let her tears fall, raising her eyes to his, looking for some answer from him, of all people.

In that moment of clarity he saw how he would become her lover. He'd offer to help with the VA, play the part of an honorable man. He would return to this apartment to shuffle the papers with the old man, pat the kid on the head, wait for her to come around. The poor woman would be dying for some parole from this purgatory, the endless beeping of that unseen machine, marking the seconds. He could see himself—it was as if it had already happened—entangled in bed with her, the furious coupling, her naked flesh, and then her gathering of clothes and rushing off again. She would lose weight, reclaim some part of her youth. They would cook meals, drink red wine. It wouldn't be difficult. And if all went well, she would be his for a time—until she grew weary of his deception, his limitations, just as his ex-wife had grown weary, and then she would realize what he truly was: another half-man.

She wiped her tears and stood up, letting the child slide from her lap. "Teto, go play with your choo-choo. Go now."

Blair grabbed his camera and followed her down the hallway to the bedroom, the mother and uncle waiting in the doorway. The antiseptic smell met him, and a stench of stale food, something rotten. He knew what to expect, but still, the appearance of him on the hospital bed shocked him. Blair had seen his share of horrors in the desert—dead bodies, burned bodies, severed arms and legs. But this man was alive. It didn't seem possible, so much of him was missing.

Blair looked away, studying the machine by the bedside—a digital display, some tubes running to the bed, disappearing under the sheets. He raised his camera and only through the lens did he truly examine the soldier. His ears were gone, just two uneven holes on the sides of his head. He had no teeth. He spoke a language of grunts, which Blair could not decipher, although his mother did, and she got him what he apparently wanted—a cracker, ginger ale, ice chips. The skin around his eyes seemed to have melted, the dead eyes staring out. A monster mask of a face. Blair forced his mouth into a blank smile, trying not to show his shock and revulsion. "Semper fi," he said stupidly.

There were some angles that would lessen the grotesqueness of his subject—the jawline, the good side of his mouth. Blair could make the image palatable, something that wouldn't disturb your Sunday breakfast. (His editor would require that, of course.) But not this time. No, Blair would not add to the litany of mendacities, all of which had led to this tableau, this rickety hospital bed. He raised the camera and adjusted the focus ring, taking headshots and closeups. He concentrated on the burnt flesh, the disfigured mouth and ears. After a few minutes he stepped back and took a final, simple shot from the end of the bed, depicting a monstrous child at sea on a giant mattress: *Hernandez, Sergeant. Improvised explosive device. Al-Iskandariya, Iraq.*

After he finished, the uncle led him down the hallway, the others following. Blair retrieved his satchel from the kitchen table. "I can talk to my editor," he told Angela, "about the VA. There's a story there for sure. Maybe we can get it straightened out. We can publicize his case, at the very least. I can't promise anything— "

The old man grabbed his hand, surprising Blair with the sudden strength of his grip. "Yes, thank you. This would mean so much, you cannot know . . ." Javier's hand was stiff and coarse, evincing a lifetime of labor (machinist, high-pressured forged steel valves, second shift, Blair would later learn). "Thank you, my friend. God bless. God bless you."

Blair waited to be released, but the old man lowered his head and began reciting a prayer in Spanish, their hands bound. He looked across the table to see the women joining in silent concentration. Blair, who did not believe in God and could not remember the last time he had prayed, bowed his head and joined these people in their hopeless entreaty, offering his own prayer for the ruined warrior Hector, for his wife and child, and for Blair himself: God be with you, my son, my daughter, let peace be with you and with all men and women, *As-salamu alaykum*, motherfuckers, amen.

Mark Powell

A WOMAN WITH A TORCH

Nayma's abuelo was up before the sun, the dim necessary light of his dressing bleeding through the beach towel hung to partition the room, pinpricks dotting a seascape of balloon-eyed sharks and smiling flounder. Nayma kept her face in her pillow and waited. She knew her abuela was up, too, out on the stoop with a heating pad on her knees. She would be sitting in her chair, extension cord run under the screen, rubbing the nubs of her rosary and saying her prayers. Through the pasteboard walls of the Walhalla Motel, Nayma could hear the human moaning that filled the gaps of whatever cartoon was playing. But it was their fingernails that got to her.

Bullshit starts early, Nayma thought. *Or maybe bullshit never stops.*

The sound was like a dog scratching itself bald, trying to scratch out its own guts, but it was, in fact, the couple next door—the early twenties man and woman and their ghostlike wisp of a daughter, all three brown-toothed and frail—the daughter haunted by malnutrition, the mother and father ravaged by the meth mites crawling in and out of their bones, an itch that signaled the impossible distance from one government check to another.

By the time Nayma got up and left her "bedroom"—you had to think of it like that when a worn-out *Little Mermaid* towel formed the limit of your privacy—both her grandparents were off to work for the Greaves family and she was left alone in the kitchen to eat her Cocoa Pebbles and finish the last of her homework for Dr. Agnew's English IV. She was seventeen and currently first in her senior class. They were reading *The Grapes of Wrath* and no, the irony wasn't lost on her. Very little was—with the exception of eight hours of sleep and little more than a passing engagement with the four food groups.

She showered and ate breakfast in the kitchenette: an alcove with a mini-fridge, microwave, and the hot plate they had to keep hidden from the motel's owner and her crazy son, an Iraq vet who twitched with the same intensity as the couple next door. She spooned cereal and flipped pages. It was quiet next door—the methheads having fallen into some catatonic stupor—and she was grateful for the silence. A few minutes to collect herself before the walk down to the bus stop where she'd ride with two dozen kids half her age, the lone high schooler in a sea of white faces because what kind of senior doesn't have a car? What kind of senior isn't riding with her girlfriends or boyfriend or somebody, right?

This kind, she had thought, in the months past when she used to try to riddle out the *why* of her days.

One cheek against the cool glass while outside grainy darkness gave way to the gathering daylight, back pressed against the torn pleather seat while they rolled past the Hardee's and the First Methodist Church, and Nayma just sitting there, books in her lap, trying to hear that small still voice that was all: *How do you put up with this shit? I mean, seriously.*

There were other places she could be. Her parents were at home in Irapuato, but home was a tenuous concept. She was born in Florida, a US citizen—her parents and grandfather were not—and had spent far more of her life in the States than in Mexico. Her parents came and went, blowing on the wind of whatever work visa allowed them entry. But for the last two years they had been working at a garment plant in Guanajuato State. It was good work (relatively speaking) at a fair wage (again, in relative terms), and Nayma had the sense that her parents were finished with their cross-border migrations. No more queuing at the US consulate. The forms in triplicate. The hassles from ICE. The rhetoric of hate—*build a wall! build a wall!*—spouted by the same folks paying you three dollars an hour to pick their tomatoes or change their babies. When she had lasted visited her parents—last summer it had been, two weeks of mosquitoes and long days watching telenovelas wherein she experienced the sort of cosmic boredom that would later haunt her with the sort of guilt you smelled in your hair—she had detected a certain relief in her parents' eyes, a sort of bounce that glided them around the edges of Nayma's life. They were done with *el Norte*.

That her grandmother was a housekeeper and her grandfather a gardener, that they had ascended to these positions from the indentured servitude of migrant labor, that they were meant to be grateful for the condescension and hand-me-down clothes. That her parents had been rounded up by the federal government, held for a week on Red Cross cots in the city gym after INS raided Piedmont Quilting, and subsequently deported with the rest of the three hundred workers Piedmont Quilting had recruited to come in the first place. That she had said good-bye to her parents through a scattering of holes punched in a plexiglass visitation window at the county detention center, that both her mother and father had contorted their bodies in such a way as to hide the zip ties binding their wrists. All this, *all this, mija*, would burn off in the fire of her success.

As a US citizen, as a brilliant minority student—*relatively brilliant*, Nayma thought again, glancing now from the graying milk of her Cocoa Pebbles to the papered wall behind which slept the methheads—she would receive some sort of generous scholarship to some sort of prestigious university and from there she would go to law school or medical school. She would spend the rest of her life in New York or Washington, DC—the capital of the universe—and make money in such ridiculous amounts as to assuage the decades of humiliations suffered by her family. That was her parents' plan, at least. Their daughter would become rich, she would become a *blanco* by the sheer aggregated weight of her bank account, and there would be no better revenge.

But first she had to get to school.

She rinsed her bowl and brushed her teeth, put her phone along with the Joads in her backpack, and stepped into the morning. The night's thunderstorm seemed to have blown out the last of summer, and in the skin-prickling cool it was disturbing to see so many children shivering in short sleeves and shorts. There were ten or so who lived at the Walhalla Motel with their mothers or grandmothers or aunts or some elderly female they may or may not have been related to, and they clustered at the edges of body morphology, either fat on Mountain Dew and pixie sticks or emaciated with need, lean as the Hondurans she remembered doing the stoop work in the strawberry fields outside Tampa. That they were cold, that their noses ran, that their hair had been shaved to their skulls (the boys, at least) or matted around forgotten Elsa barrettes or Princess Sophia hair clips (the girls, especially the younger ones) seemed most days like the results of a referendum on human negligence, something to fill her with anger at the world's injustice. But today it just made her sad.

She stood on the concrete stoop, the motel L-shaped, the rooms opening onto an apron of parking lot. Down by the highway a sign read SOFT BEDS COLOR TV WEEKLY RATES.

"Hey, girl!" she heard a voice call.

The motel office was at her far left, a block building with a pitched roof and a neon vacancy sign, a window A/C and a cupped satellite dish. It was from that direction that the voice came, and she didn't have to bother looking to see who it was. D.C. was the son of the hateful old woman who owned the motel. He cut the strip of browning grass along the filled-in swimming pool and on two occasions had unclogged their toilet when the septic tank backed up. He was of some indeterminate age—somewhere between thirty and fifty was her best guess—and possibly he was a decent guy trying to do right by his mother and the world, and possibly he was an embryonic serial killer running on Zoloft and cognitive behavioral therapy at the VA. The brim of his Braves ball cap was pulled low, and his arms and throat were inked with assault rifles and an unsettlingly precise map of the greater Middle East, complete (she had noted one day as he ran the Weed eater) with a legend denoting capitals, troop movements, and sites of major US battles.

She started across the parking lot toward the bus stop, and a moment later the pickup sidled up beside her, rattling and clunking. This was D.C. on his way to work, or maybe on his way to get his mamma a gravy biscuit from the Dairy Queen, or on his way to any number of the errands and jobs that occupied his days.

"Hey, little girl, you want a ride?"

"No."

"Why not?"

"Because I'm riding the bus." She didn't look at him. She didn't stop moving. That was her theory: no eye contact and no hesitations. He maintained the grounds at the high school—cut the grass, marked the athletic fields—and his offer of a ride was a near-daily occurrence. Without so much as a glance she knew he was hanging from the open window like a happily sloppy dog, meaty arm on the door panel.

"Well, I'm headed to the same place. You know that, don't you?"

She motioned in the direction of the children gathered ahead of her.

"Why don't you offer *them* a ride?" he said.

"Can't do it. Liability."

"That's bullshit."

"Maybe," he conceded. "It's mamma keeps track of the legal stuff."

"Whatever."

"What's that?"

"I said whatever."

He seemed to consider this for a moment.

"You know I ain't offering a ride 'cause I like you," he said finally.

"Wow. How flattering."

"I'm asking 'cause you a human being."

"I know why you're asking."

"Because you a human being and you too old to ride the bus like some ten-year-old."

"Go away."

"I mean unless you like the bus. Eighteen wheels and a dozen roses, right?"

"You're a creep."

He gave the engine a small rev. "You got too much grit in your shit, girl. You know that? Turning your nose up at people trying to be kind."

She started to tell him a third time to go away, but then she looked up and realized he already had.

She tried to read on the bus, if only to prove she wasn't lonely. But it was loud and somewhere ahead of her the window was down and a stream of air kept rattling the pages. Finally she put the book away. She was ahead anyway—there was no rush. What there was, was a bus ride that took seventy-five minutes to cover the four miles to the school. That would be four miles via the direct route, but Nayma guessed they covered a good twenty of back road, stopping at every trailer park or block monolith of Section Eight housing where poor children clustered sleepily by mailboxes and stop signs with their backpacks and dogs. Bullwinkle to Thompson to Tribble—back and forth over the bridges that spanned the wiggle of Cane Creek—East Broad to Sangamo to Torrington Road. The occasional watchful adult, a grandmother behind the screen door, a mother smoking on the stoop. The old men sat in plastic chairs and stared or took great care not to stare, depending, she often thought, on their experiences with the South Carolina Department of Corrections. The bus stopped first at the elementary school where the children bounced off, awake now, and then the middle school where they navigated blindly, faces fixed to the screens of their phones. When the bus pulled out of the middle school parking lot there was no one left but the driver and Nayma. The driver, for his part, seemed to have not the slightest notion she was there. He parked the bus and walked away without a word, earbuds plugged into his head as he lumbered toward his car.

Nayma pushed the door open and crossed from the bus ranks toward the school. She was up near the main doors, and down the gentle slope that eased toward the football stadium she could see people loitering around their cars, talking and flirting and ensuring their collective tardiness. Someone was playing

Taylor Swift. Someone else was playing Eminem. Her classmates were already self-segregating into their American lives. There were jacked-up pickups with fog lights and boys in Carhartt pants. The girls in Browning jackets of pink camouflage. There were stickers that read MAKE AMERICA GREAT AGAIN and WE HUNT JUST LIKE YOU—ONLY PRETTIER! and FFA jackets from the thrift shop—no one was actually in the FFA—and trucker hats from the rack at the Metromont (MY HUSBAND THINKS FOREPLAY IS TWENTY MINUTES OF BEGGING). Beside them were seven or eight vintage Ford Mustangs—the 'Stang Gang with their bad skin and BOSE speakers, the bass dropped to some heart-altering thump. They looked underfed and in need of haircuts, and she could practically see the crushed Ritalin edging their nostrils. Beside them were the athletes, few in number but easily identifiable by the swish of their warm-up suits. The school's dozen Black kids in football jerseys and Under Armor. Bulky redheaded lineman with arm zits and man boobs. Cheerleaders with their fuck-me eyes. The rich kids—the lake kids—were in Polos and secondhand Benzes. It was a mark of late-teen sophistication: the '90s German engineering, the chatter about diesel versus gas.

There were no Brown kids. Or very few, at least.

It hadn't always been like that. There had been a moment, brief as it was, right before the great INS raid when sixty or seventy kids made a little Mexico out of the right quadrant of the parking lot. They were mostly older than Nayma, and she had watched them congregate and laugh and play the same pop you heard in the DF. She had watched them go, too, all but a handful deported with their parents, and when they were gone, they were gone. And so too was the world they had made. There was no more gathering. The dozen or so who, like Nayma, stayed in the States had drifted to the edges of existence, a few quietly dropping out, a few quietly graduating or returning to Mexico. All governed by an abiding sense of bereavement, a mourning so softly realized it hadn't been realized at all. Nayma hadn't been part of it, but she felt it then, and felt it still. Even knowing what she knew, knowing what she was—the smart girl, the girl with a future—didn't help. Knowing didn't make her happy.

That was the thing, maybe.

She could watch them—her classmates, she meant—classify them, dissect them, in her secret heart; her real heart, the one she kept tucked behind what she considered her public heart—she could mock their choices and dismiss their lives as sleepwalking clichés. (Like her analysis was anything more than an '80s movie replayed on TBS—you could find sharper insight on Wikipedia;

these groups had their own sociological studies and trends, they had their own Tumblrs, for god's sake.) She recognized their inherent ridiculousness. But crossing toward the main doors of the school, she was also forced to recognize their happiness.

She entered the great stacked, rocked cathedral of the school's foyer with its trophy case and barely noticeable metal detectors.

Most days that galled her. Most days it sent her into fantasies of returning to Mexico, but never Mexico as it was. What she dreamed about was some idealized homeland, some creamy rainbow's end without the roof dogs and fireworks and the women holding posters showing their disappeared sons. In her dreams there were no cartels. There were no beggars or bag ladies with deformed feet or children dehydrating and lost somewhere south of Nogales and then not dehydrating and lost but dehydrated and dead, past tense. There was no room for that. But then there didn't seem to be any room in her dreams for Nayma either. She was always some ethereal floating thing, a gauze of veils hovering just beyond imagination's reach, watching.

The bell sounded and the languor of the hall began to fray, kisses, good-byes, speed-walking to first period. Nayma moved forward at the same inexorable speed. She was the senior assistant to Dr. Agnew's sophomore English course and that was where she was headed.

Bullshit started early, she thought.

But also, more accurately: bullshit never stopped.

And here was the worst of it: Dr. Agnew had scooched her desk right up against his, like she was his junior partner, his little frizzy-haired sidekick, and together they could survey the vast sea of indifference that was English II at 8:15 in the morning. Maybe that was the worst thing—though admittedly her choices here were legion. For Nayma there was a hierarchy of embarrassment, a sort of great chain of humiliation that she would sometimes finger when Dr. Agnew went on a particularly long and tangential rant about Keats or Sylvia Plath or white shoes after labor day or the way gentlemen no longer wore hats *and why is that, Nayma? I'll tell you, my dear, I'll give you a hint, it is linked—is it not?—to the decline of moderate political beliefs in the tradition of western enlightenment philosophy which has hitherto stretched from Copernicus and Francis Bacon to LBJ's Great Society and you, Connie Cayley, I don't know what you're laughing about, my dear, no ma'am, I don't, why if I found myself giggling in peach culottes with a sixty-four quiz average and an apparent inability to comprehend the mere definition of allegory in the work of George Orwell I believe*

I might be inclined to seek if not sartorial at least ecclesiastical intervention, don't you agree, Nayma?

She did not. But that didn't mean she didn't love the man.

He was the local community college's lone humanities professor until the local community college lost state funding and evolved into a start-up incubator slash pet-grooming salon with two tanning beds in the back. Now Dr. Agnew was the overeducated, overweight chair of the high school English department. A long-suffering, put-upon Log Cabin Republican who was sarcastic and erudite and slowly losing a war with his diabetes. Though Nayma had never seen him in anything other than a suit and a vintage NIXON '72 straw boater worn, perhaps, out of a sense of irony so overdeveloped it had become sincere, he was quite slovenly: shirt untucked, hair a mess, somehow barely avoiding tripping over his untied Keds as he lumbered into the room leaning on his four-stoppered cane, sighing contentedly, as if the only necessary supplement to truth and beauty was a charge account at Ken's Thrifty Pharmacy and Medical Supply. *Have you seen this year's line of Rascal scooters, Nayma? My Lord, they are sleek creations, compact and carbon-neutral. I imagine them conjured in some modernist fever dream of glass and brushed steel, let us say the aerospace industry, headquartered in Orange County, circa 1953, whisking Baptists through the aisles of Walmart, baskets laden with Chinese manufacturing. Why, it almost tempts a man to eat his weight in organ meat and simply be done with this bogus charade we collectively describe as walking.*

Today they were discussing, or Dr. Agnew was free-associating on, Emma Lazarus's "The New Colossus": "A poem, my children. A sonnet. Fourteen lines following a strict rhyme scheme and structure. Sing it with me. Give me your tired, your poor. Come on, children, we all know it. Your huddled masses yearning to breathe free." He cupped his ear. "I know you know it, my sweets."

But if they knew it they were offering no sign. That much was evident from Nayma's perch at the front of the room. Equally evident was the deep dislike radiating off the face of Stinson Wood, a dislike that appeared on the verge of crackling like sparked dryer lint into full-blown hate. He was one of the rich lake kids and, as if to prove it, had the shaggy salon-dyed blond locks generally associated with Orlando-based boy bands. In a class of tenth graders he was the lone senior, not stupid so much as lazy, entitled into a catatonic stupor he broke only to thumb indifferently through his Facebook news feed. But today he was alert; today he was all smirk, all dismissive superiority and all of it aimed at Nayma. She got this, she did, because:

A. In case anyone had failed to notice, she was decidedly Brown in a decidedly white world, and Stinson Wood—who appeared to be of Swedish extraction, or perhaps of something even whiter (an Icelandic Republican from, say, Tennessee?), should something whiter exist—didn't exactly come across as someone with what might be referred to by Dr. Agnew as an open mind bound to an open heart.

And:

B. She was ostensibly Stinson's peer, yet here she was seated at the front of the room, occasionally called upon by Dr. Agnew to provide the right answer after Stinson Wood supplied the wrong, or more likely no, answer.

It was surely both A and B, and just as surely it didn't matter. What mattered was that he was staring at her, staring with a freakish intensity that would have implied amphetamines were it not for his sociological preference for designer drugs filched from his mother's purse.

Dr. Agnew seemed to catch it too.

"Why, Mr. Woods," he said, "and top of the morning to you, good sir. What a pleasure to find you both diurnal and present. To what do we owe this rare convergence of the twain? Were you, perhaps, musing on the possibility of encountering a mighty woman with a torch? Because I am here to assure you, my son, that the likelihood of such is something just short of none, though I grant you that with some focus and persistence on your part it may yet approach not at all."

"What?"

"What? A Swedish diphthong, and an interesting one—its interest is beyond refute. Though perhaps not terribly illuminative as to our current state."

"I'm just watching her," Stinson said.

"And to whom, my child, might you be referring?"

"Her," he said, and he thrust his chin at Nayma. "Chiquita Banana there."

"You mean Nayma?"

"Whatever her name is."

"Her name is Nayma. Child, are you slow? Are you of addled mind? Did, perhaps, your mother pass to you some derivative of the coca plant, smoked, perchance, in a glass pipe, while you nestled in her womb? Mr. Wood? Dear Mr. Wood?"

But Stinson Wood said nothing. He just stared at Nayma with his lopsided grin, nodding so imperceptibly it was possible she was only imagining it. But she knew she wasn't. He was entitled. He was privileged. He was exactly the sort of person who hated people like Nayma. The nonwhite, non-male, non-southern, non-straight, non-whatever it was that Stinson Wood had been declared by the accident of his birth—it still went on, the hate, the bigotry, only it was softer now, it was subtle. It was patronizing and—the look on his face told her—it was smug.

Dr. Agnew was off discussing the poem again. "A woman with a torch," he was saying, "let's talk about this image, let's talk about this French woman standing in the harbor with her copper robe and patrician nose . . ."

Stinson had gone back to his phone, but every so often he would look at Nayma and wait for her to look back. Then he would smile that smug smile and look away, like he couldn't believe how ridiculous she was there at the front of the room with her obese mentor (was that what he was?) rambling on about the world's most irrelevant shit.

She went back to the poem. *I lift my lamp beside the golden door!* it finished, and she imagined that golden door, that place at which she might finally arrive. Did it exist? The cynical side of her said it did not. But the truth was, she believed in it. By the standards of Walhalla she appeared as un-American as you could get. But she was more American than all of them put together. She was more American than all of them by dint of her belief, and by dint of her arrival, by dint of her parents' sacrifice. By dint of—

She sensed Stinson's head snap up with a reptilian quickness. He had the sort of green eyes and pale skin that made her imagine him as cold-blooded in the actual biological sense. He was looking up now, but not at her. He was looking across the room at Lana Rogers, a freshman in sophomore English (whereas Stinson was a senior in sophomore English).

The girl looked up, Lana Rogers. She was cute and brunette and appeared just barely old enough to gain entry to the high school. She sat legs crossed in her tennis skirt, a worried look clouding her face. She had her phone in her lap and her eyes dropped to it—Stinson was texting her. She put the eraser of her pencil in her mouth and slowly lowered one hand to her lap where the phone was hidden. Not that it needed hiding. Dr. Agnew was holding forth at maximum velocity, sweeping hands, grand declarations. The girl texted back. Stinson texted again. The girl looked even more worried.

Then Lana's phone actually rang.

Dr. Agnew snapped around from the board where he had been busy diagramming the Roman street where Keats had died, but now, but now . . .

"A cellular call! My, my," he declared, "who is it that is calling? Who is it that fancies himself or herself so wondrously and spectacularly important to call during a discussion of the world's unacknowledged legislators?"

Then Nayma realized it wasn't Lana's phone, but her phone, the cheap Walmart Asus with its fifteen-dollar SIM card and factory-direct ringtone. She hadn't bothered silencing it because why should she? No one ever called. But now someone was.

"Nayma?" Dr. Agnew looked as hurt as surprised.

"I'm sorry."

"Why, I don't—"

She was up out of her desk now, the phone pressed to her stomach if not so much to mute the sound as to cradle some wound. "Excuse me. Sorry, Dr. Agnew."

She hurried into the empty hall and flipped open the phone—yes, God, it was a flip-phone—to find her abuelo yammering in a Spanish so frantic Nayma could barely understand her. Then, finally, she did: it was the Greaves woman, the grandmother. She was in the basement. She had fallen. There was blood.

Was she alive?

Yes, she was alive.

"Call the ambulance," Nayma said. Then she realized she would have to call. She got the address and hung up just as Dr. Agnew lumbered into the hall.

"Nayma," he was saying, "this is highly peculiar. I think perhaps—"

He stopped when he heard the voice on other end.

"911, what's your emergency?"

"Oh, Lord!" said Dr. Agnew and pirouetted on his four-stoppered cane.

It was like an elephant dancing, and Nayma might have applauded had she not been reciting the address. The voice of the operator carried up the block hall.

"Is she breathing?"

("Breathing!" cried Dr. Agnew.)

"Yes."

"Is she conscious?"

("Conscious! Oh, Lord!")

"I don't know."

"Please stay on the line, ma'am. Ma'am?"

But she had already slapped the phone shut, louder than she had intended.

"Oh, Lord!" Dr. Agnew said, "Child—"

But she cut him off with a look.

"Dr. Agnew," she said, "I need to borrow your car."

Nayma piloted Dr. Agnew's Oldsmobile into the parking lot of Oconee Memorial Hospital, her body hung over a giant steering wheel the size of a manhole cover, her butt slid forward over the beaded seat cover as rough as the corrugated motel roof where she would occasionally hide in plain sight. It was a little like driving a boat—not that she'd ever driven a boat; she had never even been on a boat—but that didn't stop her from imagining the car as a great yacht that rocked lightly as she turned at the traffic signal and eased nimbly around corners. She was going too fast and couldn't get the cassette of the Statler Brothers to cut off, but then she was going too slow and she accelerated until she could feel the car bouncing on its shocks. She had driven before—she could certainly drive—but never in something this big and never over forty-five miles an hour.

She glided into the parking lot, fairly sailing over a speed bump while the dashboard hula dancer bobbed wildly and across the bench leather. Dr. Agnew's papers and books fluttered and slipped. John Donne. Geoffrey Hill. Some ancient coffee-table atlas of Olde England. She shoved them all to the side and made for the main entrance, the glass doors sliding open onto the chilly foyer with its potted palms and new carpet. The walls were lined with Purell dispensers and signs explaining the importance of sanitized hands in English and Spanish. She took the elevator to the fifth-floor ICU, more or less bouncing on her heels and wringing her bacteria-free hands.

When the doors opened the smell hit her, not so much the sharp of antiseptic as something heavier and more frightening: it smelled here, she realized, like death. Up until that moment she had worried solely about her abuelos, but at that moment she felt her heart lurch for the Greaves woman, alone here with the tubes and wheeled machines and that smell she was starting to recognize as the aftertaste of human shit. She was in her nineties but somehow lived alone. *But not anymore*, Nayma thought. *Not after today.*

She found her grandparents in the waiting room, a couple of aged nervous children who fluttered to their feet when they saw Nayma. Her abuela had virtually no English, which made her, a woman who was otherwise a workhorse of devotion and faith, pathetically helpless. Her abeulo was fluent in English, educated, smart, and sarcastic. Or had been, once. He'd been expelled from the tomato fields of Immokalee, Florida, after attempting to organize what were effectively indentured servants. But the process of kicking him out—she suspected it had been more than simply driving her grandparents to the city limits and telling them to beat it—had cracked something in him, or widened a crack that already existed, so that these days he was mostly silent. There were no more jokes, there was no more laughing. He worked. He smoked. He drank one Budweiser every evening in a plastic chair on the indoor-outdoor carpet of the motel stoop.

He had never told her much about Immokalee, but she knew enough to imagine the circumstances of his life there. The town, to the extent that it was anything beyond an encampment of trailers and processing centers, was the hub of the tomato fields, the place from which migrant workers began the trek north, harvesting tomatoes in South Florida and then strawberries in the irrigated fields along the Gulf and then peaches and apples in the Carolinas. It was an eight-month odyssey of endless indentured work. Slave work, if you got down to it. Coyotes slipped the workers through the Sonora Desert on foot and into Florida in the backs of U-Hauls. When they got out they owed fifteen hundred dollars for the transport and went to work paying it back, earning two or three dollars a day while living ten to a trailer in the windless fog of mosquitos and heat and the powdered residue of insecticides so harsh they burned the skin.

Of course you paid for that too, the privilege of the trailer costing, say, ten dollars a week, and transportation to the fields—that was another two bucks. Then, of course, you might one day decide to eat something and there was yet another cost. In the end, it meant not only could you never pay off your debt, but you actually wound up in greater debt. Which meant you could very easily spend the rest of your relatively short life never venturing half a mile beyond the fields. There were periodic raids by ICE or the Department of Justice, but none of it added up to anything like justice. At best, you were deported and what was waiting for you there? Work in a textile mill if you were lucky in the way her parents were lucky: making sixty pesos for ten hours of work, sewing collars and fostering arthritis. More likely you would exist at the whim of the cartel. You might be a runner, a lookout, a mule. Until, of course, you weren't. Until, of course, a bullet placed neatly behind your right ear pierced the growing tumor the insecticides had started years prior.

So he drank his beer.

After that, he lay in bed, hands crossed on his chest as if by arranging himself for death he would save a few dollars on the undertaker. Whether he actually slept or not, she never knew. She didn't think he prayed. It was her abuela who prayed. Her abuela who kneeled on her swollen knees before the candle of the Virgin Nayma had gotten her from the "ethnic" aisle at Ingles. Her abuela who took Nayma to mass at La Luz del Mundo behind Hardee's.

But now they were both standing, silent, tragic.

She started to speak but something in their faces stopped her. They weren't staring at her, but past her, and Nayma turned to see Mrs. Greaves carted past, all wires and tubes, somebody's idea of an art project, or maybe just a bad joke.

It was the end of lunch by the time Nayma had dropped her grandparents off at the Greaves's house and made her way back to school. Nayma had fairly dragged abuela to the elevator. By the time they got to Dr. Agnew's car, her abuela was in tears and Nayma had only gotten a sidelong glance at the Greaves woman—it was all she would allow herself—but even in passing it looked bad. Her tiny self a tent of bones pitched beneath a tangle of tubes and monitors. It didn't seem fair that she would die like that. But it surely didn't seem fair to have to go on living.

She parked the Oldsmobile and headed for the front doors. You could sneak out of the school but you couldn't sneak in. The building was a well-concealed fortress of alarmed doors and hidden metal detectors and the only way in was through the entrance where, surely, someone would be waiting on her. They would suspend her, they would express their utter bafflement and complete disappointment in her, and she could try to explain but, honestly, how? And why? The college applications had all been submitted, the essays written, the recommendations sent. In a few months she would leave Walhalla and never come back. When the time came—when the money came—she would send for her grandparents. She would send for her parents, too, if they would come. The money would make them untouchable. Her US citizenship and a bank account in the high six digits. That wasn't wealth—that was protection. That was stability.

It was what she couldn't explain to the people who would question her in another sixty seconds when she walked through the front doors and confessed to having stolen Dr. Agnew's car (if she said he had freely handed her the keys he would likely be fired, and she wasn't about to let that happen). *Why did you go, Nayma? If there was a family problem, why didn't you come to us? Why didn't you let us help you?* As if by the mere comingling of their white skin and good intentions they could unravel the tangle of her life. As if skin pigment and evangelical hope would solve her problems. *Not a handout, Nayma.* (How satisfied they would appear across their shiny desks or behind the ovals of their rimless eyewear.) Not a handout, but a hand up.

Why didn't you let me help you, Nayma?

Because you can't, she wanted to say.

Because how could you solve something you couldn't begin to understand?

Her life was a construction of wildly misaligned but nevertheless moving parts that were labeled individually as money, language, citizenship—or the lack of all three—and to tinker with one, to attempt to explain one, was to risk the others, and at this point, so close to her exit, so close to the end of her sentence at the Walhalla Motel, so near the end of the next-door meth mites clawing their open sores, so near the end the creepy D.C. trying to lure her into his pickup, so near the end of so much, the last thing she was going to do was take chances.

She put her hand on the front door and took a moment to study herself in the reflection. But it wasn't her own face that caught her attention; it was the face beyond the glass. It was turning. The school receptionist was walking away from the reception desk and into the warren of hallways and offices behind her, and what Nayma realized was that she was being given a chance.

She didn't delay.

She pulled open the door and shot through, past the metal detector and the sliding second door that was—thank you!—unlocked before the door could even chime her arrival. Behind her she sensed the woman returning—excuse me?—but Nayma was already in the main hall crowded with lunch traffic.

She walked as fast as possible without running. The woman was still behind her. "Excuse me? Miss? Stop please." But she wasn't stopping, not now and not ever. She rounded the corner and ducked into the girl's bathroom—okay, she was stopping now, but this was strategic. She went to the farthest stall, locked the door, and crouched on the closed toilet seat so that her feet wouldn't show.

She waited and then came down, took a moment to collect herself at the bathroom sink. Splash her face, smooth her clothes. She put her phone on vibrate and took Dr. Agnew's keys from her pocket. That was all that was left: to return his keys, get to her next class, get through her next class, her next day, week, and so on until she could walk. Where didn't matter. Just not here.

Middle hall was less crowded. She passed the band room and the art rooms and turned right toward the English wing. A few couples were pressed along the walls, blowing little bubbles of privacy out of the otherwise public. Girls with their shampooed hair against the walls, showing their vulnerable throats. The guys were all lean. Elbows and knuckles and bristled hair. Eighteen-year-olds in letterman jackets kissing girls in cheerleading skirts. Resting their sweaty hands on hip bones. No one looked at her. She heard the guys whisper and the girls giggle as she walked past. Giggling in such a way as to let her know how different she was. Giggling to make certain she was cognizant of how ugly and Brown and plain. That there was nothing of the strawberry to her, she knew this. No strawberry-blonde hair. No strawberry sun-kissed skin. Never the right shoes or jacket or skirt, never the eyeliner that was *oh my God, so on point*. But there was something that made them giggle: the remarkable extent to which she didn't belong. Even if she did.

You're a woman with a torch, Nayma.

She tried not to walk faster.

You can do this, Nayma.

She tried to keep her head level, her eyes straight ahead. She rounded the corner—she was near the gym now, past the groping and giggling—and then she heard something. Whispers. But not whispers directed at her. These were people oblivious to her presence. They were arguing. She could tell that much. Two people—a boy and a girl. She peeked around the corner.

The hall here was long and dim and off-limits. Along one side were framed portraits of Walhalla athletes who had gone on to play college sports. Point guards and goalies and fast-pitch catchers in jerseys that read *Warriors* and *Tigers* and *Chanticleers*. Along the other side was fencing behind which were large, wheeled bins full of everything from shoulder pads to orange traffic cones. The voices, the arguing—it wasn't louder now so much as more intense—was coming from there.

She shouldn't stop.

She knew she shouldn't stop. This was a wholly unnecessary detour, yet some part of her—there was no use not admitting it—really did believe she was a woman with a torch. Someone put in the world to light the way, to take care of others, be it her parents, grandparents, whoever it was now tucked back among the portable soccer goals and arguing very volubly.

"Stop, please. Please don't, Stinson."

Stinson?

Then she knew why she had stopped: because she recognized the voice.

Two quiet steps forward and she recognized the faces. It was Stinson Wood and Lana Rogers, both from English II. Stinson had Lana backed up against the wall just like all the other boys. But unlike all the other girls, Lana wasn't kissing his throat or idly fingering whatever faux-gold chain he hung around his neck. She was pushing her fingers into his smug handsome face. She was begging him to stop.

Nayma had her hands on his jacket before she realized she was even moving. It was the white heat they talked about in books, rage, supernatural strength. The sort of thing that allowed mothers to lift wrecked automobiles off their trapped children. Except it wasn't a car she was lifting but what turned out to be a kite-thin boy who was mostly hair gel and lip—"Fucking bitch!"—and a cloying cloud of Axe body spray. She pushed him behind her, where he arranged himself, smoothed his hair, his clothes, all the while repeating to her what a fucking bitch she was.

But Nayma registered it as no more than noise.

She had one hand on Lana Rogers's shoulder, the other extended toward Stinson Wood, palm raised like a crossing guard arresting traffic.

"Are you okay?" Nayma asked.

The girl nodded but said nothing.

Then Stinson grabbed Nayma's hand and knocked it aside.

"This has nothing to do with you, Chiquita Banana."

"Leave her alone," Nayma said.

"Fucking make me, how 'bout it?"

"Touch her again," Nayma said, "and I will." And with that she watched something terrifying take place: she watched his face morph from normal human rage to something approaching a mask of smug—that word again—comprehension. It was a look that said he was suddenly realizing this wasn't a joke; this fucking Mexican bitch was serious. That she didn't get it. Yet who the hell was she to interfere with him? Did she not know how this game worked? Then the bafflement was replaced by the sort of cruelty that only comes in very deliberate calibrations.

"I will have your daddy's ass on the banana boat back to fucking taco-time by sundown," he said. "You understand that?"

"Don't touch her again."

"She wants me to touch her," he said then, a strange tactic in argument. "Don't you, Lana?"

They both looked at the girl, who said nothing.

"Don't you?" Stinson said again, but Nayma cut him off.

“Let her speak for herself.”

She couldn’t, or wouldn’t, and this seemed to fuel something deeper in Stinson, some tertiary rage that had thus far remained buried.

“Fuck you both,” he said, straightened his jacket a last time, zipped his open fly, and started down the dark hall. Halfway down he stopped and turned. “When you’re ready to apologize you know where to find me, Lana,” he called. “And you, you fucking illegal bitch. You will suffer for this. I promise you that.”

And then he was gone.

Nayma turned to Lana and was about to speak but then she was gone too, rushing past her, all unsteady legs and bed-headed hair.

Gone up the hall.

Gone around the bend.

Gone, Nayma could only hope, anywhere but back to him.

Dr. Agnew’s door was open and thankfully he was not at his desk. She put his keys by a paperweight bust of Evelyn Waugh (where on earth did you buy something like this?) and had started for the cafeteria when she heard him.

“Nayma, my dear.”

It found her like a spotlight, his voice. One of those cartoon moments where the searchlight settles on the bandit escaping prison.

“Dr. Agnew,” she said. “Your keys.”

“Yes?”

“Thank you. I’m sorry about that. They’re on your desk, right there by Mr. Waugh.”

“Mr. Waugh, my dear. As in *war*.”

“Right there by Mr. War.”

“All right, dear,” he said. “Thank you.”

She was by the door when he spoke again.

“Excuse me, Nayma.”

She stopped but didn’t turn.

“If you ever want to talk about it,” he said, “I’ve told been told I’m a good listener.”

She said nothing.

“I know what it is to need a good listener,” he said. “I also know what it is to be a stranger in a strange land. If that’s not too saccharine a thing to admit. Realizing fully that perhaps it is.”

She stood silent and still. He was moving, walking, but not toward her. He had exited through the back door into the materials room and she realized she was alone, and then she realized she was crying and couldn't stop. Crying for her mother and father and grandparents. Crying for the scared girl in middle hall. Crying for creepy D.C., who was back from the war and lonely. Crying for Dr. Agnew who was simply lonely. And crying for herself. These endless tears. These stupid, stupid tears she felt running down the copper of her robe, beneath her torch, past her book, and over her sandaled feet; these tears gathering in the vast harbor she suddenly realized surrounded her life.

Alicia Upano

ADA, AFTER THE BOMB

1

She is a beacon in the dark night, dressed from nape to heel in white. Standing at the threshold, she is a study in contrasts: her black hair blunt against her chin, the ivory of piano keys, while her red lips take shape to mouth the name of a friend inside. The bar is closed and it's well past curfew. It is January 1942. A few miles west, the Pearl Harbor shipyard remains aglow with destruction. Battleships will burn for months.

In the moments before her arrival, he served a final round of Five Islands Gin, supposedly brewed in a bathtub somewhere over the mountain range, to the small group of straggling patrons. The Blue Note is on the bottom floor of a four-story building, and it's a narrow, cramped space with just enough for tables on each side. At the back of the bar sits a little stage, a dance floor, and a jukebox. He is the young assistant to the bar's owner.

"What's wrong?" she asks. Her eyes dart from one of his shoulders to the other, as if he is finally visible. "You never seen a woman before?"

Every night, amid the big bands and cheap liquor, he sees only rayon dresses, a corner table littered with purses and gas masks. *Not like you*, he wants to say.

"That Ada girl?" a voice calls from inside. She pushes past him and joins her friend at the bar. The friend coos with familiarity. "You made it, doll. Where's Thomas?"

The young assistant watches as she pouts, demands a drink. He wipes a glass and pours. When he asks her name, she raises an eyebrow.

The friend interjects. "Let me present the great Ada Chang."

◆ ◆ ◆

Ada enjoys a small celebrity as one of the few women in the tiny jazz circuit of O'ahu, largely populated by Filipinos and their fine horns. She wants to believe she's earned her reputation—the photos of her in the newspaper, the gossip column fodder of her and her boyfriend, Thomas the trumpeter—but she fears it's just the afterglow of her father's spotlight.

George Chang is a businessman with political ambitions. In company, he introduces her as "my wayward child, fresh from enjoying the fruits of my labor," a prelude to her many failures. She dropped out of college and instead devoted herself to the dozen dancehalls in a three-block radius in Honolulu's Chinatown. He details the promising prospects he brought to their dining table. The banker fresh from Boston. The hapa gentleman with dubious royal ties to Hawai'i's lost kingdom. The import-export whiz who hailed from family friends in Kowloon.

When Ada was a girl, a piano teacher told George that Ada had great potential—not a prodigy, to his disappointment, but a talent that could be honed with practice. She was sixteen in 1935, the first time she heard Duke Ellington's "In a Sentimental Mood," and she felt as if someone heard her longing and rolled it out to her across the Pacific in the package of a perfect song.

She met Thomas during the summer of 1941, and Ada was rapt by his stories of elsewhere. From his home in St. Louis, he played his horn on the road to Chicago, through flat country, until he reached the western coast. Again and again, Ada asked Thomas to tell her about snow and overnight trains.

◆ ◆ ◆

For the first half of 1942, Ada gazes through the bartender at The Blue Note, despite her frequent after-hours visits. He pours her drinks and listens to her speak of mainland cities. Every night he believes it will be the last time he sees her, but then she appears again, always in her signature white suit. Each time the door jingles, he hopes to see her, arriving.

During one evening in June, half a year into the blackout, the bar's patrons are in a celebratory mood. US Admiral Nimitz has announced victory over the Japanese Fleet at Midway Atoll. The war, the crowd murmurs, will soon be over. The bartender finds Ada staring off toward the empty stage. "Everything will go back to the way it was," she says to him. The thousands of soldiers who flooded into Hawai'i, bringing with them their new songs and stories, thrilled

Ada. She recites the names of famous musicians who've come through—Artie Shaw, Ray Anthony, Trummy Young—as if they are holy.

She asks the bartender's name. "You ever thought of leaving, Freddie?"

"Sure," he lies.

2

The war does not end, and Ada does not leave. The Johnny Pops Orchestra comes to town for the New Year of 1943. Pops is generally good-humored, but when he first hears her play piano, he says he can tell Daddy's paid for lessons. *Loosen up*, he keeps saying. She wants to cry. At the end of the first night, Pops says only, *Good enough*.

This is the phrase that replays in her head at every measure during the five days she plays beside him. With Pops leading, she senses there's something about life itself between the notes that she's trying to capture with her fingers. It's elusive, and she's ready for the chase. During their final performance, New Year's Day, she leans into Thomas and asks, "What if we left with Pops and the boys? They're out on the Sunday steamer."

"Don't say something you don't mean," he warns. Thomas has wanted to leave for months, awaiting only a ticket out.

She gives Thomas an envelope of cash for the tickets and purchases two cheap rings for the journey. They will pretend they are married, but for now the rings remain on her dresser, because the fake metal gives her a rash.

◆ ◆ ◆

When the clock strikes midnight, signaling the new year, Freddie imagines Thomas kissing Ada, and burns at the thought.

He sits in the back of The Blue Note with a guitar in his lap, waiting for the Pops train to arrive after their Waikiki show. The band files in an hour later, and Ada and Thomas are conspicuously absent. The bassist, Chuck, pats his shoulder. "You don't seem happy to see us, brother," he teases. "Don't fret, she's coming. Her and Sir Sleazy Thomas were talking real serious."

Pops drapes his jacket on a stool, turning to the conversation. "That Freddie searching for Ada again?"

"No," Freddie says.

"Best look away," Pops says. "That dame is taken, far as I can see."

Freddie fixes his eyes on the door. Thomas doesn't deserve her, but he doesn't want to know if she thinks Freddie isn't good enough or has nothing to offer, or both. He rises to put the guitar away, but the instrument piques Pops's curiosity. "You play, brother?"

"Not really," Freddie says.

"Play us something," Pops insists.

"Yeah, Freddie," Chuck says, "play us something."

He's embarrassed. When he's alone, he'll play as he did as a boy on Maui. Nothing refined and technical as the piano. Not that big, brass sound of Johnny Pops. Nothing Ada likes. "Maybe later," Freddie says.

"You play the Hawaiian steel guitar? That's catching on all over the states. Got Hawaiian shows in every major US city. You could be somebody. Ride the wave."

Freddie laughs. "With the girls in grass skirts and the Samoan knife throwers? Not for me."

By the time Pops convinces Freddie to play a song, Ada and Thomas settle into a small table, whispering out of earshot. Pops bids them over and embraces Ada. She begins to tell him about Sunday, but he puts a finger to her lips. "Listen," he says.

The tuning on Freddie's guitar makes every note sing, twang, wrap around the sound. This is an old way of playing, passed down through generations. Not until this moment has she thought of music from this place impressive, but the instrument in Freddie's hands has the power of her piano. Ada's surprised to find her face wet by the time Pops applauds.

"Brother, that was worth the trip alone," Pops says. "You got any training?"

"My mother taught me, years ago."

Pops joins him on stage and picks up his sax. "I'm gonna play something. Listen now."

Freddie nods and Pops plays four measures. Freddie plays it back perfectly. Pops plays another bit, more complicated this time, and Freddie parrots it back. This goes on and on. "See, Ada?" Pops says. "That's what I'm talking about. You ever need a guitar player, I'd bet a handsome sum that this one could play anything. Could follow you anywhere, if you let him."

There is Freddie's toothy grin on stage and then there is Thomas boiling beside her. "But that ain't jazz," Thomas says. Ada knows him to be quick-tempered and dismissive.

"But it's something. It's something else indeed," Pops says. "You could learn a lot from him, kiddo."

Thomas's face flushes with anger, and he's on his feet. She rises to follow him, but Pops catches her arm. "Stay a while. Pops is right, you'll see."

In hindsight, Ada will recall this exchange, stretching out the seconds, trying to understand how it went wrong so fast. All she sees is Thomas's face in her mind when she discovers that the Sunday ship is overbooked. From the dock, she watches the departing ship, containing the Johnny Pops entourage and, presumably, Thomas, lost amid the thousands departing.

Every Sunday, another ship. There's more of her father's money, but she faces her own doubt: How will she go and how will she get there and how can she learn to be somebody special, a woman who can build her own life? Her options narrow into fewer moments and questions each day. The mainland coast recedes even farther into the distance.

3

She curses Pops, and Freddie joins her band. He's put down the guitar for the bass, because Pops was right. Freddie can play any instrument. The war goes on. After Midway, other Pacific victories: New Guinea, Guadalcanal. American POWs escape in the Philippines and tell the world about death marches and comfort camps. The US announces the formation of a combat team of American-born Japanese, of which 1,200 volunteer from the mainland. In Hawaiʻi, 10,000 nisei step forward. The death toll of local soldiers peaks at 37,000. Each time she leaves the apartment, Ada finds her neighbors proud, self-sacrificing.

Shame quiets her desire for more. Ada makes herself small as blackout nights turn into weeks, then months, then years. She hears no news of Thomas, but she collects clippings of the Johnny Pops Orchestra. Pops visits Europe and performs once at New York's famed Birdland. Two of the core six players are drafted in 1944, including Chuck the bassist, who returns home with a Purple Heart and stops playing and touring altogether.

In 1945, when the Japanese surrender, parties spill into streets under burning lamps. Ada invites Freddie to her father's apartment to view Honolulu, finally alight. Freddie, earnest as ever, says, "It's the happiest song in the world."

She longs to see a path in the jagged coast as clear as an illuminated runway, pointing to a diminishing horizon, the promise of earth falling away. But all she sees is what she's always known.

◆ ◆ ◆

As soldiers return—passing through on their way back to bases stateside—they appear wearier than those who left, as if there's a price to victory that no one admits. Ada and Freddie play a series of welcome-home gigs, but the evenings leave a sour taste in her mouth. On one night, early in 1946, a bar brawl interrupts one of the slow numbers, and a lover's quarrel on the dance floor during the fast-paced finale leaves an unpleasant air to the evening. There is no encore. A newspaper photographer takes their photo. Freddie leans over, intimately, as the flash goes off. Ada looks away. Did she blink in this rare moment of attention? She can already see her face in the paper next to a recipe for banana bread.

Back at The Blue Note, Ada tinkers in the empty bar with a song until Freddie joins her on the piano bench, which is not large enough for them both, and she's precariously near the edge. "You're running, Ada," he says. "Try it a beat slower."

She tries it his way, and he's right. "It's a love song. There's no need to rush." She plays it again. "That's right," he says.

The warmth of Freddie pulls her to him. He's always so sure and he says naïve and comforting things. He doesn't care whether she'll have her name in lights or whether she'll ruin her father's good name. She knows and he knows that she knows that he loves her, but still he won't dare touch her. With him, Ada feels special even when she knows she's done nothing special, not yet.

That night, Ada leads Freddie up to his little room in the attic. She wonders if he's innocent in matters of love. There've been the boys before Thomas and the occasional man after Thomas, but disrobed before Freddie, she has never been so vulnerable.

4

Now there is Ada's toothbrush in the bathroom, the smell of her in the bed, and her white suits hanging in Freddie's closet. The suits multiply, and that's how Freddie realizes that Ada's entire wardrobe consists only of seven identical suits, fine lingerie, and a silk robe so luxurious that Freddie can't help but feel inferior, for he can't imagine any future where he could make such a purchase.

Their first months together have not dampened her need to talk about her other, desired life. If she's reserved a space for him there, she doesn't let on. *She can't help it*, he tells himself. *She's been so sheltered.*

Swing is waning, even here on the island where mainland trends lag, arriving too late and hanging on well past their prime. Jazz is moving on. People don't dance as if the world will end tomorrow. They leave earlier, to their growing families in new homes. Ada despises this, but Freddie reasons it's the natural course of things. They're getting older.

When she's out until dawn, drinking helps him forget her absence, though he's been known to drink while she sleeps because he can imagine her absence. In his hands, her body feels like an hourglass, and she's sand through his fingers, the time in her running out.

Freddie likes to watch her sleep. Like a baby, she smiles when she dreams, sometimes flailing her limbs in delight. He interrogates her in the dark. *Do you see me? Am I there with you?*

A year after the war ends, Freddie lingers as Ada takes in the ornate decor of her father's apartment. The patterned rugs, the jade ashtrays, the lacquered settees. Her baby belly bumps against doorframes and closet doors as she stuffs two bags of items. What she really wants is the piano, but it will not fit in the little house on the far side of the island, a place as foreign to her as her pregnant body. This is not how she wanted to go. Freddie appears frozen, with a single hand extended over the threshold.

5

There is not enough time. A decade passes with labor strikes and a path toward statehood. Her father wins elections, his career catapulting forward, but she feels increasingly invisible except to her two children. Her eldest is a girl who takes after Freddie, not just in countenance but in disposition. Her daughter's face betrays no emotion, and yet she is loyal, always performing what's requested of her. Ada watches Freddie leave for work and return with a six-pack, disappearing to the far end of the yard with his guitar. She watches her daughter sweep the floor and hang the laundry. Her youngest is a boy, who appears to be the only happy one in the family, singing through breakfast and dancing in front of the television until his sister bullies him to sit down. His enthusiasm is total and, to his mother, exhausting.

She brings the children back to the Chinatown flat when she knows her father is out of town. They hold every framed photograph in their little hands. She wears her silk robe and teaches the kids to play Chopsticks on the piano. With her son at the window, she counts the warships in Pearl Harbor, defending peacetime. The maid stuffs them with dumplings and tea.

Her daughter, who is not impressed by much—certainly nothing Ada has offered her since birth—asks, "Is this what it was like when you were growing up?"

"I was very spoiled," she says. She doesn't believe in lying to little girls and so she doesn't tell her daughter that she is special or going places or there's enough time. But her daughter regards her with such wonder that she can't help but make a promise she knows she can't keep. "One day, I will give you a life like this, too." They stay up past bedtime and fall asleep with the lights on.

Twice Ada goes to her father's with the children, and twice Freddie's begged her home. She promises there will be no third time. Yet Freddie returns home one day at dusk to find their children standing on the stoop, the door behind them flung upon.

His daughter asks, "What are we gonna do?" His son says the suitcase under the big bed is missing.

Freddie cranes his head to the sky, pink and orange above the chiseled range. His wife, a bird, gone at last.

6

Twenty-five years after she first stood before Freddie on the dark stoop of The Blue Note, Ada finds herself in Omaha, Pops's hometown. She now knows snow, as well as slush and sleet. She's boarded overnight trains, cross-country buses, and even a ship that shimmied up and down an Atlantic coast. At a record store downtown, a man behind the register directs her to where Pops's old house stood, warning her it's gone, like the big man himself. She hails a cab, and she passes the scribbled address to the man behind the wheel. In the silence between them, the DJ reads the news in a tone as flat as Nebraska. Communist China tests its third nuclear weapon. The annual casualty count of American soldiers in Vietnam is more than 11,000. LBJ speaks of the Soviet threat and a wall in Berlin.

The cab stops on the outskirts of the city, in a suburb built on a grid. The house reminds her of the one she shared with Freddie with its detached garage, generous lawn, and large picture window. Both houses were built during the same time, she figures, after the war. From the sidewalk, she watches a curtained window, the silhouette of bodies against a television's flickering glow.

Was Pops right?

She asks herself this often. When she finally fell in love with Freddie, she thought, *Pops was right*. When she peeled Freddie up from the yard as their daughter watched through the window, she thought, *Pops was wrong*. When she boarded a mainland-bound plane, she thought, *Pops was wrong*. When she sent her letters into the ether, begging Freddie and her children for forgiveness, she thought, *Pops was right*.

She wants Pops to appear, not as an apparition but in the flesh, as if she's already a ghost in good company.

Ron Rash

L'HOMME BLESSÉ

Every month there were two or three phone queries like this one. Someone had bought a Monet at a yard sale in Weaverville or found a Grecian urn in a woodshed. One unhinged caller claimed he'd discovered the missing arms of the Venus de Milo. Others wanted him to evaluate folk art, hoping some elderly relative might be the new Grandma Moses or Howard Finster. A few showed up at the college unannounced, treasure trove in hand, sent by a receptionist or an administrator to him, Brevard's only art teacher. Most could be persuaded to seek evaluations by museums or galleries, though sometimes, out of personal curiosity or their insistence, Jake agreed to examine what they had. If nothing else, the consultations fulfilled his department's community-outreach requirement, which would help next year when he came up for tenure.

This time the art was too large to bring to campus, which meant a twelve-mile drive to an isolated farmhouse, but it was an excuse to miss his afternoon office hours, which so late in the semester meant students either arguing or begging for higher grades. He was too tired to face them. Besides, the caller was Shelby Tate, whom he'd taught last fall. A good student—smart, serious, a bit older than most. She'd mentioned the paintings in class one day. Her great-uncle had covered every wall in his bedroom with painted portraits of strange beasts, her comment garnering odd looks from the other students. Jake was curious and planned to go see them during the Christmas break, but what had happened to Melissa changed all that.

Jake locked his office and walked to the faculty lot. Across the way, a grounds crew hung a wreath above the dining room door, a reminder to stop by CVS when he returned. He headed west on Highway 19, the directions on the passenger seat. The leaves were off the trees now, revealing time-worn swells so unlike the wild, seismic peaks and valleys beloved by European Romantics such as Pernhart and Friedrich. Sturm and drang. Yet the Appalachians were daunting in their uniformity, a vast wall, unmarked by crevices that might provide an easy path out.

When the odometer neared twelve miles, Jake watched for the red realty sign marking where to turn. Gravel first, then dirt leading to a bridgeless stream. He pressed the brake, might have turned and gone back home if not for the urgency in Shelby's voice. *Please, Dr. Yancey. If you don't come now, it'll be too late.* As the car splashed across, a back wheel spun for a moment before gaining traction. The woods opened up and a small house came into view, most of its paint peeled off, the tin roof pocked with rust. A red Jeep Wrangler was parked in front of the porch. Shelby came out on the porch to greet him. Although she wore sweatpants and an oversized sweatshirt, her pregnancy was evident. Her eyes were the same light blue as Melissa's had been, which he'd either forgotten or not noticed before.

"Thank you for coming, Dr. Yancey," Shelby said, her accent more noticeable than he remembered. "I'm sorry to call you so sudden but Daddy sold this place yesterday. The new owner's going to raze this house next week."

"It wasn't a problem," he answered. "It gives me a break from listening to students complain about grades, something you never needed to do. You made an A, I recall."

"Yes sir, I did," Shelby answered, and hesitated. "I wasn't certain you were still at the college, but I'm glad you are."

For a few moments, neither of them spoke.

"Well," Shelby said, nodding toward the open door. "What I wanted you to see is inside. Watch that first porch step. It's so rotten it might give way on you."

A lantern was beside the door and Shelby struck a match and lit the wick.

"There's no electricity," she said.

He followed her into the front room. As his eyes adjusted to the muted light, Jake saw dusty pieces of furniture, a fireplace holding a few charred logs. They walked through a small kitchen and then down the narrow hallway. Shelby paused at a bedroom door on the left.

"In here, Dr. Yancey," she said, raising the lantern as they entered.

Strange beasts, indeed, Jake thought, his gaze drifting across the walls. The images were amateurish but discernable. A zebra with red spots instead of stripes, a small spiked fin on its back, a shaggy elephant with down-curving tusks, a deer with the snout of an anteater, a thin-legged boar. Plywood had been nailed over the single window frame, on it in calligraphic black the face of a lion. Except for a moldering mattress on the floor, the room was bare. But as Jake's eyes adjusted, the animals became more discernable. A mastodon, not a hairy elephant; a bison, not a boar. Despite the fin, the spotted horse was familiar too.

"I've seen these images before," Jake mused aloud.

"Where?" Shelby asked.

"A book on ancient art. They were inside a French cave."

"A French cave?" Shelby asked, clearly puzzled. "That seems so unlikely."

"Why?"

"How would Uncle Walt know about paintings like that?"

"Same as me, I imagine, from an art history book."

"But he didn't have any art books."

"Then television, or a magazine."

"Uncle Walt didn't have a television, and once he got back from World War II, Daddy says he hardly left this place. Twice a month Grandfather drove him to town to shop and cash his Social Security and VA checks, but that was it."

"When did he paint these?" Jake asked.

"Daddy says it was right after he came back from Europe."

The images did appear that old, the red and black paint flecked, the lion fading into the warped and rotting plywood.

"Maybe he saw the images over there."

Shelby shrugged. "Maybe."

"When did he die?"

"2001."

"Did he paint any besides these?"

"Not that I know of."

"So during the war, he was in France?"

"I know he was at D-Day," Shelby said and nodded at the animals. "I used to think it was what he saw in his nightmares, but if it was, why did he sleep in here all those years?"

"Maybe he needed to confront it," Jake said. "Was there ever a bed in here?"

"No, just the mattress. Daddy thinks that had something to do with the war, needing to feel less exposed. When I was a kid and we came to visit, Uncle Walt let me jump on it, like it was a trampoline. He was always kind to us kids. A couple of times I got spooked being alone back here, so I'd go back out front with the grown-ups."

"A folk-art dealer or a museum might find these walls interesting," Jake said, "but with the paintings so faded, and trying to get them out without the plaster crumbling, I doubt . . ."

"I know, but it's not why I asked you to come. Daddy's having to sell this place because the taxes are a burden. Before they tear the house down, I wanted at least one person besides Uncle Walt's kin to see the paintings, someone who might appreciate his doing them."

In the last week, the exhaustion and lack of sleep had made his emotions so raw. Now, despite the Clonazepam, he blinked back tears. Jake took out his phone, busied himself with it as he composed himself. Only one bar appeared.

"I was going to pull up some of these images."

"There's no reception out here," Shelby said and smiled, "which isn't always a bad thing. I get a few whiners about grades too—not the students, but their parents."

"Which grade?"

"Fifth," she answered. "Most of the kids are real sweet and I'll miss them when I'm on maternity leave."

"Mind if I take a couple of pictures?" Jake asked.

"No."

Jake took one of each wall before putting the phone back in his pocket.

"I'll compare them when I get back to the office. Like I said, maybe he saw photographs in France, if not in a book then a magazine or a newspaper."

"You don't have to do that," Shelby said. "The main thing was just you seeing them."

They looked at the walls a few more moments. The images were not originals like the wild bestiaries of a folk artist like Robert Burnside, nor was there some stylistic quirk. More like something copied from a book by a talented child, but as Jake stared at them he was moved that the man felt such a deep need to express what he'd endured. They walked up the hallway and onto the porch. Shelby closed the door but did not lock it.

"If you give me your number I'll text or call if I find out something," Jake said, and he paused as Shelby wrote her number on a scrap of paper. "Thank you for the card you sent after Melissa died. I should have responded but, anyway, this visit allows me to say it now."

"I've thought about calling you for months," Shelby said, "but figured you had a hard enough time without burdening you more. But with the sale . . ."

"I'm glad you called," Jake said.

He recrossed the stream and was soon on the two-lane back to Brevard.

The name of the cave lingered just on the edge of memory. Not one word like Lascaux or Chauvet, but two words. As he neared the Brevard city limits, a Subaru wagon came up fast behind him, tied to its roof a Christmas tree, its tip pointed at him like a spear. A black tide of memory washed over him.

December 14, almost exactly a year ago, he and Melissa had been decorating for a Christmas party, three other couples invited. Melissa had gotten a promotion and Jake's division chair had mentioned that his chances for tenure were excellent, so there was much to celebrate. They had gone all out: holly on the fireboard, a Fraser fir wreath. Melissa had been setting the table when the forks slipped from her grasp and clattered against the floor. She placed a hand on the table to steady herself and told Jake she was dizzy. A day later Melissa was dead. In the hospital room, he had lifted a hand heavy and cold as clay.

Shelby was one of two students who sent a card, one likely picked up at a CVS or a grocery store, the card's condolences followed by a handwritten sentence about his being in her thoughts and prayers. A brevity Jake appreciated. He'd been amazed at what people, intelligent people, could utter at such a time. An English professor, his wife beside him, quoted Tennyson's "better to have loved and lost, than never to have loved at all." Another colleague said "it's good you two decided not to have children," and yet another told Jake that at least he was young enough "to find another wife and start over," as if Melissa were simply a defective machine part easily replaced.

When he got back to his office, no one else was around. Jake left the lights off, the only glow that of the computer screen as he tapped in *cave art France*. After a few clicks, the bison, mammoth, and lion appeared. The spotted zebra was there too, though it was actually a horse. What Jake had thought a fin was instead a human hand hovering over the animal. Pech Merle was the cave's name. He pulled up an article about its discovery in 1922. Black-and-white photographs showed the first scientists exploring the cave.

When they were in grad school together, Mason Bromwich's dissertation had been on cave art, so Jake typed a message to him noting how the paintings were identical to those in Pech Merle, adding that the man who'd done them was in France during World War II.

My question is this, Jake typed. *The cave's images would be in French magazines and newspapers at that time, correct?*

Jake hesitated. The email's timing might be perceived as a subtle outreach for sympathy, for an invitation. Or seen for what it was, a request for information.

A student wants to know, he typed, and hit send.

He didn't expect an immediate reply and was about to shut off the computer and leave when Mason's response came.

Hi buddy, Long time, no hear. You need to answer your emails!! Re paintings—by details, you mean even the colors are right?

Yes, Jake typed. *Orange bison, red dots on the horses.*

Let me check a few things in some books. Need it soon?

Jake's hand paused over the keyboard.

Yes, he typed.

Give me a few minutes and I'll get back to you. You doing ok? I know it's probably not an easy time of year for you.

I'm fine.

Jake leaned back in his chair and waited. Footsteps came down the hallway, a familiar clack of heels. Jake was glad his office light was off. If not, Lila Marshall would stop and want to chat. She'd recently gone through a divorce and felt she and Jake were kindred spirits. *There are worse ways to lose your spouse than through death*, she'd once told him. Lila's office door opened but soon closed again. Her heels echoed hollowly back down the hall and she was gone. Half an hour passed before Mason's response came.

Your soldier didn't see them in a magazine or newspaper. I emailed Marc Valery and he agreed that the best sources say no color Pech Merle photographs before 1951, even in art books, much less newspapers or magazines. (That's in France or anywhere else.) The only way to know all those details would have been visiting the cave itself. M

Jake typed a response.

I doubt he'd be wandering around in caves. They were fighting a war.

Then someone's fibbing about when the images were painted.

I don't think so. The paintings appear that old.

Maybe color photographs were taken, but a GI coming upon them? It's a stretch, pal. Check troop movements. If anything they might have passed through the area.

Thanks for the help.

No problem, Jake. Seriously, you doing okay?

I'm okay.

Janice and I would love to have you come up for Christmas.

Thanks, but I'll just stick around here.

Janice promised to buy you a stocking and hang it up with Kelly's, and you know my chef credentials. What do you say?

Maybe another time.

Okay, but if you change your mind . . .

Okay. Got to go. Thanks again.

Jake sat a while longer, summoning the energy to get up, to walk to the lot, to turn the key in the ignition. The gas could wait but not the prescription, so he drove to the CVS. Inside, Christmas reds and greens dominated, but holiday cheer was absent. It was near closing and the employees looked tired and harried. The store's harsh fluorescent lights seemed designed to heighten such unhappiness. *If you don't leave, you won't get even a few hours sleep tonight*, he reminded himself.

The customer at the counter turned and dropped her prescription into a bag decorated with candy canes, shifting time: a red stocking filled with shiny foiled Hershey kisses, bright-striped candy canes, tangerines, and, at the bottom, a box of crayons. Jake must have been four, because he wasn't yet in kindergarten. He remembered the crayons' waxy smell as the colors and shapes flowed unmediated from his hand to paper. The wonder of the act remained.

Before leaving, he made a couple more purchases. Once home, he tapped in Shelby's number.

"I asked Daddy again and he's certain the paintings were done in 1945," she said. "He said the paint cans are still in his shed and prove it."

"I'm not doubting your father," Jake said. "My friend says the only explanation is that your great-uncle was in the actual cave. Did he ever hear anything like that?"

"I never heard of it, but I can ask Daddy and call you back."

"Sure, I'll be up till at least eleven."

Jake listened to a message his sister had left about holiday plans, then poured a glass of wine. He'd finished a second glass when the cell rang. He checked the number and picked up.

"Daddy said Uncle Walt never talked about the war or France to him, and hardly to my grandfather either. But there's a man in Tennessee who was in the same unit. He visited Uncle Walt a few times, came to the funeral too. Daddy had his address and made some calls. He's at the VA hospital in Knoxville. I'm thinking about visiting him Saturday. It might be the only chance to talk to someone who knew Uncle Walt during the war. Having a child, it makes things like that seem more important." Shelby paused. "You'd be welcome to come along."

Jake had no plans for Saturday morning, other than a faculty luncheon he'd just as soon miss.

"I'd like that. What time and where?"

“Knoxville’s three hours away, so is ten all right?” she asked. “We could meet at Uncle Walt’s or in Brevard.”

“I’ll meet you at your Uncle Walt’s,” Jake said. “I’d like to see those paintings one more time. And can you give your father a quick call and see if he knows which division your uncle was in?”

“He’d know because he’s got the discharge papers, but Daddy’s likely asleep now. I’ll find out tomorrow.”

As Jake finished the wine he scanned the internet for more images of the cave, finding some that were not on the farmhouse wall, including one of a man leaning or falling. Vertical lines—spears, perhaps arrows—passed through the figure’s torso. Jake read the article, which suggested interpretations based on shamanism, the image’s coloration, and its location within the cave. He shut down the computer and took the Ambien.

Jake awoke at three, feeling the same chest tightness that had sent him to the school infirmary last week. After an electrocardiogram showed nothing, Jake was given a script for Clonazepam. *Don’t hesitate to use it, Jake,* Dr. Wells had told him. He knew he wouldn’t go back to sleep so he made some coffee, then waited at the kitchen table for dawn to lighten the window above the sink. He showered and dressed; afterward, he drove to the college to teach his last classes of the semester.

On Saturday morning he arrived at the farmhouse on time, but it was 10:20 before Shelby showed up.

“Sorry,” she said. “I stopped to pick up some baby clothes from my sister.”

“No problem,” Jake said. “I can drive if you like.”

“No, I don’t mind. Plus, I know a shortcut to 40 even the GPS can’t figure out.”

As Jake opened the passenger door, Shelby nodded at a white pastry box, asked if he wanted her to put it in the back. Jake told her it was fine.

Soon they were on back roads Jake had never traveled.

“Have you met this man?” he asked.

“Once when he visited, but he probably won’t remember me. His name is Ben Winkler.”

They rode in silence a while. A green sign appeared with the words *I-40 West Knoxville/Chattanooga*, and they merged onto the interstate.

“Have you decided on names for your child yet?” Jake asked.

"It's a boy and we're calling him Brody. It's a family surname."

"I like your using a last name that way," Jake said. "My wife and I were planning to have children and wanted to do the same."

After they signed in at the front desk, the receptionist pointed to the elevator.

"Fifth floor. Take a right. It's room 507."

The door was open. Mr. Winkler sat in a recliner in the corner, a folded newspaper on his lap. A metal walker stood in front of the chair, green tennis balls on the wheels. After they introduced themselves, Winkler removed a pair of black glasses and set them and the paper on a lamp table. He rubbed the paunchy flesh below his eyes a moment, then motioned toward two plastic chairs. Shelby set the white box on the room's single bureau before sitting down.

"Pull those chairs closer," he said. "My hearing's not what it used to be."

Jake and Shelby moved nearer.

"So you're Walt's niece?"

"Yes, sir," Shelby said. "Grand-niece, that is."

For a few minutes Shelby made small talk with Mr. Winkler, asking about his health, the family pictures on the bureau. Her manner was unhurried and respectful. Though only thirty-six, Jake felt like a huge gulf existed between him and his most recent students. He wondered if Shelby's generation was the last raised to tolerate quietness and stillness. It wasn't a judgment, just a reality. Perhaps a life of unyielding distraction was better, he'd often thought since Melissa's death.

"We have a question for you," Shelby said, "about Uncle Walt during the war."

"I'll try to answer," the old man responded. "But my memory's gotten near as bad as my hearing and eyesight."

"When you were in France," Jake asked, "do you remember anything about a town called Cabrerets?"

"Hard to know," the older man said. "Most times we was too busy trying not to get shot to be looking for town signs."

"Yes sir, I can imagine so," Jake said, taking out the map he'd printed off the Internet. "I looked up the troop movements and it seems your division wasn't anywhere near there, but I wanted to be sure. The red mark I made, that's where the town was."

Mr. Winkler put his glasses back on, took the map and studied it.

"Some of us did come through there, not during the war but right after."

"Right after?"

"Yes. We had a three-day leave and took a train out of Paris. Walt hadn't wanted to go. He was in a bad way. We finally convinced him it might do him some good. The train was headed toward Toulouse if I remember right, but we got off when the notion took us. Anyways, at one stop this Frenchman come on board jabbering about something we might want to see, said he'd drive us there and back."

"It was a cave, wasn't it?" Jake asked.

Winkler took off the glasses again and set them on the table. He looked at Shelby.

"Walt told about being in that cave?"

"No sir, not that I know of," Shelby answered. "Were you in there with him?"

"Not the first time. I wanted to flirt with them French girls instead of visiting some old cave, but Walt and a couple of fellows went to see it. The others caught back up with us and said it wasn't worth the time, that they'd seen better drawings in the funny papers. When we asked where Walt was they didn't know."

A smile creased the old man's face, his eyes no longer focused on his visitors but something more inward.

"We figured he'd got one of them French girls to say *oui*," Mr. Winkler said. "Anyway, when it was near time to catch the next train, we started searching. It come to nothing until a Frenchman said Walt was in the way-back part of that cave, laying on the ground asleep. So me and another fellow went in to get him. It was spooky in there, I tell you that, and got spookier the deeper we went, and we went a long, long ways. It had to be near a mile. Darker than any place I ever been, and what light we had showing these old-time fierce animals on the walls. When we finally found Walt, he was laying on the cave floor asleep." Winkler stopped and looked at Shelby. "Your grandfather was a brave man. I don't want you to feel otherwise about him."

"I won't," Shelby answered. "You can tell us."

"We woke Walt but he wouldn't get up. One of the fellows sat down beside him and tried to talk sense to him. But that done no good. He started crying and saying that the only thing outside of that cave was death. We finally had to grab his arms and drag him. Even then he kept begging us to leave him there."

"So he was at the very back of the cave?" Jake asked.

"Deep into that cave as you could get. I didn't think we'd ever get him out. The next week Walt was headed home on a Section Eight. Some fellows in the unit thought bad of him for breaking down like that, but none of them was in that first wave at Omaha Beach. Walt was in the 116th Infantry. You know about them?"

"No, sir," Jake answered.

"Well, they was in the thickest of it. Walt and two others from his unit came off that beach alive. Our outfit had some hard tussles, and Walt fought as good as any man, but even then you could tell he was in a bad way. And every day it got worse."

"My daddy said Uncle Walt was never the same when he returned," Shelby said softly.

"None of us were, child," Winkler said, shaking his head. "It's just some could handle it better than others, or at least pretend to. My boys wanted me to go back over there a couple of years ago. They'd pay the flight, hotel, meals, everything. I told them thanks but that I'd spent most of my life trying to forget ever being there once."

The nurse who'd been waiting beside the door came into the room.

"It's time for your lunch, Mr. Winkler."

Shelby nodded at the white box on the bureau.

"I baked you some gingerbread cookies. You can have them for dessert."

"Thank you," he said, raising a trembling hand blotched purple-black. He held Shelby's hand a few moments before releasing it. "Your uncle, he was a good man. We didn't do much talking when I visited, but if you've been through tough times together, you don't have to."

When Jake and Shelby got back to the farmhouse, Jake asked if he could see the paintings a last time.

"Of course," Shelby said and lit the lantern.

They went down the dark hallway. As their eyes adjusted, the menagerie slowly emerged. Shelby set the lantern down and stepped close to the lion. She placed her hands on the plywood, wiggled it until the two remaining nails pulled free. She carefully leaned the plywood against the wall.

"What will you do with it?"

"I don't know," Shelby answered. "It wouldn't seem right not to save something, especially after today. I might put it in the nursery."

Shelby leaned to pick up the lantern. When she stood again, the window's suffusing light surrounded her. *Woman With Lantern*, Jake thought. Perhaps somewhere such a painting existed. *If not*, he thought, *it should*. For a few minutes they were silent. Though it was midafternoon, the room was darkening. The animals began receding as if summoned elsewhere.

"I guess I'd better be getting home," Shelby said, "or else Matt will start worrying."

Jake carried the plywood out and Shelby placed it and the lantern in the back of the jeep.

He opened the trunk of his car, then took out the sketch pads and boxes of crayons he'd bought at CVS.

"A gift for your son," he said. "Maybe he will be an artist like his great-great-uncle."

Shelby set the gifts beside the lantern and plywood.

"Thank you," she said, giving him an awkward hug, "not just for the gifts but for helping me find out about the paintings."

"I was glad to do it. When your baby's born, I'd like to know."

"It won't be much longer," she said, giving her stomach a soft pat. "The doctor says the third week in January."

"Cezanne was born around that date. The twentieth, I believe."

"Maybe I'll aim for that," she said, smiling.

"Would you mind if I stayed a few more minutes?" Jake asked.

"No, sir," Shelby said, looking at the surrounding woods. "In the fall when the leaves turn, this cove is such a pretty place. Even now, there's a beauty about it."

After Shelby left, Jake went back inside. He looked at the animals for a few minutes, then lay down on the moldering mattress. The springs creaked and a thin layer of dust rose and resettled. He did not realize he had fallen asleep until he opened his eyes in darkness. He felt his way through the house and out the door. In the day's last light, Jake drove slowly to the creek, stopped at the water's edge. Oak trees lined the opposite bank. In their upper branches, mistletoe clustered like bouquets offered to the emerging stars. He paused there a few more moments, then passed over.

Rachel Kadish

LETTERS ARRIVE FROM THE DEAD

When letters arrive from the dead, the postmarks are often in error. Envelopes are backdated or bear stamps from improbable places. This stands to reason; the dead are notorious fibbers. They have reputations to protect or to invent, and certain inconvenient legacies to dismantle.

In the temporary village in which they're housed before moving on, the dead close out old business, study their new obligations, and acquire necessary paperwork. Each has been allotted a certain amount of time to set affairs in order, and most work diligently, if grimly, toward this departure date, though inevitably some linger longer. (So what if they outstay their visas? Who will hold them to it?) For the most part, they remain decorous—yet even those who are, frankly, hooligans do not steal from the living, vandalize heirlooms, or poison food; nor do they murder, make appliances malfunction, shatter glass. The fantasy that the dead do such things is libel. It's not that the dead never wish harm on the living, but that their gestures are ineffective. True, they're capable of visiting the living in altered form, but most choose not to on account of the draining fatigue that results, the inner-ear problems that last days, the aching joints hardly worth what's achieved: a brief whisper that goes unheard in a noisy setting, or a brick, thrown with unfathomable effort, that nonetheless misses (the dead have execrable aim). Ultimately, even the fiercest recognize the futility of such modes of communication.

In their desire to settle their last affairs with the living, they retreat, in the end, to this post office, which promises to dispatch their messages without need for ghostly visitations. Here, at last, they press their points much as the living do: wearily, obediently, coloring within the lines of bureaucracy—because who can be troubled to do otherwise?

In the dim, dusty post office, the drowsy clerk flexes his wrist, stamps his heavy stamp. The creaking desk chair, the unoiled wheel that sticks, the sigh of the small lumbar pillow as it takes his weight. The dead, shuffling in a queue that ends at his desk, mail admonishments, rebukes, samples of tea. Their messages to the living are opaque—they know the censor in the adjoining office must be appeased. Besides, who wants to report the literal truth of their dull status in this transit village, when more newsworthy and impressive experiences await in the next phase? Still, communications must be sent—there are arguments to be settled, exhortations and endearments to convey. Nor are the dead above the occasional passive aggressive missive. The postcard reading *Wish you were here.*

(The postcard arrives in a dream. Waking, the living scramble to interpret: What lies beneath these four words? What deeper meaning may be intuited? Psychiatrists are visited, old diaries are dredged, sage is burned.)

Dreams, while the most common delivery system, are not the only one. Airplane contrails, owls, drifting smoke—anything seen out of the corner of an eye will do. Communications breach the world of the living in the form of a familiar perfume or a whorl of dust or dry leaves blowing into an alley on a windless day. A passing bus splashes mud across the new shirt purchased for a date with *her*—was it a warning from the other side? The living readily attribute such phenomena to certain departed kin, friends, or enemies—attributions that are often inaccurate. Studying the receipts noting the interpretation of their missives, the dead cannot be faulted for feeling at times maligned, even plagiarized.

At his desk with its dockets, dreaming of vacation, the clerk assesses each item with practiced skepticism. Certain things are not permitted: hazardous materials, messages that violate confidentiality laws. Surely by now the dead—the never-ending line of them traversing the long hall toward his desk—must know the routine. Yet the clientele is ungrateful. *Why was she served before me? I wasn't told my letter would be censored. My package is but a small one; it contains no harmful objects. It contains nothing that would harm a soul.*

The stamp, the creak of bureaucracy, the ticking clock. He himself works long hours, his salary is paltry—yet he makes no complaint, for who would listen? We all know a better system would be possible, if we were starting from scratch.

Please, it won't harm them. To know what I finally know, now.

Five minutes to closing, you'll have to come back tomorrow.

Now and then a message is returned to sender, unopened. Only then, as the sender makes his way toward the door, clutching his receipt, do the dead pause in their bickering and part in silence, to make way for the bereaved.

Stephen Henighan

BLUE RIVER HOTEL

The first time he shared a room at the Hotel Río Azul with a woman, he was young and the country was at war. The government celebrated the New Year by announcing that the war had ended in a victory for the army. On New Year's Day the UNGR guerrillas struck back, blacking out the electricity in eleven cities. The war ground into its thirty-fifth year. In the morning, when he caught a rattling Bluebird school bus north from the market in Chichicastenango, the edge of town was rimmed with soldiers. At each roadblock, the passengers opened their documents, then stood by the side of the road while gaunt, dwarf-like teenagers in skintight uniforms clambered into the bus's interior and prodded the barrels of their Galils at the dark-green upholstery.

The regularity of the seasons guaranteed pellucid blue January days. He drank down the clarity, even though he felt ill and exhausted, and on edge from the checkpoints. A frigid hotel in Chichi had left him with a blood-sapping cold. As they approached Quetzaltenango, the country's second city, high and remote, and only a fraction of the size of the capital, he blew his nose on toilet paper from the roll in his pocket. On the hillsides above the city, the papery off-yellow of corn stalks and the dark humus color of earth tilled for irrigation channels marked out the tiny plots of Mayan farmers. Dark-green conifers clung to the upper reaches of the hillsides. The Bluebird bus dropped him at the Minerva Bus Station, a chaotic field outside of town. He took a taxi downtown and stepped out of the cab below the park's Roman pillars and fountain. He sweated and shivered in the chill mountain air. Every other town he'd visited had been either a tourist trap or a garrison under military lockdown. Quetzaltenango, busy yet venerable, offered a Guatemalan normality.

He picked his way along crowded streets of close-packed shops dominated by battered secondhand cars, teenagers in tracksuits and blue jeans, men in open-necked shirts and pressed slacks, women in traditional Mayan skirts and *huipiles*, or sweaters and long dresses. He turned uphill on Avenida 12, entering a district where the shops were interspersed with nineteenth-century mansions that had been converted into hotels. All along the street there was graffiti on the walls, signed by the UNGR guerrillas. *El pueblo maya lucha con valentía—UNGR* ("The Mayan people fight with courage—UNGR") was splashed on the front of a hotel. The owner of a hardware store had spray-painted the stucco next to his front door with the words *Se vende concreto* ("Cement for sale"), and some wit had added *UNGR* to that as well.

The Hotel Río Azul stood at the junction of two narrow, steep streets. Inside, split-level floors were conjoined at unexpected angles, as though geological strata had been shaken, sliding together epochs and continents. Balconies hung over each of the down-plunging streets. There was a bright, enclosed lounge on the third floor, and an elevated courtyard at the back of the fourth floor that was open to the elements. The only signs of a blue river were the navy-colored plastic rectangles that were attached to the keys. The cheapest rooms were in the courtyard at the back: narrow twin-bed cubicles with the toilet located across the cold tiles of the outdoor landing.

The hotel was full. They gave him a bed on the condition that he share the room. The external courtyard looked out past the roof of the hardware store and the fall of the street at the distant snow-covered peak of the Santa María volcano. The cold bored into his bones. As he lay sneezing on his bed, he heard Doña Bendición tell a young gringa she would have to share the room. "With a muchacho?" the girl said as the door opened.

Scrubbed and blonde, she carried a backpack of no-nonsense compactness that lent her an air midway between that of an intrepid NGO worker and a hygienic Christian missionary. She confirmed both of his guesses by introducing herself as the representative of a Catholic NGO that followed up on adoptions of Indigenous children. She dropped her pack on her bed and left. He lay there reading an article in a newspaper he had found in the lobby that explained that in the Mayan calendar, January 2, 1995, was the date 12 baktun, 19 katun, 1 tun, 13 winal, 17 k'in. At night he rolled under the covers, relieved to discover that the blankets, which Doña Bendición said had been woven in the village of Momostenango, were heavy enough to protect him from the cold. The idea that this was a country where two calendars overlapped soothed him.

As darkness fell, the girl returned. He saw how young she was, only twenty or twenty-one. She was too terrified at sharing a room with a strange man to speak to him. When she got into bed, taking off only her hiking boots, she sat up in vigilance. "Is it all right if I turn out the light?" he said. Her response was a nervous whimper. He got out of bed in his woolen pajamas and flipped the switch. As the light went out and he returned toward the beds, the girl whimpered out loud. All night she murmured to herself as though praying. Each time his stuffed-up nose awoke him, the whispering was continuing. In the morning, she stood by the door. "I left fifteen quetzales on the table for my share of the bill." She opened the door, confiding a glimpse of the snowy peak of Santa María high in the thin blue sky. He knew he would never think about her again.

* * *

Coughing, he entered the hotel through the door at the top of the steps. The reception desk and the dim lobby were decorated with black-and-white stills from the surrounding mountains: closeups of the summit of Santa María, the Fuentes Georginas hot springs, corn growing in terraced plots cultivated by Maya in traditional dress. Don Miguel and Doña Bendición explained that the hotel was full because a group from the capital had booked two floors for a New Year's party. They signed him by hand in a huge ancient register where they listed his *procedencia*—where he was coming from—as Chichicastenango and filled in his *destino* as Guatemala City, because anywhere farther away was beyond human imagination. It was only the next day, after the girl departed and he staggered out to a pharmacy and bought cold pills, that he began to speak to them. The couple's three children capered around the reception desk. Don Miguel was a bony man with a solicitous gray mustache, his woolen waistcoat and dark jacket mirroring the hotel's austere decency. His wiriness and yellowish skin made him look Southern European; Doña Bendición's dark hair curled, her face was a pale tan color. Their three children, with their long eyes, high cheekbones, and straight black hair, were much darker than their parents. The inconsistency was obvious and unmentionable. It was only ten years later, when he had booked a student group into the hotel and they invited him to share a sweet, potent coffee, that he asked the question. He had allayed their discomfort with his perpetual singleness by revealing that he had a fiancée, a confession which drew sharp looks from their elder daughter. María was a short, willowy teenager whose curiosity about relations between women and men drew reprimands from her parents. Doña Bendición's curls were gray now and Don Miguel cleared his throat more often. "God did not intend us to have children," Doña Bendición said, her index finger sliding down the thin, gold cross suspended from her neck. "We were devastated by this until we understood that His plan was for us to provide a family for three children who did not have one."

The children were adopted through the Catholic Church from a Mayan village in the mountains. "Are they siblings?" he asked.

"Possibly cousins," Don Miguel said. "Their families were connected."

The past tense confirmed his suspicions. The children came from a village on the banks of a river in the mountains to which the UNGR had retreated in the mid-1980s when it began losing territory to the army's helicopter gunships. The army had entered the village, accused the inhabitants of supporting the guerrillas, and forced them to dig a pit in the muddy village square. The adults were divided into male and female. One by one, each of the village's women was stripped naked. The soldiers led each woman to the edge of the pit and raped her, then shot her in the head and threw her body into the hole in the ground. Between 12 and 4 p.m., jeering at each other as they unbuckled the belts of their tight uniform trousers, the soldiers raped and killed all of the village's women. They started with the grandmothers and ended with girls who had not begun to menstruate. Then, more briskly, they seized each man in turn, shot him in the back of the head, and threw him into the pit. Once the village's adults were dead, the soldiers slaughtered their chickens and burned their houses, their corn, their stacked firewood, and the beehives at the back of the village where two families produced honey. Later the soldiers and their officers would return to build houses for themselves on land that had belonged for centuries to a community that had ceased to exist. As homeless bees buzzed in the air, children were piled into the backs of army trucks. Their culture was eradicated; as they grew up, they would forget the Quiché language. But if given decent homes, they would become obedient citizens who were respectful of authority and the army. Don Miguel and Doña Bendición did not speak these words; others had spoken them in his hearing. He understood that this couple had been chosen to adopt because their household exemplified values that would ensure that subversives' children integrated into society. And ten years after sharing a room with her, he understood what the blonde girl had been doing at the Blue River Hotel.

On his first visit, he asked them why they had named their hotel after a blue river.

"To remind ourselves of the river of life that carries us to eternity," Doña Bendición said.

"But to signal the joy that we experience in passing down the river of life," Don Miguel explained, "we chose the color blue."

The next time he stayed there, they didn't remember him. Their business relationship began when he started booking student groups into the small double rooms that surrounded the interior lounge on the third floor and inviting representatives of local community organizations to give talks there. He was older, less skinny and unsettled, with a decent haircut. The country was no longer at war. It was the time of building democracy and implementing the Peace Accords—or, as his speakers pointed out, of failing to implement the clauses pertaining to Indigenous rights. He now spent half the year in the tourist town of Antigua, close to the capital, where he managed student excursions and provided English-language services, and the other half at home in Ottawa, working on short-term government contracts.

His parents, who had immigrated from Central Europe to swampy, boulder-strewn Ottawa Valley farmland, had called him Trevor, a name popular among Scots-Irish farming families in the region, to encourage him to integrate into their new home. At fifteen his imagination had been ignited by dreams of Latin America. He gazed at picture books in the school library, read about Mayas and Incas and conquistadors, plotted routes across the map of South America with his finger, sought ways to learn Spanish at a high school that taught only French. His imaginings isolated him from his classmates, making him believe that his emotions were unique. The conviction carried over into his relationships in university and beyond. "Why can't you meet a girl who is like you?" his mother complained, convinced that his happiness depended on his marriage to a woman whose parents came from the old country. At a superficial level his mother was so obviously wrong that only after a decade did he concede that in a deeper sense she was right: there was an intimacy he had not allowed himself. He wouldn't expect anyone to display total understanding of the cross-stitching of rural Ontario and Central America that dominated his imagination, certainly not Jasmin, whom he called his fiancée when he was in Guatemala, and sometimes, also, in Ottawa. Her parents had emigrated from Asia; her career was in finance.

She was in Ottawa on an eighteen-month government consulting contract when they met, then she moved to Toronto to work on Bay Street and was often on a plane to Hong Kong, Singapore, or Shanghai. They spent weekends in the same city for a few months each year and went on vacations together. Each time he feared that their relationship was little more than a source of reliable sex after stretches of intense work, their sensitivity to each other's needs surprised him: the lack of fuss with which a rare Saturday afternoon together was sacrificed to ensure that a report was finished, the acceptance of each other's single-professional quirks and tyrannical agendas; but also how she suddenly became more caring than he could have imagined when a contract slipped through his fingers, the warm reliability she pulled out of him when her uncle died of a heart attack and he spent two days at her side during funeral rites in Markham in a language he didn't understand. Working in different places didn't mean they couldn't be sensitive or nurturing; it didn't mean he wasn't growing as a person. Even when weeks passed during which his only glimpses of Jasmin were the sweaters, parka, toque, and scarves she left hanging in the closet of his Lower Town condo, or the photograph of her that he propped up on the counter of the colonial stone cottage he rented in Antigua, he was sure he knew her better than his friends knew the wives they had lived with for a decade.

* * *

Rhea sat next to him at a workshop in Ottawa. She was slight and fine-boned, with a feminine delicacy of skin and perception, a youthful irony, wavy dark hair, and a deep, commanding voice. He chatted with her during lunch and the Styrofoam-cupped coffee breaks without realizing that she was an undergraduate. She was more mature and definite than the students whom he led on excursions. She had traveled in all of his favorite countries, first in pursuit of Latin American theater, then to rescue giant turtles, and now in search of gender definitions: she was applying for funding to develop programs for drag-queen prostitutes in Buenos Aires. When, not quite believing her tales, he spoke to her in Spanish, she replied in an Argentine drawl, telling him that her boyfriend was flying in to visit her. He mentioned that his fiancée was in Taipei on business. After the workshop ended, they had coffee in the Byward Market and exchanged email addresses and phone numbers. Only then did he notice that they used the same phrases: "do you not" for "don't you," "laneway" for "driveway," "it doesn't care" for "it doesn't matter."

"Where are you from originally?"

When she told him, his heart went still: her village was five kilometers from his; they'd attended the same high school, years apart.

He asked her surname and recognized its local provenance. "How did you get interested in Latin America there?"

She smiled. "They had a few books in the school library."

Two weeks later, on Saturday night, leading his jet-lagged fiancée around a corner in the Market after dinner, he swerved to avoid a young couple who were kissing against one of the pillars that held up a portico where stalls were set out during the day. Jasmin's high heels danced a brief tango as she skirted the couple. He saw Rhea's white cheeks pull back from a tall, dark youth's embrace. Neither of them spoke. The next month, when she emailed to invite him to coffee, he was relieved to reply, from an Internet café down the hill from the Hotel Río Azul, that he was in Quetzaltenango.

⁂

"When I was sixteen, my father died and left me money. I knew what he would want me to with it."

Trevor's palm grew hot against his mug of beer. His mother had left the old country at sixteen, also after the death of her father. Should he ask about her father's death? He decided to ask about his life. She told him that her dad had been a lawyer and rural township councilor, a serious Catholic who might have had a future in politics had he not passed away at forty-five. "My father was a Catholic too." He, too, had died young, though not as young as Rhea's father. The harshness of the Ottawa Valley poured back like the icy spring runoff: everybody knowing everyone's business, the limitations of vision that shackled a place where time stopped in its tracks, turned in circles, as though Rhea and he *had* gone to high school together. She was in full flight, telling stories of situations her innocence had led her into and how she had gotten out of them. After her first bout of Latin American traveling, she returned to her village to finish high school. Nobody understood what she had experienced; her every divergence from accepted opinion was seen as a sign that her father's death had made her weird.

She grasped his hand across the café table, then released it. They were drinking Mexican beer in an Irish pub. It was their first meeting in six months. Her hair was longer than the last time he had seen her; in defiance of her small-boned delicacy, the picture window behind her, with the Sussex Drive traffic streaming past, embellished her silhouette to a shaggy grandeur. Over her shoulder, high up on Parliament Hill, the clock in the Peace Tower insisted that they occupied the same place and time, in spite of the generational discrepancies that reminded him that she was his protégée.

A protégée unknown to his fiancée.

"Are you all right?" she asked when he failed to reply. "Are you afraid of me?"

"I'm amazed by you." That was too strong. He didn't want to give her the wrong idea; the Argentine boyfriend seemed to be out of the picture. "I think you're one of the most impressive young people I've met in my field."

"Oh, come on. Don't be so formal. I like to be close to people who are older than me." There was a silence, as though one of them might be about to mention the dead father. She sipped her Corona. When she had returned to high school, after hiking in Peru and rescuing turtles in Panama, she was no longer capable of dating boys her own age. "In grade thirteen my best friend had an affair with the drama teacher. He was fifty. But she said he was in great shape!" The pleasure in her laughter told him that it was she, not her friend, who had slept with the teacher. "I've got to go," he said. "I'm setting up a meeting with a man in Guatemala."

* * *

He got Compañero Tino's phone number from Don Miguel. The next group of students he was guiding were third-years with two years of university Spanish who were studying the history of the civil war. Trevor made an overnight preparation trip up the Pan-American Highway from Antigua to Quetzaltenango (he called the city Xela, as the locals did). Preferring not to divulge his legal name, Compañero Tino asked for his meager honorarium in cash. They met at a stall in the market, identifying each other through an exchange of prearranged phrases, as though time had turned back to the war years of code words and underground activity. It had been six years since the signing of the Peace Accords. The country was adrift under a corrupt government, influxes of gringo money, incursions by Salvadoran drug gangs, unraveling Mayan cultures. Tino's view of these developments was that of a defeated warrior. A fine-boned man of peasant modesty, he led Trevor to the back room of the community radio station where he worked. On a creased red poster pasted to a damp stucco wall, the features of a bespectacled youth were defined in bold black strokes. *¡Oliverio Castañeda Vive!* read the lettering below. A brilliant student orator, Trevor knew, Castañeda had been murdered by the army after giving a speech.

The station's broadcasts were audible from the adjoining booth: 1970s political folk songs mingled with tinkling marimba-led ditties from the highlands and public-service announcements from cooperatives and community groups in Spanish interspersed with Quiché. As Tino interrogated him, Trevor saw how, in the context of a different time, this subdued questioning could have been terrifying; how giving the wrong answers could have led to execution. Tino stumbled over his name, pronouncing it "Tre-borr," a sound that approximated *trébol*, the Spanish word for "clover." He told Tino to call him Trébol. Addressing each other by their nommes de guerre, they settled on a subject, a date, and a price for Tino's talk. When he got back to Antigua, there was a message from Rhea. She was in Mexico City, researching gender among drag-queen prostitutes in the Zona Rosa. Email flattened her anecdotes, but enough of her personality came through that he responded by writing her a quick reply. He had work lined up for five months in Antigua. Jasmin, who had never come to Guatemala, had promised to visit him this time. In the morning, she wrote to cancel her plans for a January visit. He wrote back to settle a date in February or March.

He spent four days guiding twenty students through the highlands, visiting the vegetable market in Zunil and the weavers in Momostenango, and holding talks in the third-floor lounge of the Hotel Río Azul. Compañero Tino was the final speaker. He shuffled into the lounge and stood with his head bowed before the tall, fair students, nearly all of them young women. He said nothing. When the silence became uncomfortable, one of the students asked, in passable Spanish, "Why did you become a guerrilla?"

Tino looked down at his hands. "I became a guerrilla because when I am eleven years old I wake up, I open my eyes and see four soldiers drag my father out of our house. I will never see my father again . . ." In the spasmodic Spanish of a native speaker of a Mayan language, mingling past-, present-, and future-tense verbs, Tino related how, after the murder of his father, a spokesman for local small farmers, he fled to the mountains and grew up in the guerrillas: eating two servings of rice and beans a day; sacrificing for his compañeros; and, as he grew older, suppressing his jealousy, in order to maintain discipline, at the relations some compañeros had with the few compañeras present. He spoke of sleeping out in the rain, being trained to make broadcasts on guerrilla radio, and mourning compañeros who died in combat.

“Are you happy with the Peace Accords?” a student asked.

“No. This isn’t the Guatemala I want. My whole life, I dream of the day I will enter the capital with a revolutionary army.”

“Did you ever go back to your village?”

“Yes, to bring to justice the men who killed my father.” He paused. “Now I cannot go back.”

Uncertain how many of the students had understood the verb *ajusticiar* (“to bring someone to justice”), or realized that Tino was using this revolutionary jargon to tell them he had murdered the soldiers who had killed his father, Trevor tried to bring the talk to a close.

“Why can’t you go back?” a girl in glasses asked. Fascinated by meeting a real guerrilla, the students kept asking questions. An hour later than planned, Trevor took Tino down the street to an anonymous restaurant with tiny booths, where they ate rice and refried black beans and a leg of undernourished chicken with a slice of avocado. They drank Coca-Cola. Expressing a mournful gratitude at the students’ interest, Tino told him that his village had been razed by the military while he was away in the guerrillas; the soldiers who had killed the inhabitants had occupied their land. Tino complained of the impossibility of explaining to his son why he had spent seventeen years as a guerrilla instead of earning a living. “My son and I live in different historical periods and cannot meet. Do you have children?”

“No. I have a fiancée. But when I come to Guatemala, I don’t see her for five months.”

Tino shook his head. “Five months! I could not do that. Not anymore.” For the first time since they had met, he smiled. “Compañero Clover, you are the last person in Guatemala who lives with revolutionary discipline!”

Jasmin canceled her February trip, then her March trip. She phoned him three times a week on the cell phone he’d bought in the market. “Don’t worry,” she said. “Five months’ll be over before you know it.”

At night, he listened to the mice crawling through the rafters of his zinc-roofed stone hut on a cobblestoned colonial street with a view of the Agua volcano. His body stored the heat of the sunny days and emitted it in pangs of nocturnal lust. Though not even easygoing Antigua was a good place to be out after dark, he met up with old acquaintances in cafés in the evenings to exchange stories of the civil war, gossip about local politicians, and talk about the customs of different regions of the country. Jasmin kept phoning, growing petulant when GuaTel's connection to Canada lapsed, or when she caught him at night in a place with music playing in the background.

"I work hard!" she said, mentioning a swap, a merger, or an acquisition. "I'm beat. I need a beach. Are there beaches in Guatemala?"

"A couple." He was suppressing his emotional and sexual needs for the cause. Compañero Tino had done this for seventeen years. Yet all the phone sex in the world—and Jasmin was good at phone sex, delighting in asking in a coy voice whether he was alone—could not soothe his restlessness. Why couldn't she just get on the damned plane?

"Give me a little time. I'm on the cusp of something big. I can't bail now or somebody else will get the promotion."

He gave her the space she required, as she did him. Their relationship, always open in this way, and in this way alone, continued at night, in the real time of cell-phone conversations. His communication with Rhea was consigned to the timelessness of email. Once a day, he ducked into a street-corner Internet café and sat among Guatemalan teenagers playing video games, tourists writing messages home and drawling missionaries coordinating crusades for Mayan souls. Nothing obliged him to reply to, or even open, Rhea's messages. When he had business to deal with, he left her words preserved under glass. Yet he always replied eventually. How to identify the hour when he had begun to follow her misadventures in the Zona Rosa as though they belonged to a telenovela? The day when he had started to feel a punishing little stab in his gut if he opened his email to find no message from Rhea? The night when the abundance of her curls got tangled up with his fiancée's fine, dark strands in his lustful fantasies? The month when a communication that had been timeless elbowed its way into his daily schedule? She asked him for advice on grant applications. She was hoping to turn the drag queens into a master's thesis. *Of course before I can do that, I have to actually finish my undergrad!* She pasted a draft of her project description at the bottom of an email. Set upon by chores, he put off reading it. When he went to the Internet café later in the week, she had written again. *I'm sorry I did that! It would be so much easier if I could talk to you about it.*

He agreed this would be easier. On email, agreement morphed into commitment, so perhaps that was the instant when the momentum shifted and *if* became *when* and *when* demanded the assessment of possibilities, and the assessment of possibilities required that dates be chosen, and without knowing how this had come about, he found himself wanting, with a longing in which desire, loneliness, and an old-fashioned spark of traveler's adventure blended like the compounds that powered firecrackers during Antigua's Holy Week celebrations, to make this meeting happen. The crystalline air of December, January, and February had yielded to the wispy white clouds of March, then April, when cumulus built up like stealthy towers behind the mountains. The students he was guiding finished their semester and went home; a professor for whose research project he had been conducting interviews arrived in Antigua, declared the project completed and left with his recordings; two Guatemalan accountants to whom he had been teaching business English stopped coming to their classes. His flight home was at the end of May. He had saved some money; his only remaining commitment was to interview the Mayan mayor of Quetzaltenango for a Montreal newspaper. Free time yawned; unexplored regions of northern Guatemala beckoned. He could visit the remote north, return via Xela, and do the interview. If Rhea chose to come down from Mexico, they could meet up north and go over her grant proposal.

"Come and meet me!" he said.

"I can't, hon," Jasmin replied. "Not now. You'll have such a good time in all those jungly places by yourself."

She knew the risks of their heading into the back of the beyond together. She had heard him complain about how traveling companions wilted under the heat, balked at local food, got sick, broke out in grotesque rashes at the first insect bite, became constipated because they were afraid to use the toilets, embarrassed him by stumbling over the language. He was happiest on his own: independent, fluent, resilient, soaking up local cultures in great waves of enthusiastic understanding that perpetually replenished his enthusiasm for travel. Would he have been more forgiving if, back in the era when his habits were being formed, he had hooked up with a woman who shared his love of traveling rough?

He bit his lip and wrote: *I'm going to northern Guatemala. A meeting could be a possibility—*

I agree about the meeting, Rhea replied an hour later. *That's very important.* He thought of her riding buses from Mexico City—thirty hours on buses?—and wondered what she was expecting. For two weeks he traveled on his own in the Petén jungle. Returning to civilization in Cobán, a small city a half-day bus ride northeast of the capital from where he would ride pickup trucks across the north, he walked to an Internet café. He looked for messages from Jasmin and colleagues in Ottawa. His most recent message was from Rhea: *I'm running like a happily mad thing. On my way to the bus . . .*

As the dust-drenched pickup bounced out of the arid mountains and down into the fringes of Huehuetenango, he saw that he had entered a zone that was not Mexico, yet was no longer entirely Guatemala. Here two histories coiled together. The men in the central park wore thick black mustaches and broad-brimmed white-straw hats; when he objected to the truck driver charging him twice as much as the other passengers, the man reviled him, with Mexican-tinged venom, as a pinche gringo. He walked to the cheap hotel where they had arranged to rendezvous, took a shower, and lay down on his bed. Two hours later Rhea knocked on his door.

She was taller than the woman he had refashioned in his mind. She wore sandals, white three-quarter-length slacks, and a black tank top. He leaned toward her in greeting. As he followed her down a narrow, raised sidewalk to a restaurant, his eyes hungered for the shape of her legs. They were mopping up the last of their refried black beans with tortillas when the restaurant's power went out. "This used to happen all the time," he said, "when the guerrillas blew up the pylons."

"I know there was a war here," she said, "but I'm not old enough to remember it."

He was sitting in Huehuetenango with the girl he used to run into in the Byward Market.

After supper, they walked through the crowded, rundown streets of the Mayan market, where plastic bags and wrapping paper gusted along the sidewalks and burnt food simmered on ashy embers in the creeping dusk. They emerged onto the steps that looked out over the Minerva Temple. As large as a city block, the building was a replica of a white, Doric-columned temple in ancient Rome. "The dictator at the beginning of the twentieth century put up fake Roman ruins and shrines to Minerva. He figured that if you imported Roman gods to replace Mayan gods, Guatemala would jump historical periods and become a developed country." They sat down on the steps to look at the deserted temple in the fading light. "He forgot that histories with different starting points end up in different times."

"I have nothing against intergenerational relationships," Rhea said.

Was that what he had been referring to? He wasn't used to being with someone this intuitive. As he stared at her, she asked him if he rode a motorcycle; she was always getting involved with men with motorcycles. Touched by her willingness to tease him, he shook his head.

"No motorcycle?" she said. "That reduces your chances."

In the hotel, they exchanged a Latin embrace before going to their rooms. He was unable to sleep. Over breakfast, feeling that it was his duty to do so, he told her in a stilted voice how his relationship with Jasmin worked. He felt relieved when he had finished.

Rhea reached for her day pack. "Can I show you my proposal?"

They went to a café and worked on her application. Her prose had a purposeful lack of flab. Familiar with the committee that would assess her proposal, he suggested points she might emphasize to increase her chance of getting the grant. By midafternoon, they were finished. "I guess that's it," she said. "Time for me to be getting back to Mexico."

She slid the folder into a woven bag. She was already on her feet when he said, "Why don't you come to Xela with me?"

They stayed at the Hotel Río Azul.

He wondered whether he could pass off Rhea to Don Miguel and Doña Bendición as his fiancée. Had he told them that Jasmin was Asian? Rhea's youth would give them pause. To his relief, the owners were out when they arrived; the children were at the reception desk. The older girl, María, already had a daughter of her own, though her parents never referred to a husband. She sat on a chair with her toddler, while her adolescent brother and sister examined the register with serious gazes.

"Is a room on the third floor all right, Don Clover?" the boy, Alberto, asked.

He nodded. Alberto assigned them to one of the little double rooms around the lounge where the students had been billeted.

As he signed in and paid for three nights, María, hefting her infant, said, "Is she your fiancée?"

"Is he your brother . . . ? Your dad?" Alberto asked Rhea, his voice shrill.

"We're going to get married," Rhea replied.

The younger girl, picking up on the game, said, "Is he your grandfather . . . ? Your uncle . . . ?"

Giving him a concentrated look from beneath her eyelids, María handed him the plastic rectangle with the dangling key. Her little sister's mockery pursued them out of the lounge. On the trip down from Huehue in the recycled Bluebird school bus, he had been squeezed against the window, with Rhea next to him and a man in a broad-brimmed hat on the aisle. After an hour, the man got off and a girl, about thirteen years old, in a Mayan huipil and skirt grabbed the place for herself and her baby daughter. The baby screamed; the girl laughed and swung her around, singing to her in Quiché. He and Rhea, pressed shoulder to shoulder, murmured together like teenage classmates riding the bus to their Ottawa Valley high school. They passed rock faces, smoldering undergrowth, and ragtag streams of people walking along the roadside. Rhea told him that her father had died of a hereditary genetic disorder. If she had male children, they, too, would die at forty-five, though girls would have normal life spans. "That's another reason I keep traveling. Why settle down if my children have a 50 percent chance of being born with a death sentence?" She leaned into him as the bus went around a steep curve; this time he took her hand. For a shuddering, bone-rattling moment, they remained linked. "How old are you?" she murmured, with a naughty smile.

He told her. He had her doubled: forty-two to twenty-one. She was the same age as the students who had listened to Compañero Tino.

The beds in their room were set against opposite walls; there was enough space at the foot of each bed to prop up a backpack. An interior room, it had no windows, though there was a small bathroom and a transom of wavy glass over the door that trapped the flat light of the lounge. "My body aches," Rhea said. They went to bed early, after taking turns changing in the bathroom. In the morning, she was no better. "I think it's my kidneys." Her deep voice drowned her moan. "Too many long bus rides."

He phoned the mayor's secretary to confirm his interview. Rigoberto Quemé Chay was Guatemala's first Mayan mayor, elected by urban Indigenous neighborhoods in defiance of a racist city where Mayan people were banned from sports clubs and good restaurants. Trevor left Rhea, who wanted nothing to eat, walked down the hill, and crossed the square to the nineteenth-century city hall that looked out over the Roman columns in the park. The interview took place in the mayor's office at the back of the second floor. Quemé Chay, dressed in black, was an urban Mayan who had grown up without the Quiché language or traditional culture; he was considering running for president. Trevor asked him whether he would help rural Maya by implementing land reform. The mayor shook his head. "The land issue belongs to the past. Young people don't want to sow corn. Our future is in the cities, as entrepreneurs."

Once he had turned off his recorder, he asked the mayor if he knew the Hotel Río Azul. Quemé Chay seemed surprised that he was staying there. "Those children will inherit a business; other Mayans will create them." He flexed his lips. "You know why it is called the Hotel Río Azul."

"Doña Bendición said the river of life . . ."

"For the river that runs through the village from which their children were adopted." Quemé Chay stood up. "Give my regards to Don Miguel."

He returned to the room to find Rhea in pain. He went down to the lobby, where Don Miguel was bent over the register, and transmitted the mayor's greetings as a prelude to broaching his need for a doctor's phone number and a taxi. Don Miguel lifted the receiver of the phone at his elbow and made the arrangements. "Where is Doña Bendición?" he asked.

"She is busy." Don Miguel shrugged his shoulders. "She knows that girl is not your fiancée."

"We're only frien–"

"Do not trouble yourself, Don Clover. I am a man." Trevor had never seen him look so old.

The taxi honked at the door. He went up to the room. "I'm so sorry," Rhea said, dragging herself out of bed. "Me, the great traveler. . . . You'll never believe my stories again."

He helped her down the stairs and into the taxi. They rode to a nineteenth-century building past the lower end of the park that housed a private clinic. Rhea inched her way along the hall, leaning against the wooden panels of the vast corridor with its marble floors and twenty-foot ceilings. She was ushered in to see the doctor, who told Trevor to wait outside. When she came out, she said that the doctor had remained seated behind an enormous desk; crammed bookshelves rose behind him. She felt like a señora from a distinguished family consulting a physician about an embarrassing complaint. Diagnosing exhaustion, the doctor prescribed pills. They rode back to the hotel. Trevor ran around to three pharmacies to collect the medicine. They spent the rest of the day in the room. In the afternoon, he went out to eat rice, refried black beans, and chicken. He brought her soup.

"I've never had a man look after me before. I feel like crying."

They talked about their childhoods in the same clutch of swamp-encircled villages: his parents' desire that he marry a girl "like him," how her father's death had expelled her from the arc of her generation's experiences. "I've crossed over to the other side. That's why I'm here with you."

She was so tired that he doubted she would remember her words in the morning. That night, he slipped out of the room, went out onto the balcony, and waited for a prearranged call from Jasmin. In the cloudy darkness, the Santa María volcano was invisible. "I've been offered a really great job in Australia," Jasmin said, "and I feel I can't take it because of you."

"You said you were coming here!"

"Give me time, baby . . ."

He hung up and paced the lounge. When he returned to the room, Rhea was asleep.

◆ ◆ ◆

"Put on your bathing suit under your clothes," he said, as she stepped toward the bathroom. She had woken in the morning announcing that she felt five hundred times better. "Since you're feeling better, we can visit the hot springs."

She stopped, her exuberance contracting into watchful wariness. "I'm not used to men telling me what to wear." He remembered the blonde girl taking off her boots. Rhea hesitated, then burrowed in her pack and emerged with a cream-colored two-piece bathing suit. They ate a pancake breakfast at a gringo restaurant off the park. It was mid-May. In the implacable chronometer of the seasons, the rains were approaching. The air was damp and gray, like the unwashed, uncarded wool sold at market stalls.

He took her on the tour he gave to students. They caught a bus from the corner of the park to the village of Zunil. The vegetable market, which fascinated development students, bored Rhea. They hunted down the village's saint. San Simón, a replica of a man in garish plastic, was carried from house to house. After asking around, he tracked down the saint in a house where a family had surrounded him, begging him to petition God to give them the money to buy the land they needed to feed themselves and keep their sons at home. "All we want is the land our people used to have before the war." The father supplicated before the saint in a sibilant, anguished voice that went on and on without halting for breath, while the mother and grandmother sat on their knees before him, planting lighted candles on the floor. The sons emptied bottles of hard liquor down Simón's plastic throat.

As they left the house, he sensed her mood lightening. She gloried in the ride up the mountain in the back of a pickup truck. They gripped the metal frame fixed to the half ton's box. As the pickup climbed, the valleys filled with mist that streaked across the road and prickled their eyebrows with cold dew. "This is like the cloud forest in Costa Rica," Rhea said. He saw that, at least for part of the year, this was a cloud forest. He had brought student groups here, but always in the dry season; only now, seeing through her eyes, had he grasped the mountainside's rainy season identity.

The hot springs were nearly deserted. They floated, lulled to the verge of sleepiness. Their fingers, bobbing side by side, grew wrinkled. They were basking in the soupy, sulphureous water beneath the black overhanging cliffs when the soldiers arrived.

There were thirty of them—tiny, tight-uniformed youths whose arms looked too spindly to wield their Galils. He gripped Rhea's shoulder, seeking her substance, afraid that he had carried her back to the era of his first visit to Guatemala.

The young men laughed and clowned around, returning him to the present. An officer imposed order: half of the soldiers stood at ease in the mist, their Galils level at their waists in a phantasmagoric recollection of the war, while the other half stripped to their underwear and waded into the springs. Rhea was shocked by the military presence; Trevor felt oddly reassured. At the time of his first visits to Guatemala, being surprised in a swimsuit by the military could have meant death; now it was an irritation.

They dried off, dressed, and rode down the mountain in the back of a truck, then walked across the village to catch the bus back to Xela.

"I said I'd stay for three nights," Rhea said. "I'll leave tomorrow. I have to get back to my drag queens."

They ate supper at a Mexican restaurant. Rhea's banter about the Zona Rosa oppressed him. Afterward, they rambled through the silent park in the darkness. The morning newspaper had announced a lunar eclipse. To their astonishment, high above the Roman columns, they saw clouds sliding by curved degrees over the moon until the lunar surface was blotted out; celestial bodies born at distant points fell into alignment. As they climbed Avenida 12, she slid her arm through his. At the reception desk, Doña Bendición handed them their key in silence. They climbed to the third floor, entered the stuffy room, and lay down on their beds.

"You look pensive," Rhea said. "What are you pensing?"

His breath hurt his chest.

"Whatever I'm pensing," she said, "I'm going to come and pense it over there." She crossed the room and lay down on his bed with her back to him. "I know this is wrong because of Jasmin," she murmured, "but I know when someone is like me."

He clasped himself against her back. They adjusted their hug, then adjusted it again. At long intervals they gave each other chaste, close-mouthed kisses on innocuous body parts. He kissed her shoulders, her elbows. Their bodies clambered together with infinite slowness, as though wallowing through a zone where time had been suspended. After forty minutes he reached under her low-cut black T-shirt and caressed her back; he ran his hands down the backs of her legs. He was back in the Ottawa Valley, in a grade twelve class where they were studying *Wuthering Heights*, except that this time he understood what Cathy meant when she shouted, "I *am* Heathcliff." Each caress peeled away layers of concealment, each stripping stroke brought the merging of their essences closer. He pressed down harder on her flesh as he slid his palms over her back. Rhea's breathing quickened, synchronizing with the motions of his lightly sweating hands.

"What I'm pensing now," she gasped, "is that I've intruded on a lot of situations and caused a lot of problems." She rolled over. "That's what happens when you're attracted to older men who already have lives." She sat up, the corners of her eyes glistening. "This time I'm going to keep my clothes on. I'm sorry."

His breath caught in his chest. "There's no doubt," he said, "that in moral terms you're doing the right thing."

"That's a first. Me doing something moral in a relationship!"

"Just my luck to run into you when you decide to be moral."

Having intended these words as a joke, he heard their bitterness cut the night. Rhea became angry. "You're the one who laid out every detail of your relationship with Jasmin over breakfast in Huehue. How do you think that made me feel, after I'd ruined my health coming all that way to meet you? I wanted to be welcomed, not pushed away."

"You know I had to do that."

"Did you? Did you really? She's here in the room with us!"

He bowed his head.

"It would have been so much better," she said, her voice faltering, "if you had let me pretend that this high-flying career woman wasn't going to out-compete me for you. Then I could have fallen in love with you, and if you'd gone back to her afterward, we would have had our moment . . ."

They spent the rest of the night, dressed in makeshift pajamas, sleeping in each other's arms. Now and then they woke to run their lips over each other with pursed affection. He felt the compactness and burning heat of her body. Near dawn, he dreamed that he was embracing the adoption girl and felt a lurch of revulsion at her scrubbed blondeness.

In the morning, they took a taxi to the Minerva bus station. The bus to Huehuetenango was parked in a muddy trench. Rhea watched the *ayudante* load her backpack onto the roof. He kissed her on the lips. She opened her mouth until their lips met around an oval-shaped space that was locked between them. She turned away, then veered toward him again and gave him a hard kiss on the neck. She disappeared into the bus. And that should have been the end of that story.

◆ ◆ ◆

It was inevitable that they would flirt over email, she suggesting that he visit Mexico City that summer, he inviting her to call him when she was in Ottawa. Then, equally inevitable, the tone of her messages changed: *I have a lover, a lover who loves me and whom I can love every night . . .* She danced around the specifics of her relationship until just before her return to Canada. Then what had been implicit was made explicit: Rhea's lover was a middle-aged woman. Her fleeting backpacker affairs, her long-distance relationships with older men, the absence of a serious boyfriend in her life, fell into place. She had been able to acknowledge the intergenerational dimension of her desire before the same-sex dimension. One night, she phoned and they met for coffee in the Byward Market, in an Eastern European place on a side street concealed from the Peace Tower, where the maps on the walls depicted vanished national borders revered by Trevor's parents. He expected Rhea to bring her lover, a woman from rural southern Mexico, but she came alone. She seemed just the same: her hair tousled, her virile voice vying with her soft-toned sensitivities, her mind continuing to nourish itself on Latin American politics and literature. With the help of her grant money, she had finished her undergraduate degree by submitting independent-study projects long-distance. She was going back to Mexico to live. "To Mexico City?"

"No, to Tabasco. That's where Guadelupe's from. Her whole family's there."

He wanted to say: *Tabasco's too rural, nobody will accept* you. Realizing that any objection he made would be suspect, he asked: "What does your mother say?"

"She says Guadelupe's too old for me." She smiled. "Focusing on generational difference is her way of not dealing with lesbianism." She scrutinized him. "Are you still with Jasmin? Are things the same between you? Was I right to say no?"

"Yes, yes, and no," he said.

"Which, from my point of view, means yes, yes, and yes."

Her emails stopped. Sometimes, in the middle of the night, when Jasmin lay naked beside him, he would wake and hear himself saying, in a voice inside his head: *No, Rhea. Not Tabasco. Not those endless swamps, more water than land, Mexico's Ottawa Valley, as ingrown as the Ottawa Valley fifty years ago and much, much poorer; you can't live a same-sex life there—or any life you'd want to live.* Who was he to make such judgments? After a point, time and understanding fused. What his mind ruled to be impossible, might be feasible in her reality.

He stopped spending part of the year in Antigua. He found a desk job in the civil service, on contract at first, and then permanent, and had an affair, which felt stupid even as it was occurring, with a woman in another department. This gave Jasmin the pretext they both sought to end their relationship. Within six months, she was engaged to a Chinese-Canadian banker from Toronto; he heard later that she had a daughter. Trevor settled down as an Ottawa bureaucrat, one of countless stolid men who came off farms in the Ottawa Valley, shed their overalls for ill-fitting suits and landed government jobs. He was comfortable, yet he resented his job security even as he clung to it. Unlike other men he knew, who struggled to pinpoint the moment at which their lives had declined into ordinariness, he knew exactly when and where his nerve had failed him.

◆ ◆ ◆

A decade later, the phone on his desk rang. The display screen showed a cell number of which he had no record. He sweated as he heard the tones that had responded to his passion. "I'm in town," she said. "Could you meet me in the Market for a coffee?"

He left work and walked through the construction and the Rideau Street traffic. On the maps on the café's walls, the national boundaries from bygone eras were fading. She sat at a table at the back, petite yet well nourished, looking fresher and more beautiful than he could have imagined after all these years. "Oh, you're all gray!" she said, lifting her cheek for a kiss.

"You look great."

As Jasmin smiled, an alertness to her body combed his skin. He observed her shape, sheathed in her blue pantsuit and high-necked white blouse. They had been together for seven years, and he remembered little about their conversations. In the middle of telling him about her daughter, who was eight, she asked, "Are you still with her?"

Thinking she meant the woman in the other department, he said, "No, that didn't last— "

"I knew you weren't going to stay with *her*. I mean the other one, the young girl . . ."

"I don't know what you're talking about."

"Come on, Trev, who ever knew you better than I did?" Her eyes refused to release him.

"She fell in love with a woman," he said, hoping this would put an end to this subject.

Jasmin laughed. "Oh, Trev, that was really bad luck!" She sipped her coffee. "Are you in touch with her?"

"The last time I wrote to her, four years ago, I got a reply telling me that she had promised her lover not to communicate with anyone from her past."

"She was looking for a mother, not a father." Jasmin savored her coffee, regarding him with an expression that rankled him. He didn't remember her showing any interest in personal psychology. He wondered what her husband was like. Or was it her daughter who had changed her? "Listen, I'm not here to make you feel bad. I actually wanted to ask you a favor. I have the most incredible mother-in-law. . . . A rich lady who collects art. When she decides she wants something, there's no stopping her. She used to get on planes and go and buy whatever she wanted. But she's too old now. She's gone crazy over Mayan weaving. She has to have blankets— "

"There are a couple of good import stores— "

"My mother-in-law only uses middlemen she appoints personally. The village she's been reading about is called Momo— "

"Momostenango. Yeah, that's one of the best weaving villages."

"Could you go there for me, Trev? We'll pay your expenses and a finder's fee. I know you'd do a great job and make my mother-in-law happy."

"I haven't been to Guatemala in years."

"Maybe it would do you good to go back. We'll make it worth your while."

Mergers and acquisitions. Their merger had ended, but he remained her acquisition. Straightening his shoulders, he said, "I always thought you were going to be the person who would make me stop going to Guatemala. I never imagined you paying me to go back again."

Jasmin smiled.

◆ ◆ ◆

He returned to Quetzaltenango in a downpour. It was December 10, 2013, the date 13 baktun, 0 katun, 0 tun, 17 winal, 14 k'in. Time's order lay broken. It rained in the dry season, rain falling nonstop at the coldest time of year. The Santa María volcano was invisible. The Mayan farmers on the hillsides above the city—those who still had land—faced hunger as their crops washed away, along with the immemorial order of their calendars. Trevor got out of the tourist minivan from Antigua next to the park and sat down beneath the Roman pillars. He wheezed with fever. A decade's absence had drained his body of its Guatemalan immunities. Having allowed his vaccinations to lapse, he had renewed them all at once. His body ached, he was popping Imodium to keep his bowels under control, his stomach felt bloated, his breath was short, and his head throbbed from the altitude. Remembering an eclipse he had watched from this park, he wondered whether he had the strength to carry his backpack up the slope of Avenida 12.

The climb exhausted him, reminding him that he was fifty-one. Would Don Miguel and Doña Bendición remember him? In his feverish weakness all he wanted was a bed. He crossed the street and went in the door. Instead of opening into the wood-paneled lobby, the steps funneled him up a narrow staircase to a landing at the top. He was on the third floor, but it was not the third floor he recalled: a wall ran through it. A tired young woman and an adolescent girl sat behind a makeshift counter. He asked for a room and was shown a box where the single bed occupied most of the floor space, the carpet had been clawed away in patches, and a film of brown water covered the bathroom floor.

"No?" the woman said as he stared at the sight in confusion. "Gringos don't stay here."

"I remember when lots of gringos stayed here."

She snorted and turned away.

He stumbled toward the stairs, hesitating as he felt the woman peer after him. He walked down the narrow staircase and out onto the street. Crossing to the opposite sidewalk to get a better look, he saw that the Hotel Río Azul sign had moved. What used to be the main entrance was blocked off. The building looked dilapidated. He stumbled down the hill to the park, spotted two blond young people and trailed them to a new hotel called The Black Cat. He went in the door and asked for a room. Without thinking, he asked in Spanish. The pony-tailed receptionist struggled to reply, then switched to Australian English. "It's chock-a-block, mate," he said, "but if you're up to sharing with another bloke, we might squeeze you in."

He shared a room with an aging hippie from Washington State. "The Guatemala I know is gone," Trevor muttered.

"I hear you, man."

They went downstairs to the restaurant. The menu, in English only, featured pizza and chicken wings, hamburgers and huge salads. Trevor, wary of his stomach, ordered ginger ale and garlic bread. They sat at a table with half a dozen travelers from different countries who chatted in English. They had all come up from Antigua in tourist shuttles; they rode from one English-speaking hotel to another in transportation restricted to foreigners by US-dollar ticket pricing. None of them spoke Spanish; none of them knew that Guatemala had suffered thirty-six years of civil war or wondered why there were Roman pillars in the park. Events impressed them as spectacles, not as cause-and-effect along a strand of time. As he made a faltering attempt to tell the girl on his left about the civil war, only to see her glance flicker away in boredom, he felt as despairing as the Maya he had glimpsed along the edges of the enlarged, four-lane Pan-American Highway trying to flag down buses that no longer stopped to pick them up.

After supper, he paid to use one of the computers in the lobby. Calling up Rhea's email address, he wrote: *I'm back in Xela. You and I shared more than we realized . . .*

He sent the message, knowing it was foolish. He read his other messages and answered some of them.

His breath cut short: Rhea had replied.

He clicked on her message: *Rhea ya no usa esta dirección. Guadelupe.* ("Rhea no longer uses this address. Guadelupe.")

What the hell did that mean? He typed: *¿Rhea todavía vive en Tabasco?* ("Does Rhea still live in Tabasco?")

He waited for a reply. At last one came: *Se fue.* ("She went away.")

He typed: *¿Adónde fue?* ("Where did she go?")

Quién sabe. ("Who knows.")

He sent three more messages without receiving a reply. He woke in the morning feeling healthier, though not five hundred times better, or fit enough to make the trip to Momostenango. Needing to talk to someone, he left the hippie snoring beneath a black eye mask, stepped out of The Black Cat, and crossed the park. He found his way through back streets to a small door. He thought it was the right door, even though the gaudy, digital-looking logo overhead was unfamiliar. He stepped inside to find a reception desk. "I'd like to talk to Compañero Tino."

Giving him an odd look, the woman at the desk asked him to wait. He stood listening to a soundtrack of Mexican *norteño* music and *pop-en-español* ballads. After a few minutes, a light-boned young man who wore a white dress shirt and a dark jacket came to the desk. He introduced himself as Oliverio Morales. "You asked for my father?" When Trevor nodded, he said, "My father is deceased."

"My most sincere condolences. I knew him a long time ago. Was it sudden?"

The young man looked uncomfortable. He opened the counter and led Trevor to a back room. "What's your name, señor?"

"Your father called me Compañero Clover." This was the room where Tino had interviewed him. The walls had been replastered and whitewashed; red tiles covered the floor. The same logo that hung over the front door blazed from its place between speakers on the wall.

"My father's life ended because of his drinking. He suffered badly during the internal armed conflict." Oliverio paused. "After he died, I bought out the other members of the cooperative, then sold the station to this company from Miami"—he waved at the logo "—and they hired me back as manager." An elusive smile. "Of course, the content had to change."

"But you cover local news? I used to stay in the Hotel Río Azul— "

Oliverio looked disconcerted. "That was a great tragedy. Five years ago, Don Miguel and Doña Bendición were coming back from a shopping trip to the capital. They died in an accident on the Pan-American Highway. The children began to fight, María— "

María. The woman who had shown him the room had been María. "But they were all adopted from the same village."

"I see you know the family. And, though you are too polite to say so, I'm sure you know it's the same village my father came from."

"A village that was destroyed— "

"Joining the guerrillas at eleven saved my father's life. If he had been there during the events that followed, he would have been killed. Only very young children were spared. Like María. We're cousins. But Alberto and the younger sister were the children of one of the soldiers who killed my father's father— "

"Who were orphaned when your father and his compañeros executed the soldiers."

Oliverio winced at the verb *ajusticiar*. "Please excuse me, Compañero Clover, but nobody talks like that now." He caught his breath. "You know that when my father killed the soldiers who murdered my grandfather, he left the bodies on the riverbank where the whole village would see them? It is difficult for me to accept some of the things my father did." He shook his head. "When the children were growing up, they thought they were victims of the same tragedy. But in recent years, with all these people dragging out the details of this history, they learned that they came from families that had killed each other. When the parents died, María and Alberto got lawyers and the hotel was divided. History taught them hatred. That's why your hotel is falling to pieces."

"You hold history responsible for that?"

"That's why I was happy to get rid of the political programming." Oliverio leaned back in his chair, mouthing the words of love that sighed from the broadcast booth. "I'm finished with history, and so are you. All you'll learn here is that love lasts forever."

* * *

"I knew you would come back," María said the next night when he walked into the Hotel Río Azul. All day he had roamed through the city, then the park, in dwindling circles that encompassed markets and shops, huipiles and school uniforms, bursts of Quiché and pseudo-classical architecture. A cold drizzle fell. He fortified himself with two Gallo beers before climbing Avenida 12, where the hotels' front walls were splashed with political graffiti he was too out of touch to understand. When he emerged onto the partitioned landing that served as a reception area, María stood alone behind the desk. She wore a baggy, hooded sweatshirt that was too large for her. "You remember me, don't you?"

"I didn't recognize you the other night," he said, insisting on the formal *usted* even though she had addressed him as *tú*. "My most sincere condolences on the loss of your parents. They were an important part of my life."

"We haven't seen you in years," she said, in a strange hankering tone that made him wonder how old she was. Almost thirty? Was it possible that María was almost thirty? And that Rhea was thirty too? As he regarded her with the curiosity owed to the last surviving thread of a vital seam of his life, she said, "I'm glad you remember my parents fondly. I no longer know what to think of them. They gave me a good life when I was a child. I was their beloved daughter until I got pregnant. Then I became a lascivious Indian who was unable to control her desires. They favored Alberto; I knew he'd get the hotel, even before we learned we weren't brother and sister."

"You got part of the hotel."

"He got more of it. We're both in debt to lawyers and he's doing as badly as

I am. The people who used to stay here—backpackers; decent, modest Guatemalans—those people don't exist anymore. All I get is drunks and whores. The people who travel now are rich. They want luxury hotels. The gringos want everybody to speak English. In a year or two Alberto and I will both be out of business."

She stepped out from behind the counter. He watched her lank, shiny-black hair spill over the thrust-back hood as she stepped past him and closed and bolted the door at the top of the stairs. She returned—she looked a foot shorter than he—took his hand, and said, "When I was a little girl, I used to listen to you talking about your fiancée in Canada and I dreamed that someday a man would make me his fiancée. Maybe even take me north." She led him down a hall, pulled a clutch of keys out of the pouch at the front of her hoodie, and opened a door. They entered a windowless room where muted light filtered through a glass transom.

"Why didn't you show me this room the other night?" he asked. "I would have taken it."

"I didn't recognize you. These days too many gringos with backpacks look around here then go to The Black Cat. I thought, 'Well, fuck him. If he's not going to stay here anyway, I'll show him a really terrible room.'"

They sat down on the right-hand bed in the gloom. "The time you came here with that girl—"

"Your daughter was already born then, wasn't she?" he murmured, yielding by addressing her as *tú*,

"Yes, I knew then that no man would marry me in church, because I already had a child. And I knew that girl wasn't your fiancée. You confirmed for me the way the world really was. That men who had fiancées went to hotels with young girls."

"It was more complicated than that."

"Yes, it is always complicated, isn't it? If my mother were still alive she might not welcome you back."

He heard their breathing in the near-darkness. She had brought him to the room he had shared with Rhea. Or a room that was identical. It was shabby now, but less decayed than the room she had shown him two nights ago. The silence went on until María said, "I'll welcome you, if you like."

She reached up to kiss him. He closed his arms around her, feeling wrapped in her strong scent. He was aware of the rank milkiness of his own odor. Was she convincing herself that she was possessing the shining gringo of her teenage fantasies? He slid his hands down the brief space of her back. This was the second time he had caressed a woman's back on this bed, the third time he had shared a room at the Hotel Río Azul with a woman. As María stood up, slid her hoodie over her head, then shucked off her T-shirt and unhooked her bra, he thought that this would be the first time he had had sex with a woman in this room. He rolled alongside her onto the narrow bed, hauling her against his cushioned gut. "I'm glad you came back," she said. "These days, the only men who are interested in me are men I don't want."

He slid his tongue over the tiny dents inside her collar bones. As he took her small, firm breasts in his mouth, his libido cranked up, his body stumbling in its wake. The headache from his cold, the Imodium plug in his bowels, his queasy stomach and unsteady breathing, warned that his flesh was his antagonist. The torpor in his veins stoked moral qualms. As true as it might be, at a submerged level, that each of them was delving for compensation for emotional losses, that she as much as he would be gratified by their encounter, at a more blatant level he was a tall white man who was about to take advantage of a small Mayan woman, reenacting a pattern of exploitation that had been recurring in Guatemala for five hundred years. Even as they kissed and he felt drawn into her body, his mind tripped on the assumption that his privileges were a match for her easy availability. Racial assumptions such as these underlay the atrocities that had dispatched María from her village.

He fell back on the bed, almost nudging her onto the floor. "You're very beautiful, María, but I'm an old man now. *Ya soy viejito*. It's better if I keep my clothes on."

"Don't you want me?"

"Of course. But I don't think it would be right."

"You can't do it because you're thinking about that girl. She's here in the room with us."

"Then why did you bring me to the same room?"

As María's distrustful eyes observed him across the pillow, he wondered how she had known that this was the room he and Rhea had shared. She couldn't have remembered from all those years ago! Yet he was almost certain this was the room. The thought released an access of tenderness toward her; they embraced like two survivors from a disaster. "Where's your daughter?"

"Playing video games in her room."

"Her life will be better. Now that the war's over—"

"The war is not over!" María sat up fiercely, as though unaware that the top half of her body was naked. "Never let anyone tell you the war in Guatemala is over. If the war had not happened, I would live in a village and I would speak Quiché. My village would exist, I would have my culture. . . . All these people floating around like bees in the cities, bees who cannot return to their hives, who cannot return to the village and are not accepted in the city because they have the faces of *indios*, who cannot be city people and cannot be peasants—that is the war continuing!" As she ran out of breath, he thought of Compañero Tino's son, of her former brother Alberto. "It is the same for my daughter. She belongs nowhere. That is the war continuing."

María slid off the bed. She put on her bra, T-shirt, and hoodie. "I will accompany you . . ."

"I'm sorry, María." The words had never felt so inadequate. The apology required by María, by the hotel, by the country, was of cosmic proportions.

They stepped into the corridor. He had shared a room at the Hotel Río Azul with a woman for the last time.

They entered the partitioned-off lobby. She unlocked the door to the staircase. "You know she came back."

"Who?"

"Your girlfriend."

"She came *here*? To this hotel?" The thin air made him faint. "When?"

"Two weeks ago. She looked at lots of rooms before deciding where to stay. That's why I remembered. . . . She talks like a Mexican now," she said with a laugh. "On the day she left, she asked me if you still stayed here."

"Did she say where she was going?"

María stepped behind the desk and opened the large, handwritten register he remembered from her parents' time. She flipped through pages and pointed out a line with Rhea's name. In the register her procedencia and her destino were both entered as *México*. His wrist trembled as he took María's hand. Leaning over, he kissed her on the cheek like a brother or a cousin. He held her for a moment, then let her go and walked back to The Black Cat. Tomorrow he would go to Momostenango to bargain with the weavers. Once he had shipped Jasmin her purchases, he would cancel his flight home and get a bus to Mexico.

Jonathan Blum

THE WHITE SPOT

When I was nine, my parents went through a bitter custody battle over me. In the end, the judge decided that I should live with my mother Mondays through Saturdays and go for visits with my father every Saturday night and Sunday. Back then, my father was on call at the hospital seven days a week, and he had no one to look after me during the hours he had to work, so he started bringing me to the hospital with him on Sundays and keeping me in the break room on the same floor where his patients were located.

The break room was only about the size of two closets. It had a coarse plaid sofa, a low-hanging spherical leather chair, a coffee maker and mugs, a sink, some cabinets, a telephone, and a laminated poster above the telephone that was called Screening Guidelines for Invasive Carcinomas, which was put out by The American Academy of Pathology. That first day in the hospital, which was my first time in a hospital since birth, I tried to sit up straight on the plaid sofa and read one of the sports biographies I carried with me everywhere, but I couldn't concentrate at all. My mind kept wandering, wondering what my father was doing—where exactly he was and who he was with.

My father never talked about his work—not during his residency, not now—but I knew a few things about what he did. This was because, starting a couple years earlier, I had skimmed through the back sections of two of his medical books and seen pictures of sick pulmonary patients. I had seen many pairs of lungs that were removed from their bodies after death and photographed. One such pair, which had belonged to a person with emphysema, had an oozing gray coating over the usual healthy red color. Another pair of lungs had holes, caused by black carbon deposits that were the result of smoking. I had also seen a smoker with a gangrenous, partly lopped-off foot, a smoker with a gaping hole at the base of his throat, and a smoker with no tongue in his mouth.

In my own shy, optimistic way, I took pride in the fact that my father treated lungs. Lungs were vital—and underappreciated. I thought of them as the unsung heroes of the human body. Unlike the much-celebrated heart and brain, no one ever talked about the lungs, and yet we couldn't last four minutes without them. They took in and released breaths every three seconds or so, usually without our ever noticing. They moved oxygen to the bloodstream and removed carbon dioxide. They kept us going, even when we were sleeping.

After I had been daydreaming for more than an hour, my father, who was a big man—six-foot-two, a hundred and ninety pounds, with curly black hair in a white lab coat and brown Wallabes—came back into the break room, sat himself down in the low-hanging chair, and crossed his legs, his feet close to mine. The air conditioner wasn't working right that day, and there were beads of sweat on my father's forehead and odoriferous spots under his arms. His breaths were quick and confident. He had just seen all his patients, and he had to write up some notes. As he went through page after page of triplicate paper with a blue ballpoint pen, checking boxes, scratching words, signing his name quickly at the bottom of each page, I half-hid my eyes behind one of my sports biographies and pretended to read.

I was very curious what my father was writing on those pages—one white, one yellow, one pink—but I didn't dare ask. I had decided it was best not to talk to him at the hospital unless he talked to me first.

Finally he asked, "How's Roberto Clemente?"

"He died trying to help earthquake victims in Nicaragua," I said.

"Yeah, I remember that," my father said. "You ready to get out of here?"

My father got called into the hospital almost every Sunday. Sometimes these calls were for what he called real emergencies and sometimes they were false alarms. His beeper would usually go off while we were at his apartment playing chess or squaring off at our favorite game, Encyclopedia, in which we picked a single volume of the encyclopedia, opened it up at random, and quizzed each other about the facts inside. After my father's beeper went off, he would usually say, "All right, kid. Let's go."

Some weeks my father only saw one patient; other weeks he saw many. Sometimes he went down to ICU; other times he did rounds only on the pulmonary wing. Just hearing him refer to the people he saw as *my patients* excited me; it meant that he was the one in charge of their care. I didn't dare ask him what he did when he saw his patients, although there was nothing I would have liked to know more. I just stayed in the break room, reading, while he was gone.

One Sunday morning, my father got called in earlier than usual. We stopped in the hospital cafeteria on the way. At the register, a ponytailed woman with a flappy chin smiled when she recognized my father, then asked him who was this fine young gentleman he had brought with him today. The woman was surrounded by a pot of chili and oyster crackers, a jar of Little Debbies, some loose cold cuts and cheese slices, and a box of mayonnaise packets. After telling the woman my name, my father bought a couple cinnamon buns, which the woman heated up in a microwave that was spattered with drops of soup. My father ordered a coffee.

As we rode up the elevator, I counted floors.

When we arrived at the break room, my father tousled my hair and said, "You're a good kid, coming in here every week and not complaining. You want to learn how to read a chest X-ray today?"

I couldn't believe my good luck.

Almost two hours later, after he had seen all his patients, my father came back to the break room, carrying his clipboard.

"Let's do it," he said.

He and I walked down the hall toward the pulmonary wing. He saluted nurses. I ran my fingers along the wall. We passed paintings of muhly grass and Tampa vervain. Soon we arrived at a narrow opening in the wall. Inside was a small alcove with a wall-mounted X-ray viewer. Screwed into the wall next to the viewer was a plastic box in which dozens of loose X-rays were haphazardly stuffed. Behind that wall was a closed door.

My father disappeared through that door, then came back a minute later with a small pile of X-rays in shabby paper envelopes.

"Okay," he said. "First you need to know how to read a normal piece of film."

He put an X-ray up on the screen and flicked on the viewing light. At the center of the image was a pair of long black regions, not quite symmetrical; one had a sharper, more curved bottom than the other.

"The lungs," I said.

"That's right," he said.

At first the two lungs in the X-ray made me think of lakes or pools, then of wings or windows, and then of the tombstones you see in cartoons.

"Can you guess why they're black?" my father asked.

I shook my head. My shyness amounted to a terrible fear of saying the wrong thing.

"'Cause they're mostly air," he said. "But you don't want them too black. That could mean air is getting trapped."

After my father had pointed out the features of a healthy lung, including the soft webbing of bronchi, he directed my attention to the white areas that framed the lungs: the ribs, clavicle, vertebrae, trachea, shoulder bones, arm tissue, diaphragm, and heart.

He then slid over the normal chest X-ray and said, "Now we're going to look at some pathology."

He posted an X-ray on the viewer, next to the normal one.

"What's different from the normal X-ray?" my father asked.

This was an easy one.

"One of the lungs is white," I said.

"That's right," my father said. "The left lower lobe is white. In this patient's case, the small air sacs in the lungs, known as alveoli, have gotten clogged with dense liquid. The patient has pneumonia."

"Could the patient die?" I said.

"Not necessarily," my father said. "We'd have to know some other things. Like the status of the infection. And the age of the patient. But probably not," he said.

My father put up another X-ray.

"What's wrong here?" he asked.

This one was harder. I shook my head.

"Look at the lungs," my father said. "Healthy lungs are elastic. When we breathe, they expand and contract. But with certain diseases the lungs lose their elasticity. They hyperinflate. Look how narrow the heart is. You see the flat, low-set diaphragm? These lungs are too big and too dark. Dark, I told you, means air is getting trapped. The blood's not getting enough oxygen. This person has emphysema."

"Could the person die?" I asked.

"Yes, they could," my father said.

"When?" I asked.

"Anywhere from eight months to a year, maybe two years. Depends what treatment, if any, works."

I thought about this answer, wishing I understood death as well as my father did, as well as my grandparents did.

"Here's something that'll make you pause and wonder," he said. "By the time emphysema patients get to me, they generally have one foot in the grave. They're lifetime smokers. Their lung function is impaired or badly impaired. And yet these same people, who know that the only *possible* way to stop their disease is to stop smoking, go right on smoking. They sometimes sneak cigarettes in their hospital beds when no one's around. You can smell it halfway down the hall. What do you think of that?"

My father got out another X-ray.

"One more?" he asked.

"OK," I said.

He put the diseased X-ray up next to the normal one. The two looked virtually the same.

"Look closely," he said.

I couldn't see any difference.

"Here, below the clavicle," he pointed. "This opacity. This white spot."

I saw what he was pointing at. But because the spot was dense and white, like the bones and tissue nearby, it didn't look that different from the white in the normal X-ray.

"I see it," I said.

"That's cancer," my father said.

I didn't dare ask if the person could die from it. Of course they could. Instead, I wondered what my father saw when he looked around him every day. How much more did he see than an ordinary person did?

"Is there any way to get rid of it?" I asked.

"For most people," he said, "by the time it's detected, they're already a goner."

"How fast do they die?" I asked.

"Ninety percent of the patients I see with lung cancer die within a year of diagnosis. Often it's just three or four months. But I never tell them that—unless they ask."

"Why not?"

"Don't you think people deserve the chance not to lose hope?"

I thought about this. I then asked my father to show me another X-ray that might or might not have a white spot. Then another. And then another. I wanted to be able to identify the spots as quickly and accurately as he could.

Finally, I got the hang of it. I identified three cancerous spots in a row.

"Now imagine having to break news like that to a patient," my father said.

The words startled me, because up until that moment, finding the white spot had been something exciting, like discovering buried treasure.

"All right," my father said. "Enough for one day. Let's get out of this place."

Within a few weeks of reading X-rays, I could tell the difference between healthy lungs and chronic bronchitis, tuberculosis, pneumonia, emphysema, and cancer. I saw collapsed lungs and severe asthma. I saw a rare lung disease with a long name that mainly afflicted younger people.

One Sunday, on the ride over to the hospital, my father told me he was sick of looking after patients seven days a week. He needed a break. But he didn't have anyone he could call who could cover his patients on Sundays.

"I'll cover your patients," I told him.

He laughed.

"You know, that gives me an idea," he said. "How would you like to come around with me today and visit patients? You could just poke your head in the room and say hi. It would probably cheer them up. A nice kid like you."

"Any day," I said.

So the plan was hatched. I would walk the halls of the pulmonary wing with my father; he would tell me when to come into a room and when to leave.

"You're going to see some people who're in bad shape," he said. "Can you handle it?"

"Of course," I said.

"Actually, I think I'll start you with one patient today and we'll go from there."

When we arrived at the hospital, my father went down to ICU. He had a guy there who was barely holding on.

While I was in the break room waiting, I wondered what it was like for my father to lose his patients all the time, even when he did the exact right thing you were supposed to do to treat them.

When he returned, he pinched my shoulder and said, "All right, let's go."

We walked down the hall toward the pulmonary wing, my short legs unable to keep pace with his longer ones.

"This lady has emphysema," he said under his breath.

He wouldn't show me her X-rays; that would be an invasion of privacy.

"But you have a good idea, from experience, what her film would look like."

The lady's door was almost completely closed. Facing us was a work of art by a four- or five-year-old, some trees and flowers made out of paper plates, markers, Popsicle sticks, crayons, glue, and pieces of colored yarn.

"All right, here we go," my father said.

He knocked on the door. A woman's hoarse voice croaked, "Yes?"

"Halloooo, Mrs. Grinnell," my father said, his voice ringing out. He pushed open the door and put on a smile.

He stopped and then I stopped at the foot of the bed. An old woman with gray hair that had turned a dingy yellow was propped up in bed. She looked pale and worn out, as if the muscles in her face could no longer follow instructions for what to do. Stuck deep inside her nostrils were a pair of small, flexible tubes, which were attached to a green tank on the floor that had some kind of valve on top of it. The old woman was wearing a blue hospital gown and watching a game show on TV, in which the audience was *aah*-ing because the contestant had made a mistake.

"How's your shortness of breath today, Mrs. Grinnell?" my father asked over the game show. The woman was sucking in air every few seconds. "Is the oxygen helping?"

My father went over and took the remote control from the bedside and muted the game show.

"I believe so, doctor," she rasped, then sucked in air.

"You believe so? Yesterday you characterized your problem with shortness of breath as being a 2, 1 being the worst. Is it still a 2? We're trying to prolong life here. Are we making headways?"

The woman gathered her thoughts.

"Who's the boy?" she rasped.

"He's mine," my father said. "Can't you tell?"

In fact, my father and I didn't look a great deal alike. There were lots of ways I was probably never going to equal him; physical strength and size were just a couple.

"You want to show this lady what kind of head you've got on your shoulders?" my father asked me. "It's crammed with knowledge," he confided to the woman.

I cracked my knuckles to show readiness.

"All right," my father said. "What's . . . um . . . 24 times 48?"

"1,152," I said without missing a beat.

"31 times 13?"

"403."

"What's the capital of Iceland?"

"Reykjavik."

"Who was the twenty-first president?"

"Chester Alan Arthur. Republican from New York."

"What year was Tampa founded?"

"Indians started living here 2,500 years ago. But after the Spanish arrived in the 1600s, most of them died of diseases. Today's Tampa started forming in 1824, after the United States purchased Florida from the Spanish."

"All right, now you ask him one," my father said to the woman. "Try to stump him. See if you can."

"I may be up to a 2.5," the woman croaked and gulped air.

"That," my father said, "makes me happy. That," he said, "is what I like to hear."

My father told the woman he was going to keep her on oxygen twenty-four hours a day for the next couple days and see what happened. He was also going to start her on a medication that would help open her breathing passages and promote air flow.

The woman coughed deeply; her lungs sounded as if they had holes in them through which a wet substance was trying to escape.

"Just lay off the tobacco," he told her. "Or else."

An old man in a plaid shirt and a silver crew cut, clearly the patient's husband, entered the room and slowly made his way over to the far side of the bed. He seemed as though he was trying not to look worried.

"I'll check on you tomorrow," my father said to the woman and her husband.

"Bye," I waved.

The following Sunday, my father let me visit a few patients. Mrs. Grinnell had been released, but there were plenty of others to see. A few doors down from Mrs. Grinnell's old room, we went to see another patient with emphysema. On the way, my father whispered, "This guy's finished. Three months max. He's not responding to anything."

Upon being quizzed by my father, I told the man the four nucleobases that DNA nucleotides are made up of—cytosine, guanine, adenine, and thymine. I told him the average life expectancy of an American in 1780 (36), 1880 (40), and 1980 (73). I named a major-league baseball player who turned a childhood disability into an advantage—Mordecai "Three Finger" Brown.

After that, we saw two other patients with emphysema, neither doing well. I told them both a joke my father loved whose punch line was, "Yeah, the food is terrible. And such small portions." Once the joke was finished, I took a small bow.

Then we saw a guy with chronic bronchitis who, my father said, might just walk out of this hospital in pretty decent shape, though if he doesn't lay off the cigarettes, he's sliding down the same chute as the rest of them.

"Ready to get out of here?" he finally asked.

The following week, my father said he was going to test my maturity. He was going to bring me in to see a patient who was dying of lung cancer. Tumors everywhere. She was on a ventilator, which eased her pain, but by next week there wasn't going to be anything left of her to ventilate.

We stopped at a soda machine on the way. My father dropped in some coins, which rattled in the machine's innards. He punched the machine twice and two cans of Mountain Dew came flying down. We both took long drinks.

"This is a lady you're not going to be able to cheer up," my father said. "I've been seeing her for months. Nothing amuses her."

We went inside. The patient, who was propped up in bed, had a thin netting of white hair, anger lines across her forehead, and the most liquid eyes I had ever seen. They were blue and welling up and staring at me, piercing me. She was wearing an oxygen mask over her nose and mouth that was connected by a tube to a red, peeling canister beside the head of the bed. Another tube led from a ventilator on wheels down into a hole in her neck. The ventilator kept making a whishing sound.

"Good afternoon, Mrs. Szabo," my father said. "Jó napot."

I was shocked. My father never spoke Hungarian, his parents' language. On the two or three occasions per year when we left Florida to visit my grandparents in Wilmington, Delaware, my father did everything he could to block out his Hungarianness and Jewishness.

"Look who I brought," my father said, examining the ventilator settings and jotting down notes on his clipboard. "My son, Jay."

Mrs. Szabo stared at me with stern brows and liquid blue eyes. She looked as if I had somehow just personally offended her or was about to.

I looked at my father. I didn't want to say the wrong thing.

"Mrs. Szabo's family is from the city of Pécs in Hungary, isn't that right, Mrs. Szabo? In the beautiful Carpathian Basin. Not far from my mother's home village."

Mrs. Szabo's chest rose a little when she inhaled and fell soon after. I could see the outlines of her toes underneath the bedding.

"Mrs. Szabo came to the United States as a young girl. On the eve of the First World War. Her family was poor and uneducated. They were looking for opportunity. Her father found work as a coal miner. In Western Pennsylvania. Hard life, but, income-wise, he did better than he would have done in Hungary. Raised four kids. Spoke Hungarian in the home."

My father's voice sounded like it was tinged with malice; I had never heard him speak that way.

"His dream was to make enough money in America to be able to go back to Pécs and buy a plot of land and plant orchards. He wanted to have a family business that shipped out fruit to the rest of Europe. Sour cherries in the summer, apples in the winter."

My father continued, "Mrs. Szabo's told me all about her family." "Their ups and downs. Their hardships and disappointments. But she's never asked about mine. Even though I have a Hungarian-Jewish surname. Maybe she doesn't want to hear about mine. What do you think, kid?"

Mrs. Szabo's liquid blue eyes stared out across the oxygen mask. They looked like they were permanently geared up for a fight.

"Hungarians don't like to hear our stories, do they, Mrs. Szabo? The way we Jews go on and on about our miseries, you'd think we were the only ones who ever suffered. Well, I want you to know how *my* parents came to the United States."

The ventilator went on whishing.

"This is where you come in," my father said to me, crossing his arms.

"When we go see my parents," my father said to the woman, "the kid just sits there at the table for hours and listens. Soaks it all in. Me, I can't sit still for half a minute. I go for jogs. I listen to rock and roll on headphones."

He turned to me. "What year was my mother born?"

"1926," I said.

"And tell Mrs. Szabo about my mother's life when she was a young girl."

"Like what happened on the way home from school?" I said.

"Yes, like that," he said.

"On the way home from school," I said, "two girls in her class would kick her and make her nose bleed and say, 'Rotten Jew. You will all die.'"

"And what did my mother do?"

"To get them to stop," I said, "she did their homework for them. And gave them money every week. It was a time of Depression in Hungary."

"And what else do you know about that time?"

"Her two favorite people were her older brothers, Lajos and Sanyi. Lajos taught himself how to make leather so that he could make her a pocketbook for her birthday. The next year he made gloves."

"Mmm," my father said. "And what happened after that?"

"Hitler's armies entered Hungary."

"When?"

"March 19, 1944."

"And when did the Jews have to start wearing the yellow star of humiliation?"

"April 5, 1944."

"And when were the Jews in my mother's village forced into the ghetto?"

I lowered my eyes, which I now realized were filling up with tears. I couldn't remember the date. I would have rather said no date than the wrong date.

"Tell Mrs. Szabo about the ghetto," my father said.

"All two hundred Jews from the village were forced to live there."

"Two hundred out of how many people total in the village?"

"Seven thousand."

"You see how much he listens?" my father said to Mrs. Szabo. Her liquid blue eyes seemed to be burning with rage.

"They all had to sleep in the temple," I said. "Or else jam themselves into three small houses around the temple. Everybody said, 'Something bad is going to happen.'"

"And what happened?" my father asked.

"First, Lajos and Sanyi were taken away to forced-labor camps. With some of their friends."

"Right, right," my father said. "And after that?"

"All two hundred Jews from the village, including my grandmother and her parents, were shipped off to Auschwitz. It was a three-day ride with no food or water."

"Oh, Mrs. Szabo doesn't want to hear about Auschwitz. We Jews, obsessed with talking about Auschwitz."

My father, standing beside the ventilator, bowed his head gloomily, placed his hands behind his back, and squirmed.

In fact, at Auschwitz, my grandmother's parents were sent right to the gas chambers. On arriving, my grandmother's mother said to Mengele, in German, *We are mother and daughter and we would like to stay together*. He separated them. If my grandmother had insisted on staying with her mother, she would have been sent to the gas chambers too.

"This kid could tell you stories—100 percent true—of what went on there," my father said. "But weren't there some good Germans at Auschwitz? I once heard my mother say she'd have never made it out if not for the German who put an extra piece of bread in her pocket or the ones who took care of her in the clinic when she got diphtheria. At any moment, they could have just gassed her."

Mrs. Szabo's eyes were boiling over with rage.

"What happened next to my mother?" my father asked.

"By miracle, she got sent to Lenzing. With three hundred other girls."

"What was Lenzing?"

"A subcamp of Mauthausen. In Austria. She did factory work. The girls all became skeletons."

My father's beeper went off. He silenced it. A nurse popped her head in the door. My father raised a finger and she disappeared.

"I hope we're not taxing your patience, Mrs. Szabo," my father said. The old woman's eyes were burning inside the masked pouch of her face. "We Jews. Can't stop broadcasting our troubles to the world.

"So what happened after that?" my father asked me.

"The Americans liberated Lenzing on May 5, 1945."

"And where did my mother go?"

"Back to Hungary," I said. "By train."

"And here we get to the part of my mother's story that you're really not going to enjoy, Mrs. Szabo. Mrs. Szabo is a true Hungarian," my father said to me." "She goes back to Pécs once every three years. As often as she can afford. Speaks fluent Hungarian. If there is such a thing as an American with a Hungarian world view, Mrs. Szabo has it."

The old lady's eyes narrowed. Her chest rose and fell more slowly, as if she were starting to fatigue. For some reason, I found myself picturing what her chest X-ray must look like, white spots everywhere. And if she was at death's door, why weren't any of her loved ones here?

"What happened on the train ride back to my mother's village?"

"She met a boy. The boy who became my grandfather. He had been doing forced labor in Germany, repairing railroad tracks. He went back with her to her village."

"And what happened when they arrived?"

"There were no Jews there," I said.

"And what did she do?"

"She went and knocked on the doors of some people she had known. And they all said to her, 'No Jews live here.'"

"How long had she been gone?" my father asked.

"A little over a year."

"And what happened next?"

"She went to the temple. And the temple was now being used as a warehouse. And she went to the homes of some family and Jewish friends, and all the homes were occupied by other people. And she went to the Jewish cemetery, and the cemetery had been cleared and replaced by a lumber yard.

"Finally, she went to see the man who was the publisher of the village newspaper. She said, 'All I want is to find my brothers.'

"'We have no Jews here,' the man said.

"'Jews have lived in this village for over five hundred years,' my grandmother said. 'May I take out an ad in your newspaper in order to find my family?'

"The man agreed. But nobody answered the ad."

"Continue."

"Two days later a cousin arrived. She told my grandmother that both her brothers were dead. Lajos had been shot by a firing squad after he injured his foot on a long march in Austria. Sanyi perished in a camp in Yugoslavia.

"My grandmother broke down in tears and said to my future grandfather, 'I cannot stay in this country another day.'

"They began making plans to come to America. My future grandfather had five sisters in Wilmington, Delaware."

Once again I realized that I was about to cry. What if I had made some factual mistakes in the telling of my grandmother's story that would invalidate everything I had said? The idea upset me terribly. My grandmother had warned me more than once that non-Jews often don't believe our stories, so don't make errors.

"How many members of our family went to the camps?" my father asked me.

"Forty-two."

"And how many came back?"

"Three."

"Gratulálunk!" my father said to Mrs. Szabo. "You see? That wasn't such a hard story to have to listen to. Now we can both go back to forgetting all about it."

Mrs. Szabo's eyes were closed, wet at the edges. My father went over and put his hand on her shoulder.

The following week, as my father and I were driving to the hospital, he told me that Mrs. Szabo had died.

"That old Jew-hating buzzard," he said. "We showed her what was what."

Up until that moment I had never given much thought to how anyone could hate a group of people so much that they would want to get rid of them all. When my grandparents told their stories, that was never posed as a question. It was just a given. People hated Jews.

Now that I had kept my composure while visiting a patient at death's door, my father brought me in to see his sickest cases.

I usually kept quiet and put on a cautious smile. While my father examined and interviewed the patients, he would go on quizzing and quizzing me.

A few weeks later, my father found someone to cover his patients on Sundays. In exchange, he would cover for the other doctor on Saturdays.

While my father told me this, he looked at me as if I would be automatically relieved that I wouldn't have to come into the hospital with him any longer. Now we could do fun things together on Sundays. Watch football. Go fishing. Barbecue. Get out of town. We wouldn't have to be afraid that anything we did would be interrupted by a call from the hospital.

But I wasn't ready to stop going to the hospital. I was learning things there that I could not learn anywhere else.

On my last day at the hospital, I told my father I didn't want to stay in the break room at all. I only wanted to be with him. So he let me trail him everywhere. He even let me wait for him outside the double doors he used to enter the ICU.

By now, I had known four people, including Mrs. Szabo, who had died while in the hospital. Naturally, in every case, the room was reassigned to another emphysema or cancer patient who was in similar need of being cheered up.

Toward the end of the day, we approached Mrs. Szabo's old room. When I glimpsed inside, I saw a barrel-chested man with tufts of silver chest hair who was staring up at the ceiling. He gave a deep, wet cough. Then another. He cleared his throat, brought up mucus, spit the mucus into a tissue, and took a deep, gasping breath. My father bent over and whispered to me that this guy was not going to be able to stop smoking for all the tea in China.

"I give him six months."

Josie Sigler Sibara

THE MAN ON THE BEACH

I have often paid the price of sleeplessness for my father's crimes, the crimes of all of Germany, though I had never set foot in that country when I again encountered the idea that became so compelling to me in the summer of my thirteenth year.

On a scorching August evening in my fortieth, I was walking down Sunset on my way to a Dodgers game. I was alone. The two things I loved best about living in the States, the baseball and the uncloseted men, didn't always go hand in hand. Especially not in 1986. Who could invite a friend to succumb to such amusements while the Reaper floated down alleyways wearing love's clothes? Outside a secondhand shop, I stopped to examine the offerings on a shelf labeled with a cardboard sign that read *free books*. The first I touched, with its glossy cover and effusive blurbs in bright-yellow font, looked like it had been printed in some conspiracy theorist's garage, but I did not put it down. It was about Nuremberg. Nazis who fled.

I tucked the book under my arm and walked on, throat tight. In the stadium, I stowed it beneath my seat. Days before, at my friend Aleks's funeral, I had promised myself again that I would face the legacy I had spent two decades avoiding. A familiar promise, usually made upon waking from a nightmare I didn't fully understand. By morning, I would bury again the reason I felt guilty, ashamed, deserving of death. But I had begun to understand the brittle, patient terror of knowing you will lose everyone you love in a fell swoop. I was expecting two things that week: the results of my own test and another funeral.

The Dodgers lost. It was the outcome I favored in those days. I felt rocked in common sorrow between the strangers who flanked me. I considered leaving the book under my seat. But I didn't. I walked back home, put the book on my bedside table, stripped to my shorts, and lay down. After a failed attempt to drift off, I rose, feeling the tremors of a dam about to burst. I shook myself a martini, but instead of turning on the television as I often did, I sat in the living room before an open window and began reading. The writing was awful, but I was keeping my promise, wasn't I? By the second chapter, which opened with a brief and stilted biography of Hitler, I found myself nodding off. I was about to close the book when a footnote caught my eye, a single word: *Patagonia*.

My skin suffered the rush of time as I passed backward through it to land in my own body crouched before Nahuel Huapi in November of 1959, my breath hanging in the frigid spring air. Across the lake, clouds rolled down the snow-capped peaks and hovered just above the trees. I had gone farther out along the shore than usual that Saturday morning and been rewarded by the discovery of a small cove enclosing a rocky beach. I pressed my father's heavy binoculars to the bridge of my nose and watched an imperial cormorant dive and disappear. I imagined the bird swimming, searching for freshwater crabs in the depths, the fluffy white feathers of his breast smooth and flowing in the water. At last, he surfaced and perched on a rock near the shore. He spread his wings wide, rare behavior for an imperial. The flesh encircling his eye was an even deeper blue, if possible, than the shimmering expanse of that fjord.

They're prettier than the black-eyed variety, no?

The voice, its tinny vibrato like a current of electricity, startled me. I turned to see an old man wearing round glasses, one hand pressed deep in the pocket of his baggy wool trousers, the other clutching the binoculars that hung at his paunch. His eyes were startlingly blue. His stringy black hair was parted in the middle and longer than most Argentinian men wore it, his beard chestnut with tufts of silver. He had spoken to me in German, but seeing my face, my dark eyes rather than just the back of my blond head, he tried Spanish instead, constructing a simpler sentence.

Superior creature, isn't it?

I've never seen a Magellanic or a red-legged, I said in German, shrugging. But it's not actually the imperial's eye that's blue. It's just the lid.

I hear they can dive to fifty meters, he said.

Cormorants could dive *almost* that deep, about forty meters; however, they rarely did, according to my father, who had been an avid birder. But I did not contradict the man, as I had something better to share.

The Chinese use them for fishing, I said. They put a metal ring around their necks so they can't swallow the big fish they catch. Doesn't seem fair. But it works.

This, too, was something my father had told me, and I tried to get the tone right, casual, as I said it.

The man pulled off his glasses. He put his binoculars to his face with a trembling hand. He seemed familiar. I might have seen him at a banquet in Bariloche when my father was still alive. Or perhaps the man was a customer at the chocolate shop where I worked sweeping floors and washing molds. We watched together until the imperial flew off in the graceless wobbly way they do, like a child first learning to ride a bike. Then the man settled his binoculars back at his paunch.

Do you go to the German school? the man asked. He began to cough, deep and rattling.

I used to, I said when he was through. I go to the *escuela* now.

Three years before, my father drowned in that lake, and at thirteen, I still believed his death had been an accident. After he was gone, my mother, who did not want to return to live with my grandparents in Buenos Aires, used what money we had to buy a small chalet just outside San Carlos de Bariloche. The following year, I began going to public school, where I did not fit in, although I went by my middle name, Eduardo, instead of Reinhard, as I still do. I missed the *Aléman*, though I hadn't belonged there either. The most popular boy, Franz Achter, who was kind when we were alone, called me a *cabecita* in front of the others. Argentina had for a century taken in men like my father to whiten the country, and my grandparents had welcomed him to marry their brownest daughter for the same reasons. Anyway, school would soon be out, and then I could spend the long summer days exploring, reading, dreaming.

Ah, the man said, as if he had heard my thoughts.

This made me nervous. Arturo, a boy at my new school, had told me that the *Nahuel*—by this he meant not a regular jaguar but a man turned into a jaguar through sorcery—could listen in on your mind. That was how a Nahuel found you even if you hid. Then he transformed, crouched, and pounced. But the man looked too weak to pounce. And I prided myself on being a scientist who did not believe in such things, anyway. Yet sometimes when I pictured my father's last moments, I saw him heroically fighting off a Nahuel that nonetheless dragged him into the water. I held my hand out at arm's length. The sun was two fingers' width above the highest peak on the other side of the lake, which meant it was 10 a.m. My mother had probably woken. I walked to the water's edge and dipped my fingers to wash off any grit that might scratch my father's lenses. The cold shot up my arm, made the bones ache all the way to my shoulder. Nahuel Huapi never froze, but it was filled with melted glacier. Whenever I touched that lake, I imagined the moment my father had inhaled his first and last breath of it. I capped his binoculars.

Adios, I said to the man.

Auf Wiedersehen, the man said.

I hiked along the shore, tripping in my haste on the tangled roots of a lenga beech that had broken from a ledge to seek the lake. Water poured over the tops of my boots. I retrieved my bicycle and began to ride toward the city, pushing at the pedals with drenched feet. Even as I turned down the dirt road that would lead me home, I could not stop picturing how the man's eyes had glinted in the light as he said good-bye. *Could a Nahuel have blue eyes*, I wondered, *given that jaguars had amber?* I rode faster.

The day I met the man on the beach, or perhaps one shortly after, I leaned my bicycle against the wall of the chalet after a morning spent exploring, went inside, and kicked off my sodden boots. I placed the binoculars on one of the shelves in the entryway, where I kept all of my father's tools, clothes, and books. The chalet had been built for a caretaker, but my father's friend, Karl Müller, who owned the larger house up the road, decided after all that he required privacy more than caretaking. Herr Müller had helped me cut down a tree for our Christmas with my father's axe, which he also taught me to sharpen. I ran my hand over its blade and then the badges on my father's cap. The first looked like a great cormorant spreading its wings over an angular black piece of driftwood; the other was a skull with a hopeful, winning smile, thigh bones crossed behind it. I had found these things buried in a trunk after my father died.

The kitchen smelled of freshly brewed coffee. I poured myself a cup *con leche*, drank it, and went to the bedroom where my mother was sitting up in the bed, propped by pillows. I crawled in next to her and pressed my face to the cool fabric of the quilt. She stroked my hair and inhaled—she said she liked the smell of the outdoors that came in with me.

See anything good today? she asked.

I told her of two birds I could have seen in the forest, a firecrown and a parakeet. I never revealed I went to the lake, because I didn't want her to be afraid I would drown too. I often intimated I had not gone past the cypress grove at the end of our road.

Did you eat anything? I asked, eyeing the untouched tostada on a plate on her bedside table.

Chocolate, she laughed. What else?

I stopped at the grocery each afternoon to buy cheese, beef, and tomatoes, but mostly, my mother and I lived on chocolate. No matter how carefully Signor Buzzato and I set the molds, some of the chocolates did not come out uniform, and these he did not want to sell. I brought them home. My mother and I not only drizzled chocolate over our *medialunas* but ate it at lunch and dinner as well.

In truth, my mother was too sick to eat anything heavy or spicy. I did not know exactly what was wrong with her; then, the stigma of cancer was like that of AIDS in my own time. Some say Perón never told Eva her diagnosis, though the people knew. My grandmother said that someone had scrawled *¡Viva el cáncer!* on a building in a rich neighborhood. Eva Perón's death was my earliest memory of an event beyond my own family, and it gave me the idea that even powerful women sometimes just went weak and let go. Lying on my mother's bed in a shaft of late-spring sunlight coming in the window, I understood at some great depth within me that she was dying, but I resisted diving. My mother, however, was like those Chinese fishermen, sending me down to gather things too big to swallow.

She had begun telling me about my father, covering the easy parts first: how my grandfather died in the first war when my father was just a baby, how my father grew up in a Germany starved by an unfair treaty between nations. But right around the time I met the man on the beach, my mother told me about my father's decision to attend a special school, which marked a turning point in my father's story.

Junkerschulen was for training *Schutzstaffel*, she said.

She could scarcely pronounce the words, let alone explain the concepts behind them; they sounded like icebergs jutting from the rolling sea of her Spanish.

The school for German officers? I asked.

Boys at the Aléman often boasted of what great men their fathers were. Meanwhile, I had only a vague idea of my father's work in Germany during the war. Of why he had come to Argentina. He never spoke of the past. If my mother was the fisherman, he was the ring around my neck, the reason I failed so well, once I was grown, to remember.

The school your father went to opened right as he turned eighteen, she said. There weren't a lot of other jobs for a young man. Maybe he could have been any number of things. He was brilliant and talented. But once he was trained . . .

Yes? I asked.

Well, he had to go forward, you see.

Forward where? I almost asked. But I nodded and shrugged. It was terrifying to know. I heard the silences in the history lessons about the war we got at school. At the Aléman, they did not teach the Holocaust at all. No one had ever explained to me and my comrades that our town's most upstanding citizens were murderers. But they did not have to explain it for us to know. We could feel it in the striding steps of the doctor, in the crisp cuffs of the postmaster's suit, and it made us cling to any pride we could keep in our fathers at all costs.

He had to go into the *Totenkopfverbande* when they appointed him, become a guard.

Head of a dead man, my brain translated before I could stop it. *Death's Head Unit*.

I should go, I said. I'll be late.

On Saturdays, I went to the shop after lunch instead of in the late afternoon as I did on school days. I mopped the floors and bleached the counters before helping Signor Buzzato melt chocolate for the week ahead. That spring, the Signore had trained me to stir the chocolate so he could tend to the customers who came in for *merienda* during the Christmas season. Each time he turned the wide, flat paddle over to me, he wiggled his eyebrows and his mustache in unison, pointed at the bulge of muscle under his rolled-up sleeve, and said, Only muscle will win over your little sweetheart, *amigo-amico*.

He meant my friend Emelia. On weekdays Emelia walked from school to the shop with me. When I worked the counter, usually so the Signore could go out back for a hand of cards and a cigar, Emelia would talk with me while she ate her pastry or drank a hot chocolate. She never came in on the Sabbath, though I wished she could sit with me while I stirred as it gave me too much time to think.

I wasn't to let the chocolate burn. I swept deep with each stroke, running the paddle's edge against the bottom of the vat each time to loosen the film of sugar that stuck there. My arms were sore after ten minutes, though the process took an hour. It did help to imagine how my own thin arms would look with muscles like the Signore's. But it wasn't Emelia I wanted to impress.

On an early summer afternoon near the time in question, a sudden warmth filled the air, and I broke a sweat while stirring. So I turned down the burner as I had seen the Signore do and propped the back door open for some cool air. Franz Achter was in the alleyway. He leaned—one knee bent, his foot on the wall, his shirt untucked—against the bank building several doors down on the other side.

I had seen him once that winter in the same alleyway. He and his friends had knocked me to the ground and taken the bag of ill-formed chocolates I was bringing to my mother. When Franz punched me in the mouth, my teeth gashed his knuckles. He placed his bloodied hand on my neck and pushed my face into the snow, leaned against the small of my back while one of his friends kicked my side. That day when I got home, my mother put her fingers in my mouth and nudged each tooth to make sure none were loose; it seemed as if she was hunting for the bits of Franz that might have remained between my teeth, so I pulled away. She held my head, made me look into her eyes, and said, Who did this to you?

I would not tell her.

But I did check to make sure Franz was alone before I said, Guten Tag.

Hey, he said, hooking his thumb at the back door of the bank. I'm just waiting for my father.

Herr Achter was an important man in our city; at those banquets I hardly remembered even then, he had sat at the head of the main table, presiding over the festivities.

Standing in the alleyway alone with me, Franz looked embarrassed, just as he had when we were paired up in fifth grade to dissect a frog together. His hand had shaken so badly as he tried to slit its rubbery belly that I had to take over the scalpel. He had swallowed hard each time I separated out some small organ and pinned it to a white corkboard; I thought he would cry when I quartered the tiny heart.

I left Franz in the alleyway, went back into the kitchen, got a ladle, and filled a mug with straight melted chocolate. Checking to make sure the Signore was still busy at the counter, I motioned Franz over.

What? he said, but he was already strolling toward me, his shock of blond hair falling in his eyes.

I handed him the mug.

¡Zarpado! he said.

I watched Franz's throat as he drank the entire mug in long, hard gulps.

Gracias, he said. Haefer, you're all right.

He handed me the mug.

Come back sometime, I said, trying not to plead. I'm alone in the kitchen on Saturday afternoons.

You want to see something neat? he asked.

Sure, I said.

He lifted his shirt, grabbed at his belt with both hands, and tipped the buckle up so I could see it. I almost dropped the mug. It bore the same cormorant as my father's badge, but I was paying more attention to the three moles that formed a triangle on Franz's ridged stomach just above his navel.

Copado, I said. I have a few things like this too.

Franz nodded and said, It's my father's. He doesn't have very much of this stuff because he lost a lot of it after the war.

I reached down and ran my hand along the edge of the buckle. My finger grazed his skin, catching on one of the curly, coppery hairs beneath his navel.

Eduardo! Signor Buzzato barked behind me.

I turned. The Signore was frowning. Franz yanked his shirt down.

Sorry, Signore, Franz said, clasping me on the shoulder, making my stomach spin. I was just catching up with old Eduardo here. We don't see much of him these days.

The chocolate is burnt! the Signore said, his face red.

I'm sorry, I said.

Franz smiled before he walked away and the chocolate filled the lines between his teeth, ringed his lips like blood. It reminded me of how my mouth had looked the day he punched me. I followed Signor Buzzato back into the kitchen.

Now listen, the Signore said, and he pulled the towel from the front of his pants and slapped it down on the counter, which was one of his favorite modes of self-expression.

No one doesn't have history, he said. No one. But if you want to keep your job, you'll learn to keep it under wraps. Do you understand me?

I thought he was upset because he had caught me touching Franz, but he went on: I don't want to see any of that Nazi *mierda* anywhere near this store. That kid has no idea what it means.

I let out a long breath, relieved.

My father, I said. My father had a badge like that too.

I'm sure he did, the Signore said. But you don't have to go reminding people.

On that stifling August night in Los Angeles in 1986, the book in my lap and an empty martini glass on the table beside me, I willed myself to soak up all of my mother I could: her strong, slender hands; her hair like a thick, dark waterfall; her courage. I willed myself to recall each detail of Signor Buzzato, who had no son of his own, who knew the truth about my father yet trusted me, who tried to show me how to become a man. I willed myself to stay with Franz in the alleyway, to remember the feeling of loving someone before you knew what it meant that he gave you pain while you gave him sweetness.

I spread my arms wide before the open window. But no breeze came to cool my feverish chest. It was hot out, I reasoned, and I was upset. I did not have an actual fever. Still, I got up and went into the bathroom, where I shook the thermometer and tucked it under my tongue. In the mirror, I examined my neck, the back of my arms, my sides. I had tried to avoid this activity—what good could come of it?—but the memory of twisting my young body to see the bruises the tip of the boy's boot had left all down my left side, so similar to the tumors I feared would soon appear, broke me.

Who did this to you?

Six months before, I had driven up the coast toward Santa Barbara to catch a boat to Anacapa for the weekend with another marine ornithologist and three graduate students from the University. For seventeen years, ever since I'd come to California for graduate school myself, I had been observing the Brandt's cormorant of the Channel Islands to determine the long-term effects of the Dos Cuadras oil spill on breeding. It had been a while since I'd been out in the field, having spent a great deal of time that semester not only in the classroom but also on the pavement while a friend drew a chalk outline around my body and in hospital rooms that smelled of death. Some ornithologists had begun surveying cormorant populations using aerial photography, which meant a bird in the hand wasn't always. The salty air of the Pacific felt good against my face as the small vessel made its way toward the Islands.

We arrived in the late afternoon, just as the sun was going orange and sinking in the sky. While two of the graduate students went off to set up with Dr. Bradley, another, Gabriel, helped me position a mist net near a large colony on a beach half a mile from where we'd docked. I was grateful for his help, having left my own graduate students behind in a bid for time to myself. Gabriel spoke to me in Spanish. He was from Chicago. His mother was Mexican, but his father was Norwegian, he said, flicking his thumb between his ice-floe eyes. He reminded me of home. He was tall and his long reach allowed him to untangle knots high in the net. He did this with fast, nimble fingers and tucked his black curls behind his ears with a similar motion. The birds' guttural grunts filled the air, felt solid as pennies or baseballs.

They've got their love-dress on, Gabriel said, admiring the brilliant turquoise of their throat patches.

Within minutes, a cormorant flew into our net. We pulled on our gloves. Gabriel took its neck between his first two fingers and slid its back into his palm; I freed its feet and tail, snipping a line of net caught on its wing. Unlike the cormorants of my boyhood, the feathers on the breast of the Brandt shimmered as if it ate a steady diet of emeralds. It glared at me with eyes the color of a lagoon in a dream. Its heart beat wildly as I measured its wingspan and examined the gonads. The bird turned its head to the side like a Catholic wife as I swabbed a sample from its cloaca for Dr. Bradley's immunity study. The Newcastle virus had spread among inland cormorants; he worried it would eventually reach the coast. I clamped a ring around the bird's ankle. Even after so many years of netting birds, I hated this part: what must it be like to go about the rest of your life tethered to something you never agreed to? When I was through, Gabriel walked to the water, stepped up and out onto an arch striated with volcanic ash, turned his long body to the wind, and let the bird go. It flapped its wings to right itself, skimming its feet over the surface of the water. Then it flew upward and dove into the waves, its throat patch like a bit of sky falling.

I set up my small tent in an inlet near a cliff for shelter and readied my stove; it was bound to be a cold night. With the nets set, I would not sleep. Too much risk a bird would be hurt by trying to free itself. Gabriel strapped on his head lamp and unrolled his sleeping bag in my tent.

We can take shifts, he said, shivering, breathing into his cupped hands.

The sun set. I freed two gulls in the next hour. Another hour passed and Gabriel emerged bleary-eyed to sit watch. I went into the tent filled with his sweet musky odor. I did not fall asleep. Two hours later, when it was my shift again, Gabriel came to the door of the tent. I sat up. He crawled in and knelt before me. He unzipped his parka and pulled his shirt off. It had been over a year since I had touched a man's chest. I tried to resist, but finally, I buried my face against the flat, hairless plain between Gabriel's nipples. Where our cold skins met they burned; the whole time, I was half aware of a living thing caught in a net and struggling. We got up to free cormorants and returned to our island on the island, that separate existence we hoped would not follow us back to shore. Just before sunrise, he kissed me, pulled his parka on, and left the tent. He spent the day working with Dr. Bradley, and a young woman named Frances helped me. I never saw him again.

Who did this to you?

I did it to myself. That was what I thought at thirteen, and I still believed it at forty. As I returned to the living room, a sob erupted from my center. I did not want to die. I did not want to die slowly like my mother. But I did not want to die like my father either, like my friend Aleks, who shot himself in the temple the day he learned he was positive.

Haefer, I said to myself, *you're all right. You're all right.*

Once school let out that summer, I woke early each morning and rode toward the wild part of the lake, a wide flat mirror in the first gray light. Several times I made my way to the special beach. I could not help looking over my shoulder for a Nahuel while I was there. Once, I spotted fifty or so imperials raft feeding—floating together close enough to touch wings—which gave the fish no chance against them. Their young had hatched; I found half of a shattered white eggshell in a footprint I thought must have been the man's. On my fourth or fifth trip, shortly after Christmas, the man was there when I arrived. He stood at the water's edge, his head bowed. I thought he might be praying and I did not want to interrupt him, so I waited. A moment passed, and he turned to look at me as if he'd known I was there all along. He motioned me over with a bent forefinger. I walked toward him and he shifted so I could see the cormorant lying on the rocks, its beak crushed and its left wing broken.

Take a look, he said, scratching at his beard with the hand that seemed to have a tremor.

As I passed him, I caught a whiff of some strong chemical odor—shoe polish, perhaps. I crouched to examine the bird, sad for its death but excited to see it up close, to flex the unbroken right wing. Its belly was gashed open, its glistening brown-purple entrails spilling out. Had it simply been dashed against the rocks? Or had another animal, an eagle perhaps, preyed upon it? Or a Nahuel?

Behind me, the man began to speak what sounded like nonsense, though it wasn't:

When, spite of cormorant devouring Time,
The endeavor of this present breath may buy
That honor which shall bate his scythe's keen edge
And make us heirs of all eternity.

What? I said.

It's Shakespeare, he said. It means honor is the only thing that outlasts death.

Oh, I said. Is that true?

The man's strange blue eyes widened and he paused before he said, I believe so.

I pictured my father's honor as a solid metallic triangle exiting his chest and hovering before him in the depths, reassuring him of everlasting life while his heart ran down like a clock, and then floating to the surface, a bit of jetsam I might be able to gather in my hands.

Time is a cormorant because the bird eats everything in sight, the man said, rubbing his beard again and beginning to cough.

My father blames the kelp gulls equally for that, I said.

I loved to hear my father's story about the gulls so much that I did not realize he did not like to tell it. Once when I was four or five, small enough to sit on his knee, we were discussing the story of Jonah, and I asked if whales had any enemies. My father made the mistake of telling me something he had seen off the coast of Argentina once before I was born: a flock of kelp gulls descended upon a right whale calf and ate her alive, tearing off strips of flesh the length of a man's arm—

My mother had looked up sharply; having been delayed by her slow German, she had at last caught what he was saying. My father choked on his words. I begged him to tell me more. Finally, over the years, I dragged out of him the worst of the details: the whale screaming each time she surfaced, the blood and blubber floating in the water, how she finally failed to rise and her dark shape faded into the depths.

Or, I said to the man, I mean, he *blamed* them.

The man, who had finished coughing and was gathering a wad of phlegm in his handkerchief, brought his binoculars to his face.

Where is your father? he asked with a grimace, as if he knew the answer. Perhaps because he could look inside my mind.

I swallowed and said, He died.

Mine died when I was about your age, he said, and he angled his gaze toward Isla Huemul. That was where Arturo said the Nahuel lived, keeping camp in the ruins of the failed nuclear fusion project Perón had authorized there. The man did not sound as sad as I thought he should about his father. Would I be less sad about my father when I was an old man? I did not think so. Perhaps he was numb. My mother had recently explained to me the way that time and getting used to something could make you numb.

Where do you live? I asked.

Still looking through his binoculars, he held up a shaking thumb, pointed behind us, and said, My house is at the end of that path. The beach is my private one, but you're welcome anytime. You're quite the ornithologist. Someday we can look at the colony on my property if you like. Though I'm not a fan of it, you might be.

I had not realized I was trespassing. The man, regardless of his oddness, took me seriously. He had lost his father young too, and so he might understand what it meant that I had lost mine. I came to the beach several more times over the next few weeks of that summer, and though I remained disconcerted by some of our interactions, I grew used to him, and I even felt a strange allegiance to him.

Each afternoon when I returned home from my summer adventures, I sat with my mother and listened to her tell my father's story. So at last I learned he was a guard in a labor camp.

Dachau, my mother said.

I had heard of it. Patrik Tagert's father had worked there too. It did not mean much more to me than that, but I felt this knowledge lift and shine like a spider's thread in the breeze and drift toward other threads, other hauntings in my brain about the men in our town.

My mother went on: Over the gate, your father said, there was a sign that read, *Arbeit macht frei*. Work will set you free. When he was a young man, your father believed that sign. Believed what he was told, that the work they were doing would change the country for the better.

Like the *descamisados*, I said. Arturo told me all about it, how they sat in the Plaza de Mayo—

No, no, not like that, not that kind of work, my mother said, shifting in the bed. I could not tell if she was in pain or if she did not like what I had said.

But the Jews had done nothing wrong? I asked. I thought of Emelia, whose parents had come to Argentina before the war. Her mother and father were decent and kind. They knew my father was German, yet they did not leave me on the doorstep when I came knocking.

It wasn't only Jews, my mother said. It was also others. Revolutionaries. And men who . . .

What?

You know, *maricónes,* she said, looking away.

I tried to swallow but something tightened around my throat, leaving too much saliva on my tongue.

Never mind that, she said. The point is, when he got here, he saw that he was wrong, and though he kept many of his friendships from his youth, he kept to himself. That was why we stopped going to the banquets, you remember, where they celebrated Hitler's birthday? Your father truly repented.

Repented what? I asked.

The guards were not always kind to the prisoners, she said.

I sighed. My mother was not saying all she knew, not even saying all I knew. Surely my father had not done the things I had heard whispers of at the Aléman. But he had clearly done something my mother wanted to hide from me.

What you have to understand is that Hitler had an . . . addictive kind of charisma.

Like Perón?

A little. In the time before we left Buenos Aires, Perón was becoming like a savior to the workers. Maybe it wasn't perfect, but it was quid pro quo. Your vote for your wages. Hitler was always just evil. And he made his men take vows of loyalty to the death.

Why couldn't they just break their vows?

Because vows make words into something real that you can't get out of.

Dad knew him . . . Hitler . . . personally?

She did not answer that question, but went on to tell me that when he first arrived, my father had served for a time in the part of Dachau where they kept officers who resisted or disobeyed.

Even though he had his doubts, your father saw how they were treated, how they were punished.

How were they punished?

My mother's black eyes bore into mine before she said: A man could be tortured for disobeying. Your father did not stay there long, but he never forgot it.

The word, *tortura*, *folter*, *tortura*, *folter*, played in my head in both of my tongues—how my mother said it, how my father would have—as I rode my bike to the chocolate shop that afternoon. What did these words even mean? What exactly did my father fear they would do to him? What had he done?

The week, perhaps even the day, I had this conversation with my mother, Emelia came to the shop. Signor Buzzato called me to the front. I was sweating from the intense heat of the kitchen.

The lady would like a *submarino*, and I have business to tend to, he said, pulling the towel from the waist of his pants and slapping it down on the counter. He left to go out back, although I had seen no evidence of a card game in the alleyway.

I made the drink for Emelia, heating the milk and plopping a bar of chocolate into it. I placed it before her and she inhaled the aroma. Her hair was wet and her shoulders sunburned.

Hot weather, hot chocolate? I said.

¡El parásito! she said. I've been at the beach. The water was freezing.

After talking about nothing awhile, I worked up the courage to ask why her parents had left Germany.

They were killing us, she said, rolling her eyes. You know that. If they had stayed, I would have never been born. They were lucky to get passage to La Paz because Argentina closed its borders—something my mother never forgets. They moved here and started the store. But they never got to just be . . . unafraid.

Unafraid, I repeated.

She began to explain to me in a fast, breathless way a story she had obviously heard from her parents more than once: Maybe Perón had not liked Jews, because although he had friends who were Jews, he also had friends who hated Jews, but the fact is he allowed Jews to hold political offices, own businesses. Emelia's father said absolute power corrupts absolutely and Perón had absolute power, so it could have gone dreadfully wrong at any turn, but it was actually better before the coup. Some said it was getting better under Frondizi, but he thought the Jews had never had problems in Argentina, apparently forgetting about the pogrom of the *Semana Trágica*, not to mention those closed borders. Anyway, clearly Jews had problems, because Perón had let in all these Nazis, so how could they not have—

She cut off there. She, like me, did not have many friends, and we needed each other.

Anyway, she said, we have a book that talks more about it—you know, extermination—than they told us at school. If you really want to know about it, you can read it, but you should know my father told my mother it was the worst thing he'd ever seen. He hid it from us, so of course we had to look at it.

Yes, I said. I want to see it.

Come over later, then, she said, just as Signor Buzzato came back in. He raised his eyebrows at me to say *congratulations* and Emelia raised her eyebrows at him to say *you're ridiculous*.

That evening at Emelia's, once I had endured the pleasantries of her mother and sisters, we went into her father's office, where she said we were going to play *Escoba*. She got out the cards and dealt them on the coffee table. But once her mother stopped hanging around outside the door, Emelia closed it and climbed onto her father's desk chair, one foot on its back, teetering as she stretched to reach the top bookshelf and fumbling around behind a Joseph's Coat so long-dead its leaves had gone gray.

She put the book in my hands. I could tell from the way it opened that she had turned to the page before us many times, rows of bodies piled on top of each other so you could not figure out whose limbs were whose, spindly trees touching the sky in the background. In the foreground, a young girl, her face turned toward the camera, screamed her outrage even in death. *The liberation of Belsen*, the caption read.

I just think sometimes, Emelia said, that could have been me.

I could feel the warmth of her thigh against mine, smell her sunburn, as I flipped forward, looking at photographs whose contents are familiar now, though I had never seen them before. The men holding the guns wore hats like my father's. Their uniforms bore the same badges and pins. Bile rose in my throat. Could my father, who had loved me so well, really have killed other children, burned their bodies? When I reached the end of the book, I flipped back to the beginning.

Do you mind? I asked Emelia.

No, she said.

I skipped the first few pages, which were all text—then I had only a bit of English—and turned to the first page with a photo. My heart slammed sideways in my chest and, as if it were a cannonball, my whole body jerked. In the photograph on that page, a younger version of the man from the beach stood leaning against a desk, his arms crossed, looking at the camera. *Hitler in 1936*, the caption read. I gagged.

Are you all right? Emelia said.

I couldn't breathe, couldn't answer, and Emelia pounded me on the back.

I know him, I managed to choke out.

Eduardo, Emelia said. That's Hitler.

I know, I said.

I had seen photographs of Hitler before, though not many; I grew up in that brief era before his image became as ordinary as it was when he was alive and on newsreels all the time. I knew the man on the beach had looked familiar, but I had never been able to place him until that moment.

Hitler died, Eduardo, she said. He shot himself. There's proof.

She flipped forward a few pages to show me the body. The dead man had the same mustache, but he was not the man on the beach, nor the man in the first photo.

How can you be sure that's really him? I asked.

Emelia appeared concerned, but not for herself as I thought she might be. For me. I've looked at it a million times, she said.

I flipped back and examined the portrait more closely. Perhaps I was mistaken. The picture was in black and white, so I could not tell if the eyes were blue—yet they had the same intensity, a thing you could not escape. The man on the beach had the same forehead, the same weak jaw, the same flaring nostrils. He had a beard, and his hair was darker and longer, but of course, those things could be changed. So I told Emelia about the man on the beach. How at first I thought he was a Nahuel—she rolled her eyes at this—and I knew that wasn't true, but he definitely made me feel strange. I pointed to the year of Hitler's birth beneath his portrait, 1889. The man on the beach was just about the right age.

There were witnesses, Eduardo, Emelia said.

What if the witnesses lied? I said, thinking that if my father had managed to get himself halfway around the world to hide, certainly Hitler could have managed too.

I think they double-checked, Emelia said, sarcastic, tapping his date of death.

An idea crept over me then, and my body jerked again. What if the man on the beach is . . . you know . . . *der große Deutscher*? I said.

The boys at the Aléman—Franz Achter included—had sometimes whispered of a man who had been extremely powerful in the Fatherland and lived in Bariloche but never showed his face. Until that moment, I had afforded the whole business about as much credence as Emelia gave the Nahuel. None of those boys ever said directly who the Great German was, but couldn't it be Hitler himself?

I asked Emelia, I mean, who else could *der große Deutscher* be, really?

Plenty of people! she said. Look around you! Anyway, Eduardo, that rumor's sick. It feels like those people *wish* Hitler was still alive. But he isn't.

How can you be so sure?

Emelia took the book, closed it, and said, I just *am*.

The morning after I read the footnote in that other book, the one that suggested Hitler had faked his death and escaped to Patagonia, I drove to Silver Lake to visit my friend Lucas, who had pneumonia. I pulled up in front of the small blue bungalow to see his sister, Sarah, and his lover, John, embracing on the front stoop. I wedged my impala into an impossibly small space and made my way toward them.

He's gone, John said over Sarah's shoulder, moisture pooled in the dark circles around his eyes. I heard what lay beneath that simple statement: *And I'm gone. And maybe you're gone too.*

After I held each of them briefly and awkwardly, I went inside and stood next to the bed where Lucas's body lay wrapped in a white sheet. I wished I could see his face, but I did not uncover him. I told myself I preferred to remember him in life, not death.

It was what I had told myself about Emelia too.

I had last seen her during the Christmas holiday of my final year in graduate school. I was visiting my grandmother, whom I would also never see again. Emelia was living in Buenos Aires with her boyfriend, a young professor of economics. She made me dinner in their small apartment. It was just the two of us; her boyfriend had a meeting that night. She asked me questions about my life in Los Angeles and I evaded answering.

Are you happy? she asked me at last, exasperated, pushing her hair back off her face with her hand and staring at me with her wide, gray-green eyes, just as she had when we were twelve years old.

Mostly, I said. Are you?

Things have changed here, Eduardo. Since the coup. It's no place to raise a child.

A child? I said.

Eduardo, she laughed. You never notice anything.

She pulled up her thin white cotton shirt so I could that see her belly was slightly rounded.

Bad timing, she said.

I suppose so, I said, and we continued to eat.

That night, after she hugged me good-bye, as I was about to walk out the door, she grabbed me by the forearm. I turned to face her.

Eduardo, she said.

Sí?

If I were you, she said, stressing the word, when I made it back to Los Angeles, I wouldn't . . . maybe you could find a way to just stay?

Of course she knew about me. I nodded and kissed her forehead.

Two months later, Emelia and her boyfriend were disappeared. All her mother ever learned was that they came to Emelia's apartment in the early hours of a Sunday morning.

The year after, I married a woman who reminded me of Emelia. It was brief and unhappy. I got my citizenship, got my divorce, and tried never to think again of my wife, Emelia, or what I had learned about the pregnant women who were disappeared: the junta took them to prisons, chained them to the wall, waited for them to give birth, and then killed them. Prominent military families raised their babies.

In 1986, standing before the body of my friend Lucas, I finally allowed myself to wonder if some small piece of Emelia still walked in the world, believing, as I had for a while in my own childhood, in a different history from the one that was my own. A little girl, perhaps, with Emelia's clear eyes, who would someday learn the parents she loved had murdered the ones she'd never known. I reached out and uncovered Lucas's face; I looked at him—at his eyebrows, his earlobes, his cheekbones, his lips. Then I replaced the sheet and waited with John for the coroner to come.

As I rode my bike through the city that evening in 1960 after Emelia showed me the book, I saw death everywhere; every house a barracks, every streetlamp a showerhead spewing gas. I looked into the eyes of a little girl in her mother's arms at a crosswalk; the woman turned her back to protect her child from a Nazi guard with his gun pointed. I saw the guard shoot her and her daughter, saw them fall to the ground and bleed. My father was the guard. My father had done these things. And was I any better? I had let myself get so comfortable with murderers that when Hitler himself sidled up to me on a beach, I chatted with him as if he was my grandfather. Maybe Emelia was right. Maybe it wasn't him. But what if it was? What could I do? Who could I tell? Anyone who would believe me already knew and was on his side.

I turned off the main road, legs pumping, face hot with a creeping hatred for my own existence. I slammed my way into the chalet. I began to take my boots off but then stopped. The entryway, I realized, was my first task. I pulled my father's knapsack from the shelf and began tossing his things into it.

When I got to his dagger, I held it before me in both hands. I slid it from its sheath. The blade was dull. I took out the file that Herr Müller had shown me how to use and slid the dagger along it. The two sang when they met. I pictured how easily it would cut through the water's surface, dive, bury itself in the lake's bed. I did not allow myself to imagine opening *der große Deutscher's* neck, but I must have suspected already that if justice was to be done, it would have to be by my own hand.

Duardo? my mother called.

I did not answer.

She called again, and I heard her struggling to get out of the bed. She stood before me, a silhouette clinging to the frame of the kitchen door.

What are you doing? she asked.

Making things right, I said. Getting rid of him.

She stepped into the room, tried to reach out to touch me, but I elbowed her away. I kept sharpening the dagger. She watched silently until I sheathed it and tossed it into the knapsack, on top of my father's hat. I opened the door and then paused, turned to look at my trembling mother, her hair lifting in the breeze that came in. For a moment, she looked young and well. Time tumbled backward, so that in the shadows behind her, I saw my father as he had been years before too, kneeling on-shore, drawing me toward him with his finger, which he placed over my mouth. He turned my body toward a familiar driftwood log upon which was perched a bird nearly as big as me. It was black with a white frill around its neck and fringed wings, a wise old turtle face, hooked beak, comb the size of my palm.

Condor, my father whispered.

The bird looked at us with its yellow eye before it lifted itself—a miracle of physics—and took flight over the lake, its wingspan twice as long as my father was tall, the white feathers amid the black like the keys of a piano. We watched it soar.

Once in a lifetime, my father had said, and he squeezed my shoulders.

My mother leaned against the wall and said, There is nothing we can do to make things right, Eduardo. All we can do is try to understand.

I do understand, I said. He killed people? Tortured them?

She covered her mouth.

Tell me the truth, I said.

She nodded.

The truth! I yelled.

He was transferred from the officers' unit at Dachau to the medical unit, she said.

Medical, I said, confused. So he was caring for the sick?

No, my mother said, wringing her hands, working up her courage. He was assigned to aid the medical team in restraining its subjects.

Restraining them?

Your father worked with them during the cold-water experiments.

What? I asked.

They were worried about German soldiers on the front who were freezing to death, German pilots who fell into the ocean, she said. So they froze the prisoners to try to figure out how to warm them.

My father, using whatever force necessary, brought the prisoners from the medical barracks into the room where they would be frozen. The doctors, I've since learned, inserted a probe into each man's rectum to measure his temperature. My father held them down, tied their hands to their opposite elbows, and helped submerge them in icy water or put them outside naked in thirty-below weather. After my father was promoted, he ordered a lesser officer to do so.

Your father tried to be kind, my mother said. He often spoke to them as—

They died? I snapped, incredulous she could proffer this as if it made my father's crimes less, not more, heinous.

Some, she said, and then, quietly: the Russians lasted hours.

I shook my head. My father had the gall to talk to a man while he murdered him, but not the mettle to spare my mother from knowing of it.

Her hands spread before her like a supplicant by then, and she told me the rest of his tale: When the camp was liberated, US soldiers gave the prisoners guns and told them they could kill the guards. My father hid in a closet in the medical barracks, snuck out in the night, and then passed himself off as a prisoner. He made his way to Spain, got a false passport, and took his passage by sea.

How could you do it? I asked.

Do what? she said, shivering.

How could you . . . be with him?

At first, I didn't know.

But after?

We had you, Eduardo, she said, which now seems to me her only real crime against me, but at the time, it softened me as much as what she said next: You can't help loving who you love.

Even though he was a murderer.

He wasn't a murderer. He had to do what he was ordered to do, no matter how objectionable.

No, I said. He could have given his own life.

My mother put her hand on my arm and said, He did, Eduardo.

I saw my father's death for the first time as it had really happened: one winter morning he went to the frigid lake, stripped off his clothes, walked into the water, and drowned himself.

Not soon enough, I said to my mother, and I walked out the door. I got on my bike and rode away.

What will you do, Eduardo? she called after me. *Por favor!*

I did not answer, because I did not want her to see me cry. It wasn't until later that I realized she was afraid I might kill myself too.

The weight of my father's things in the knapsack pulled against my heaving shoulder blades as I rode. I was still crying. Near the cypress grove, I slammed on my brakes, digging my rear tire into the dirt. I laid my bike down and stepped into the trees. I needed to catch my breath, to think. Was I really going to go to the lake in the dark and drown all the parts of my father I had left? Would that even fix anything? What else might I do? I dragged my forearm over my damp face. I looked up into the coppery light that filtered through the branches and spilled onto my chest, a final warmth in the cooling air. This shifting, late-evening light reminded me of Franz. What might he give to have a dagger like the one whose handle I could feel pressing against my back through the canvas of the knapsack?

I mounted my bike and headed not to the lake but to Franz's house. The sun had set by the time I found myself leaning my bike against the brick wall that surrounded the Achters' porch. The light over their door still burned. Moths dove in desperate circles, banging their heads against the glass lantern. I started up the stairs. The noise of Herr Achter turning the page of the newspaper made me jump. I had not seen him sitting there. He looked a little surprised to see me too. But he recovered quickly, relaxing back into his chair and shaking the paper to rid it of creases.

Franz is upstairs, he said. Go on in.

I put my hand on the handle, but I did not open the door. I turned to look at Herr Achter. What had he thought of my father, who had not married a German woman, who had cut himself off from his former comrades? Did they understand he had killed himself because of what they had done? How could Herr Achter just sit on his front porch reading a newspaper like he had never swatted a fly? I balled up my fists. I imagined punching Herr Achter in the face.

But like my father, Herr Achter had not really pulled the trigger on his own gun, had he? Hitler had made him do it. And Hitler was still alive. I realized then what I had to do, saw I had come to the Achters' to make sure the man on the beach was Hitler before I killed him. Herr Achter would certainly know.

I opened my mouth, but I failed to formulate an actual question.

Herr Achter peered at me over his paper and said, somewhat impatiently, It should be open.

I sputtered, unable to think of a question that would not make Herr Achter suspicious. It would be safer to ask Franz. So I tugged at the door, found the stairs and climbed them. In his room, Franz was reclining on the bed, one arm behind his head. He leapt up when he saw me in the doorframe.

Haefer! he said.

I have something for you, I said, opening the knapsack and drawing out my father's hat, coins, sash, and pins. I handed Franz everything except the dagger, which I slid into my pocket while Franz ran his fingertips over the badges on the hat, just as I always had.

Where did you get this stuff? he asked.

It was my father's, I said.

Why are you giving it to me? he said, suspicious for a boy used to receiving things.

I could not say that once I killed the man on the beach, until his identity could be proved, I would go to prison, and we might not see each other for a long time. I could not tell Franz I loved him.

Here, this too, I said, pushing the knapsack toward him.

Danke, Franz said, taking it in his hands.

I nodded and shifted my weight from foot to foot, preparing to ask Franz about *der große Deutscher.* But Franz spoke before I did.

It's dark out, Franz said. Do you want to stay tonight? My mother won't mind.

I knew I should just ask Franz the question I needed answered and head on. But the man would not be on his beach at night, I reasoned. I needed a place to sleep, and I could not go back home.

Sí, I said.

Should I call your mother? Frau Achter asked when Franz delivered me to the kitchen.

She knows I'm here, I lied.

Frau Achter not only insisted that I stay, but she insisted that I eat. I chewed on a wurst while she fussed in the background, warming rolls. I could tell by this and the softness in her eyes that she knew about my father's suicide. Her care made me feel like a child, and this gave me pause. The man had to be brought to justice. I had no doubts about that. But maybe I should not be the one to do it. Maybe I should just tell Frau Achter. But she would tell Herr Achter. And he and the other men of our town would protect the man. How would I forgive myself if I let the chance pass to end it once and for all?

Franz brought me a pair of light-blue pajamas and I changed into them in the bathroom while he changed into his in the bedroom. I came in as he was buttoning his shirt. My throat tightened. I cleared it and, trying to sound offhand, said, Say, Franz, is there really a *große Deutscher*?

Franz, who had been setting up his sleeping bag on the floor, swiveled his head to look at me. Why? he said, exhaling audibly through his mouth.

No reason, I said. I thought if anyone would know, you would.

Franz stood up, walked to his door, put his hands to either side of the frame, and looked into the hallway. Then he said, I know there's one.

How do you know?

Franz whispered, Because I live with him.

What? I said.

Franz gestured toward the front porch.

Your *father*? You think your father is *der große Deutscher?* But I've seen his face!

That story is just how he protects himself, Franz hissed. Think about it, Haefer. Who else could it be? Who do you know who's more powerful than my father?

I did not use Emelia's logic on him because Franz's eyes shone so with pride. The Signore was right. Franz could not grasp the horror of our fathers' crimes. It made me sad for him. And sad for myself because Franz could not help me. I would have to rely on the strength of my own conviction.

Copado, I said.

Franz puffed his chest out and said, I know.

I got into the sleeping bag and turned on my side. Frau Achter turned off the hallway lights moments later. Franz turned over and sighed. Soon the buzzing of the porch light ceased and his father's heavy boots thunked up the stairs. Then it was quiet but for the distant noises in any city. Franz slipped from his bed and knelt beside me on the floor.

What? I whispered.

Comrades should stick together, he said, and he crawled into the bag with me.

He pressed his back to my chest. My lungs felt as if they'd explode with the sudden intake of air when he reached around behind him to put his hand down the front of my pajamas. I reached around him to feel his heat in my hand.

So it was true. I was what I had suspected I was.

You can't help loving who you love, my mother had said.

But if our fathers had known, then they would have put us in the camps. They might have killed us. As I closed my eyes that night, I saw the man in my mind's eye. Yes, I was sure it was him.

Franz was not in his bedroom the next morning. As I pulled on my pants, the dagger in my pocket thudded against my leg. I went into the bathroom to rinse the stains out of the borrowed pajamas. I rolled up the sleeping bag and went downstairs, where Frau Achter offered me a pastry. I bit into its sweet softness and went into the dining room, where I expected to find Franz. I wanted to tell him good-bye. But Franz was not there.

He's out with his father, Frau Achter said.

My legs weakened and I sank into a chair. What if Franz told Herr Achter what we had done?

But do stay and have more breakfast, Frau Achter said as she pulled a rag from her apron and wiped the dining room table until I could see her reflection in its wooden surface.

I swallowed the ball of dough that had caught in my throat. If Franz told, wouldn't he be telling on himself too? No, I reasoned. He would not tell.

Where did they go? I asked.

The community center, she said.

Code words for *Nazi Club*. Code words for danger. What had Emelia said about her parents? *Unafraid*. I would never be unafraid. Never free. None of us could ever hope to be unafraid until I did the task that had been set before me.

Danke, I said as I stood and walked toward the door.

No need to rush, Frau Achter called after me, but I was already mounting my bike.

I rode to the wild part of the lake and hiked to the beach. I stood on shore, felt myself cupped by the Andes, just as my father must have the morning he died. I knew the man might not come to the beach at that hour or even that day. I would have to go to him. I made my way over the rocks to search for the path the man had mentioned. I found the worn-down place in the brush and stepped into the swallowing woods to ascend a gradual slope. In moments, I was standing before a large red chalet with yellow flowers in the balcony pots. It was enormous, though you could not see it until you were standing right in front of it. The man was sitting under an umbrella at a table in the yard with a woman whose hair was drawn back into a gray bun. He was eating a grapefruit with a sharp little spoon.

Buenos días, the man said.

The woman turned and her eyebrows rose in surprise.

This is the young ornithologist I told you of, the man said. He squinted as he moved out of the umbrella's shade, which made him look even more like the photograph in Emelia's father's book.

Oh, the woman said, but her expression did not change.

My spine seemed to be unbraiding, notch by notch, from fear and loathing. I could not just run up to the man and kill him in front of his wife.

I came to see the colony, I said, trying to keep my voice even. Remember? You said you'd show me.

The man seemed a bit taken aback, but he wiped his mouth with his folded napkin, put it down on the table, and said yes. He gripped his cane and lumbered to his feet. He coughed from the exertion.

Are you sure? the woman asked him.

He nodded.

I followed the man across the lawn. In the distance, a worker knelt in front of the hedges, trimming them as if it were a regular day in the country. Did he know whom he served? Could I really be the only one who had realized? Or was I just the only one who cared? Or . . . was I wrong? I swallowed.

On the far side of the grand chalet, we came to another path and started up it. It was rockier than the path from the beach, and the man missed his footing once, slipped, and teetered. Without thinking, I reached out to steady him. I pulled my hands away fast. They burned where they touched his forearm.

Danke, he said, and he began coughing. A small trickle of blood came from the corner of his mouth. For a moment, I returned to who I had been just a few weeks before; I allowed myself to imagine he was a Nahuel, a jaguar who killed for food, not a human who murdered out of hatred. But he was, in fact, in my mind at that hour, very likely *the* human who had killed more out of hatred than any other.

I heard the colony before I saw it. Each call was a door that needed oiling. Even the man's coughing was blotted out once we came out from the trees onto a cliff that jutted out over the water. A thousand cormorants, maybe more, had built their nests on that rock face. Several swooped through the air, landing only to shove others aside. Fuzzy, brown fledglings stuck their heads into their parents' mouths to root around for fish. Sometimes they shoved so deep for what they sought, the sharp angles of their beaks were visible through the feathers of their parents' throats.

The man warbled over the din, Milton portrays Satan transformed into a cormorant, sitting on the Tree of Life. Of course, he was referring to the great cormorant, not imperials.

I flinched at the word *Satan*. I had no idea who Milton was, but he was wrong.

They seem more like Christ, I said. I put my arms out, You know, on the cross?

I suspect it's because greats are black, he said, as if he hadn't heard me, and maybe he hadn't.

Where I grew up, they are thought of as pests, he said.

Where was that?

Austria, he said.

My heart churned in my chest. It was him.

The man stepped down in front of me and stared out at the water as if he were thinking of home right at that moment.

We exterminate them there, he said.

Fumbling, I pulled my father's dagger from my pocket and unsheathed it. The man coughed. I stepped up onto a rock beside me and half a meter behind the man. I could see the top of his head, the small bald spot and strange gray roots beneath his shoe-polish hair. I took a deep breath. I brought the dagger up, eyeing the age spot on his neck where I would stab him. The cormorants grunted restlessly as the crowd at any execution. The man kept his back to me, which should have made my task easy.

Yet I hesitated. Would I stab my father, who was guilty of many of the same crimes? But my father was dead, and why should this monster live on while his victims were bones in their unmarked pits? Was death even enough to punish the man? What exactly would I have to do for it to be enough? My hand shook on the knife, like Franz's had that day in fifth when I flayed the frog's lungs, pulled out its intestines, popped the tiny gonads. Could I do that to a human? Any human?

Come on, Haefer, I said to myself. *If you don't do it—*

An imperial landed a few yards away on the cliff. The bird began gagging. I sensed the man watching too, as it ejected a pellet, that small, neat package of death, the things it could not digest. It wasn't so easy for humans. This man's death would lodge itself inside me for the rest of my life. A breeze came and goosebumps rose on the man's neck. I sheathed the dagger, slid it back into my pocket.

I have to go, I said. My mother is expecting me.

I walked away, down one path, over the lawn, and down the other. I hiked back to my bike. Before I got on it, I threw the dagger as far out into the lake as I could. It hardly made a splash. At home, my mother tucked me into the daybed in the living room where I slept as if I had the flu, and when I woke, she brought me a plate of chocolates, which we ate together.

The following autumn she died. I boarded a train headed east through Río Negro to Buenos Aires to live with my grandparents. My last thought as I stood at the station in Bariloche, the town where I was born, was this: If I were in my father's Germany, this train would be taking me to Dachau. Then I did not think of it much again for a very long time.

Although, every now and then, I found myself diving deep. In my first year of college, when I read *Love's Labour's Lost* and encountered the passage about the cormorant, the one the man had quoted, I heard his tinny voice in my head, but I could not place it. I did not let myself place it. In my early thirties, I once spent a weekend with a man from the Cape; his father, a German immigrant, knew two men in their neighborhood who had been high-ranking Nazis. I stared out at the Atlantic while the man spoke. I almost told him my story. But I choked it back down.

Forty-eight hours after Lucas died and on the day of his funeral, I drove to the clinic to get my results. Back then, they never told you over the phone for fear you would do what my friend Aleks had done if you were positive. As I sat in that examination room, I had a sensation similar to the one I'd had on that train rumbling toward Buenos Aires two and a half decades before: If this room were in Dachau, my father would be coming to freeze me to death. But that wasn't why I was shivering.

Reinhard? the young male nurse said as he poked his head around the door.

I clenched my hands on the edge of the hard table.

It's Eduardo, I said.

Sorry, he said.

He held up his clipboard and with no ado said, You're negative.

When he was done counseling me about safe-sex practices, I drove to the beach in Santa Monica and watched the gulls fight over a box of French fries.

I looked out at the water. I took off my shoes to feel the hot sand between my toes. Charles Waterton, the explorer, told the following tale about the cormorant: He was once a merchant who freighted a ship with wool. The ship struck some rocks and sank. The cormorant dives eternally in search of his foundered vessel. That cheap book was my vessel.

Did I believe it? Did I believe the man had really been Hitler?

It's not impossible. Hitler employed a doppelgänger; maybe he was the one who died in that bunker. But when I Google the topic, the ads on the sides of the pages I turn up also claim that spontaneous human combustion is a real concern. I'm nearly seventy now, the age Hitler would have been that summer. Last December, a group of Norwegian bikers found the remains of what some thought was a Nazi submarine on the coast of Argentina, but the photos reveal a hull far too small for a voyage so long.

The only thing that can be proved was that I once met a man on the shores of Nahuel Huapi; he was born in Austria, he liked to quote literature, and he had a bad cough. I wanted to kill him and almost did. But when I tried, I learned that every man who kills another human being for any reason does it himself. And I was not capable of it.

The year I was born, some of the guilty were tried and convicted at Nuremberg. I've watched the films of the hangings, and in each man's face, I saw my father. But when I finally visited Dachau and stood in Block Three, I refused to picture him there. I took a note from Emelia: my father did not deserve to exist, even in my imagination, so close to the mass graves of those he murdered. It was February. When the sun reached its highest point in the gray sky, I opened my coat and stripped off my scarf, let the burning, cold wind touch the skin of my neck and chest. Nothing I offered could make up the difference between my existence and those never born.

ACKNOWLEDGMENTS

All the Names They Used for God: "All the Names for God" by Anjali Sachdeva

Bellevue Literary Review: "Bon Voyage, Charlie" by Dan Pope

Iowa Review: "Letters Arrive from the Dead" by Rachel Kadish

Kenyon Review: "Coffins for Kids!" by Wendy Rawlings and "The White Spot" by Jonathan Blum

London Magazine: "A Small Dark Quiet" by Miranda Gold

The Massachusetts Review: "Ada, After the Bomb" by Alicia Upano

The Missouri Review: "The Resurrection of Ma Jun" by Denis Wong

Obsidian: "The Time Is Nigh" by Camille F. Forbes

Ploughshares: "Blue River Hotel" by Stephen Henighan, "Down to the Levant" by Joshua Idaszak, "L'homme blessé" by Ron Rash, and "The Man on the Beach" by Josie Sigler Sibara

Witness: "A Woman with a Torch" by Mark Powell

Special thanks to Colleen McGrath, Elise McHugh, Clarence Lo, Amina Gautier, Christine Sneed, and the University of Missouri for making this anthology possible.

CONTRIBUTORS

JONATHAN BLUM is the author of *The Usual Uncertainties*, a short-story collection, and *Last Word*, a novella. He teaches fiction-writing classes online and can be found at jonathanblumwriter.com.

ROBERT OLEN BUTLER has published eighteen novels and six volumes of short stories, one of which won the 1993 Pulitzer Prize. Among his many other awards is the 2013 F. Scott Fitzgerald Award for Outstanding Achievement in American Literature. Apropos of this volume, he was a finalist for the Dayton Literary Peace Prize. He teaches at Florida State University.

CAMILLE F. FORBES is the author of the biography *Introducing Bert Williams: Blackface, Burnt Cork, and the Story of America's First Black Star*. A Hambidge Center and Kimbilio Fiction fellow, she has been published in *Obsidian* and *Callaloo*. She holds a doctorate in the history of American civilization from Harvard University and is an associate professor in literature at University of California San Diego.

MIRANDA GOLD is a novelist and creative writing teacher living in London. Her first novel, *Starlings*, was published by Karnac Books in 2016 and reprinted by Sphinx in 2019. Her second novel, *A Small Dark Quiet*, was published by Unbound in 2018. She is a creative writing tutor at Crisis Skylight and is collaborating with New River Press on an anthology of work by people who have experienced homelessness.

STEPHEN HENIGHAN's sixth novel is *The World of After* (Cormorant Books, 2021). He is also the author of four books of short stories, including *Blue*

River and Red Earth (Cormorant Books, 2018), and six books of reportage or criticism. He has translated novels into English from Portuguese, Spanish, and Romanian.

JOSHUA IDASZAK's work has been published in the *Kenyon Review*, *Ploughshares*, *TriQuarterly*, and elsewhere. His fiction has won the *Poets & Writers* Maureen Egen Writers Exchange Award and *Boulevard* magazine's short fiction contest and has been named a finalist for the *Chicago Tribune* Nelson Algren Award. He holds an MFA from the University of Arkansas and has received support from the Fulbright Program and the Sewanee Writers Conference.

RACHEL KADISH's most recent novel, *The Weight of Ink*, was awarded a National Jewish Book Award. Her work has been read on NPR and has appeared in *The New York Times*, *Slate*, and *Paris Review*. She has been a fellow of the National Endowment for the Arts and lives outside Boston, Massachusetts.

PHONG NGUYEN is the author of three novels: *The Bronze Drum* (Grand Central Publishing, 2022); *Roundabout* (Moon City Press, 2020); and *Adventures of Joe Harper* (Outpost19, 2016), winner of the Prairie Heritage Book Award. He is also the author of two story collections: *Pages from the Textbook of Alternate History* (Mastodon Publishing, 2019) and *Memory Sickness and Other Stories* (Elixir Press, 2011), winner of the Elixir Press Fiction Award. He is the Miller Family Endowed Chair in Literature and Writing at the University of Missouri, where he currently serves as the director of creative writing.

DAN POPE is a 2002 graduate of the Iowa Writers Workshop. He has published two novels, *In the Cherry Tree* (Picador, 2003) and *Housebreaking* (Simon & Schuster, 2015). His short stories have appeared in numerous print journals, including *The Gettysburg Review*, *McSweeneys*, *Iowa Review*, *The Bellevue Review*, *The Bennington Review*, *Shenandoah*, *Harvard Review*, *Crazyhorse*, *The Greensboro Review*, as well as many anthologies, including *Best New American Voices 2007* (Harcourt) and the *Pushcart Prize Anthology* (2020).

MARK POWELL is the author of six novels, including *Small Treasons* (Gallery/Simon and Schuster), and has written for the *Oxford American*, *Garden & Gun*, and the *Daily Beast*. He has received fellowships from the National Endowment for the Arts, the Breadloaf and Sewanee Writers' Conferences, and twice from the Fulbright Foundation. He directs the creative writing program at Appalachian State University in Boone, North Carolina.

RON RASH's latest book is *In the Valley* (Doubleday, 2020). Winner of the 2010 Frank O'Connor International Short Story Award, he teaches at Western Carolina University.

WENDY RAWLINGS has published three books: *The Agnostics*, a novel; *Time for Bed*, a short-story collection, and *Come Back Irish*, another short-story collection. Her work has appeared in *AGNI*, *Creative Nonfiction*, *The Kenyon Review*, the 2016 Pushcart Prize anthology, and other magazines. She directs the MFA program at the University of Alabama and loves some people and all dogs.

ANJALI SACHDEVA's short-story collection, *All the Names They Used for God*, is the winner of the 2019 Chautauqua Prize and was named a Best Book of 2018 by NPR. She teaches at the University of Pittsburgh and in the low-residency MFA program at Randolph College.

JOSIE SIGLER SIBARA is the author of *The Galaxie and Other Rides* (stories) and *living must bury* (poetry). She has been the recipient of an NEA Fellowship and a James Jones First Novel Fellowship. Her most recent fiction appears in *Ploughshares*, *Crazyhorse*, and *The Master's Review*.

ALICIA UPANO is the winner of the 2018 James Jones First Novel Fellowship and the 2016 Poets & Writers Maureen Egen Writers Exchange Award Hawai'i (fiction). Her creative work is published in *Asian American Literary Review*, *Bamboo Ridge*, *The Massachusetts Review*, and *The Southern Review*, among others. Born and raised in Hawai'i, she has lived in Asia and on both US continental coasts and now resides on O'ahu with her family.

DENIS WONG was born in New York City. His stories have appeared in *Gemini Magazine*, *Hyphen Magazine*, *The Margins*, *The Missouri Review*, *Cha*, and *Wasafiri Magazine*, among others. Wong received his MFA in creative writing from the City University of Hong Kong. He currently lives and teaches in New Jersey.